A Place in the Sun

A Place in the Sun

The Journals of Corrie Belle Hollister
BOOK FOUR

MICHAEL PHILLIPS

A Place in the Sun

Hendrickson Publishers Marketing, LLC
P. O. Box 3473
Peabody, Massachusetts 01961-3473

ISBN 978-1-59856-688-8

Printed in the United States of America, by Versa Press, East Peoria, Illinois

First Hendrickson Edition Printing — January 2012

Cover Photo Credit: Mike Habermann Photography

To Michael Oliver Cochran

A Note to the Reader

The idea for the story of Corrie was born two decades ago in the living room of a Eureka, California, home. Michael Phillips had gotten to know Judith Pella from a Bible study they both attended, and their common interest in writing began the conversations that ultimately resulted in a collaboration and the launch of The Journals of Corrie Belle Hollister series.

Then these talented and dedicated novelists had the idea for a totally different historical series, The Russians, and decided to work on the two projects simultaneously! Their enthusiasm and discipline got them through the first two novels in both series, but reality raised its head—they decided that each would continue on with one series. As it turned out, Michael was captivated by courageous Corrie and the frontier setting not too far from his home, and Judith loved the drama, complexity, and the intensive research required by the Russian story. So this is the reason Michael Phillips' name appears solo after book two of the series.

Judith and Michael went on to collaborate on several other historical series over the years. They love to hear from their readers.

The authors may be contacted at:

Michael Phillips
P. O. Box 7003
Eureka, CA 95502
macdonaldphillips.com

Judith Pella
judithpella.com

Contents

Election Day

CHAPTER ONE

$\mathcal{P}$a walked out of the schoolhouse with a big smile on his face.

He took the stairs two at a time and ran over to where the rest of us were standing by the wagon. "Well, I reckon that's that," he said, still smiling. "Now all we gotta do is wait!"

Of course, since the rest of us were under twenty-one, we couldn't have voted, anyway—at least not Zack or Tad. But neither could Almeda, even though she was the one who got everybody for miles around interested in the political future of Miracle Springs by jumping into the mayor's race against Franklin Royce. People soon enough found out that she didn't consider being a woman to be a handicap to anything she wanted to do!

And so she stood there waiting with the rest of us while Pa went into the schoolhouse with the other men and voted. When he rejoined her, their eyes met, and they gave each other a special smile. I was well on my way past nineteen to twenty, and I'd been through a lot of growing up experiences in the last couple of years, so I was beginning to understand a little about what it felt like to be an adult. But even as the oldest of the young Hollister generation, I could have only but a bare glimpse into all that look between Pa and

Almeda must have meant. If the Lord ever saw fit, maybe I would know one day what it felt to care about someone so deeply in that special way. For today, however, I was content to observe the love between the two persons I called Father and Mother.

A moment later Uncle Nick emerged from the schoolhouse, and came down the steps and across the grass to join his wife Katie and fifteen-month-old son Erich, who were both with us.

"Well, Drum," he said, giving Pa a slap on the back, "we come a ways from the New York days, I'll say that!"

Pa laughed. "Who'd have thought when we headed west we'd be standing here in California one day as family men again—and *you* with a wife and a son!"

"Or doing what we was just doing in there!" Uncle Nick added. "I reckon that's just about the craziest, most unexpected thing I ever done in my life! If only my pa, old grandpa Belle, and Aggie could see us now!"

A brief cloud passed over Pa's face. He and I had both had to fight the same inner battle over memories of Ma. We had both come to terms with her death—not without tears—and were now at peace, both with the past and the present.

As to the future—who could tell?

A lot would depend on what Rev. Rutledge and the government man from Sacramento found out when they added up all the votes later that day. For the moment, Pa and Uncle Nick had cast their ballots in the long-anticipated election for mayor of Miracle Springs, and in the Fremont-Buchanan presidential voting. I couldn't have known it yet, but my own personal future was as bound up in the latter election as the former. I had already invested a lot in the Fremont cause, and

I couldn't help but feel involved in its outcome—almost as involved as in the local election for mayor.

But for the moment, the future would have to wait a spell. As Pa had said, there was nothing else to do *but* wait.

We piled in our two wagons. Pa gave the reins a snap, and off we rumbled back to our home on the claim on Miracle Springs Creek. Pa and Almeda sat up front. In the back I sat with my lanky seventeen-year-old brother Zack, who was a good five inches taller than me, thirteen-year-old Becky, and eleven-year-old Tad. Emily, now fifteen, rode with Uncle Nick and Katie, carrying her little nephew.

That was election day, November 4, 1856, a day to remember!

But there'd been so much that had happened leading up to the voting, I reckon I ought to back up a bit and tell you about it. . . .

*A*fter I got back from my adventure in Sonora six weeks earlier, I was certainly surprised by Almeda's unexpected news.

I had just filed my story on the Fremont-Buchanan race with Mr. Kemble at the *Alta*. After that and Derrick Gregory and the double-dealings of that ne'er-do-well Robin O'Flaridy, I sometimes wonder if *anything* could surprise me! But I'll have to say I was sure excited when I got home and Almeda said, "You'll never believe it, Corrie, but your father and I are going to have a baby!" An adventure, a baby, and two elections were almost more than I could handle!

Three or four days after I returned from Sonora, we got the first inkling that Franklin Royce, the town banker, was up to his old mischief. One afternoon Patrick Shaw rode up to the house. One look at his face, and you could tell right off that he was in some kind of trouble.

Neither Pa nor Almeda had to say anything to get him talking or ask what the trouble was. It was out of his mouth the instant he lit off his horse.

"He's gonna run us off our place, Drum!" he said. "But me and Chloe and the kids, we ain't got no place else to go. What am I gonna do, Drum? I don't know nothing but ranching, and with a family and the gold drying up everywhere, I can't pack up and try to find some new claim!"

"Hold on, Pat," said Pa. "What in tarnation are you talking about?"

"He's fixing to run us out, just like I told ya!"

"Who?"

"Who else—Royce! There it is—look for yerself!"

He thrust a piece of paper he'd been holding in Pa's direction. Pa took it and scanned it over quickly. He then handed it to Almeda.

"He says we got thirty days to get out!" Mr. Shaw's face went red, then white. If he hadn't been a man, he probably would have started crying.

Almeda read the paper over, taking longer than Pa, her forehead crinkling in a frown.

"It might as well be an eviction notice," she said finally, looking up at the two men. "And if I know Franklin, it's no doubt iron-clad and completely legal."

"What happened, Pat?" Pa asked. "How'd you get into this fix?"

"Well, it ain't no secret my claim's just about played out. I wasn't lucky enough to have any of your vein run across to my side of the hill. Though I suspect Royce thought it did, the way he's been after my place."

"What do you mean?" asked Almeda.

"Why, he's come out offering to buy the place three or four times the last couple of years."

"And so now he figures he'll get your place without paying a cent for it!" said Pa, the heat rising in his voice.

"A few of my cattle got that blamed infection last spring when my pond had the dead skunk in it. It spread around the herd, and I wound up losing thirty or forty head. I missed a good sale I was gonna make, and so couldn't make a few payments to the bank."

"How many?"

"Four."

"So how much do you owe him—how far behind are you now?"

"I pay him a hundred sixty-seven a month."

"So you're—let's see . . . what, about six, seven hundred behind," said Pa, scratching his head. "I'll help you with it, Pat. I can loan you that much."

"No good, Drum! I already thought of that. I knew you'd help if you could, so when Royce delivered me that there paper, I said to him, 'I'll get you the $668—that's how much he said I was in arrears, is what he called it. I told him I'd get it to him in a few days, because I knew you'd help me if you could. But he said it wouldn't help. He said now that I defaulted, the whole loan was due immediately, and that if I didn't come up with the whole thing in thirty days, the claim and the house and the whole 250 acres and what cattle I got left—he said it'd all be his."

"How much is your loan, Mr. Shaw?" Almeda asked. "What do you still owe the bank?"

"Seventeen thousand something."

Pa let out a sigh and a low whistle. "Well, that's a bundle all right, Pat," he said. "I'm afraid there ain't much I can do to help with *that*. Nick and I couldn't scrape together more than three or four thousand between us."

"What about me, Drummond Hollister?" said Almeda, pretending to get in a huff. "I'm part of this family now too, you know! Or had you forgotten?"

"I ain't likely to do that anytime soon," replied Pa smiling.

"Well then, I insist on being part of this. Parrish Mine and Freight could add, perhaps, two or three thousand."

"I appreciate what you're trying to do," said Mr. Shaw, his voice forlorn. "But I could never let you loan me that kind of money, everything you got in the bank. It don't matter anyhow. Between all of us, we ain't even got half of what it'd take!"

"Yes, you're right," sighed Almeda. "And it wouldn't surprise me one bit if your loan had a thirty-day call on it even if you weren't behind in your payments. Franklin as much as told me that's how he structured all the loans around here. Of course, I couldn't say for certain without seeing the loan document, but my hunch is that your getting behind is only an excuse for the foreclosure, that legally he is perfectly justified in calling your note due at any time and giving you no more than thirty days' notice."

A little more talk followed. But there wasn't much more to be said. Mr. Royce had the Shaws in a pickle, and nobody could see anything they could do about it.

Almeda's Decision

CHAPTER THREE

*T*he next surprise came a couple of days later.

Almeda had been rather quiet ever since Mr. Shaw's visit. The terrible news of what Mr. Royce had done seemed to weigh on her, and I knew she felt almost desperate to find some way to help him. Yet there just wasn't enough money to get him out from under the call on his loan.

It was getting on toward late in the evening, Pa was sitting with Tad and Becky in his lap reading them a story. I was trying to draw a picture of Zack from memory. Zack had taken Rayo Rojo for a ride that afternoon, and for one moment, just after he'd mounted, she reared up on her hind legs. Zack leaned forward, his feet tight into her flanks, one hand flying in the air, and his eyes flashing with the closest thing to pure delight I'd ever seen. The sketch wasn't turning out too well, but I didn't want to let myself forget the mental picture of that wonderful moment.

Suddenly Almeda's voice broke out loudly, as if she had been struggling all day to keep the words in and couldn't hold back the dam a second longer.

"It's just not right for a man like that to be mayor!" she exclaimed. "Drummond, I'm sorry for acting rashly, and I hope you'll forgive me, but I just don't know what else to do. We've just got to stop him, that's all there is to it! Pregnant or not, and despite his threats, and even if I am a woman—I don't know what I can do but go ahead with it! It *must* be done for the good of this community—I am going to run for mayor after all!"

For a few seconds there was silence. Everyone stopped and looked at her. Pa was still holding the book steady on his lap, but his and Tad's and Becky's eyes all focused intently on Almeda where she stood over by the stove.

"If that don't beat all!" Pa said finally, shaking off the two kids from his lap, climbing to his feet, and walking over to her. "Sometimes I wonder whether I married me a wife or a hurricane! Well, if I'm gonna have me a new son or daughter, he might as well have a ma for a mayor to make up for the fact that his pa's such an old man!" He smiled and gave Almeda a big hug. I knew he was proud of her decision, even though maybe it wasn't the same one he would have made if he had to decide.

So many things immediately began to run through my heart!

What about all those threats Mr. Royce had made about what he would do to Almeda if she didn't keep out of the race? He said he'd cause trouble for Pa and Uncle Nick with the law, that he'd investigate the ownership of the land and their claim! All along we'd worried about what Royce might do to all the miners and ranchers and people around Miracle Springs who owed money to his bank if he didn't win. The incident with Patrick Shaw showed that he wasn't fooling, and I didn't see how Almeda's running would help, even if she won.

Worst of all, he had threatened *me* too! He had told me to stop interviewing and talking to people about the election, and as good as said that if I didn't, he would let it be known to powerful slavery people that I was a pro-Fremont reporter, and that I would be in danger. And after what had happened in Sonora I knew it was no empty threat! The powers behind the scenes in the national election were real . . . and *were* dangerous! For all I knew Royce might be somehow connected to Senator Goldwin and his people! After my story appeared in the *Alta* exposing the falsehood of Mr. Gregory's claims against Fremont, they might try to track me down and do something to punish me. I was still so new to this whole world of politics and news reporting, I had no idea what to expect. And I certainly didn't want Mr. Royce getting me in more trouble than I was already in!

With all this worrying about Mr. Royce and his threats against *me*, I hardly even remembered at first what he'd said about opening a supplies outlet and freight service of his own, and putting Parrish Mine and Freight out of business.

But Almeda hadn't forgotten. She weighed everything, and over the next few days talked to Pa a lot. They prayed, and in the end they both concluded that her decision to run was the right one after all, and that they had to go ahead and see the election out to its conclusion on November 4.

I think Almeda felt a little like I had with the Fremont story, that there was more at stake than just the outcome of the election itself. She felt that it was her duty to fight against what Franklin Royce stood for, to fight against his underhanded and deceitful methods. She felt she was standing up for what was *right*. Even if she lost, she felt she needed to take a stand in the community for what was right and honest and true.

It was not an easy decision. Everything Royce had said was true. He *could* hurt her and her family if he chose to. He *could* put Parrish Freight out of business. He *could* challenge Pa and Uncle Nick's ownership of their land. He could hurt a lot of other people in the community, just like he was doing to Patrick Shaw, if he decided to start calling loans due. Franklin Royce was a powerful man!

But in the end Almeda and Pa decided to take the risk— because it was the right thing to do. Maybe it wouldn't help the Shaws keep their claim and their ranch and their home. But they had to do something to show that Royce couldn't just do whatever he wanted without any opposition. A man like that simply shouldn't be allowed to work his will in a town and come to power without anyone standing up to him. Sometimes you just have to do what's right, no matter what the consequences.

Realizing all the risks involved for Pa and Almeda in their decision, within a day or two of Almeda's surprise announcement to the family, I made a decision of my own.

I decided to start up again with my article on the Miracle Springs mayor's election. And whether Franklin Royce liked it or not, I was going to pick up where I'd left off interviewing people. I *would* write at least one article, maybe two, on the election. There wasn't much time left before November, but what there was I would use. And I wouldn't settle for one dollar an article either! If Mr. Kemble wasn't willing to pay me at least three or four dollars, I'd submit it to another editor—even the *Globe*, if I had to! But I was sure the *Daily and Weekly Times* in Sacramento would print it. Sacramento was closer, and both Mr. Royce and Almeda were a little bit known there.

So I dusted off my writing satchel, read over the notes from interviews I'd done earlier, and tried to figure out how

I could go about telling people in the rest of the state about this election in what Mr. Kemble would call an "unbiased" way. Then I started going to visit folks again to find out their thoughts, now that the election was getting close and Almeda was back in it.

*O*ne thing I was learning about being truthful was the importance of being out in the open with folks—not only being honest in what you said, but coming right out with things so that nothing was ever said or done behind another person's back. I don't think there's anything more destructive among people than thinking and saying things about someone that you're not willing to tell them to their face. And I knew that if I was going to be a writer—especially if I was going to write about people—I had to show integrity in this straightforward way.

So I figured there was only one place to begin my article about the election, especially if I was going to be fair and unbiased.

Therefore, that very afternoon, I rode into town, left Raspberry with Marcus Weber at the stable, and crossed the street to the bank. I went straight to Mr. Royce's office, knocked on the door, and walked in.

If he was surprised to see me, he certainly didn't show it. But neither did he smile.

"Mr. Royce," I said, "I would like to talk with you, if you don't mind. Either now, or some other time."

"Now will be fine, Miss Hollister," he replied, still sitting behind his desk, still not smiling or showing any sign of emotion. He motioned me to a chair with his hand.

"I imagine you know," I said, "that my stepmother has decided to remain a candidate for mayor after all."

"So I understand," he replied. "It is of course her decision to make, but it is an unfortunate one that will, I fear, have most unpleasant consequences."

The squint of his eyes as he looked steadily into my face confirmed his meaning. I took a deep breath to steady myself.

"Well I have decided to go ahead with what I was doing too," I went on. "I am going to write the article or two I was planning about the mayor's election. And to do a good job I am going to have to continue talking to people around town and interviewing them."

"I am very sorry to hear that," said Mr. Royce. But his tone held a threat. "It would deeply grieve me to see a promising young writer such as you find herself on the wrong side, shall we say, of powerful interest groups and individuals who—"

"Look, Mr. Royce," I said, "I know you're trying to scare me by making it sound like I'm going to be in danger if I don't do what you say. But if Almeda can do what she's doing in spite of all the trouble you could cause her and our family, then I figure I can too. I'm going to do it whether you like it or not, and you might as well just stop trying to frighten me off by talking like that."

He stopped, his mouth half open, shocked that I would cut him off and dare to speak so brazenly.

I probably shouldn't have interrupted him, or spoken quite so boldly. But he was starting to make me angry with all his cool words and hidden threats, sitting there behind his big fancy desk as if he owned the world and could tell everyone else what to do! And I knew he was especially annoyed that Almeda and I were causing him so much trouble. He wanted us to stop interfering with his plans and the powerful grasp he used to hold on to everything around him. I'm sure he figured he could scare us into submission. Well I didn't like it! My face got red and my voice sounded a little edgy, but I couldn't help it.

For a second or two he just stared, probably wondering whether he should threaten me further, or stand up and throw me out of his office! But before he had a chance to do either, I spoke again. And this time I went on and said everything I'd come in to say. I didn't want to give him a chance to cut *me* off.

"Now, doggone it, Mr. Royce," I went on, "I'm gonna try to be fair in this article I'm writing. It's not going to be something that's supposed to make people favor Almeda. I want to present both sides and talk to folks who are gonna vote for you *and* for her. My editor Mr. Kemble said he didn't think I could write a fair and unbiased article, being so closely involved like I am. He said I couldn't be objective—he called it a conflict of interests."

I paused to take a breath, but only for a second.

"But I'm going to prove him wrong, Mr. Royce," I said. "I'll show him that I *can* write an unbiased article about the election that will interest the people who read his newspaper. I intend to be fair, but you're not making it very easy for me to think unbiased thoughts when you're telling me and my Pa and my mother the things you're going to do to us if we don't just quit and let you run for mayor all by yourself. What would folks think if I wrote about what you said to us?"

"I would deny every word," replied the banker coolly. "It would be my word against that of a teenage girl desperately trying to sway people in favor of her father's wife. No one would believe a word you said."

"You might be right, for all I know," I said. "I don't want to write those things, and I'm not going to write them. What I came here for was to interview *you* and to ask you to give your side on some things. Whether you believe me or not, I want to write what's fair and truthful about you as well as Almeda. And it would be a lot easier to be fair to you if you'd give me a little help instead of talking mean like you're doing."

I stopped. Judging from the expression on his face, people didn't normally speak quite that plainly to Franklin Royce. And if I'd stopped to think about it, I probably wouldn't have either. But I'd done it, and it was too late to take my words back now!

He sat just staring back across his desk at me. The office was completely silent. His face didn't give away a hint of what he was thinking. I'd heard Pa and Uncle Nick talk about poker faces, and if this was one of those, then I understood what they meant!

Finally Mr. Royce's voice broke the quiet.

"What do you want to know?" he said. The red was gone from his cheeks and the meanness from his tone, although he was obviously not pleased with the whole affair.

"Why do you want to be Miracle Springs' mayor?" I asked, getting out a sheet of paper from my satchel and inking my pen. "What made you decide to run?"

He cleared his throat, but kept looking at me almost warily. The question *sounded* like what a newspaper reporter would ask, and yet he didn't quite believe it was coming from the mouth of a girl he wasn't sure he trusted.

"I, uh . . . feel that the town, growing as it is, must look to its future, and who could be better qualified to lead such a diverse community forward than one like myself, who has been such an intrinsic part of helping in its growth up till now?"

I wrote quickly to get down all his words.

"So you feel you are the most qualified person to be mayor?"

"I do."

"Because you are the town's banker?"

"That of course is a large part of it. In that role I have, as I said, helped this community grow. I have helped to finance much of the building, most of the homes. I have a stake in the community because of who I am and what I have done. As mayor I will always be looking out for the best interests of its people."

Again there was silence for a while as I wrote. Mr. Royce was getting used to the idea of an interview. He was starting to sound like he was delivering a campaign speech.

"Your opponent, Mrs. Hollister, could no doubt say the same thing about her history in the community and all the ways *she* has helped the miners," I said. "What real difference is there between you and her?"

His eyes narrowed for an instant, and I knew he thought my question meant more than I intended.

"Of course she could *say* it," he answered with just an edge of derision. "But there is a clear difference between a thirteen thousand dollar loan to build a house or buy a spread of acreage, and a store where you buy a fifty-cent gold pan or a five-dollar sluice box or pay a few dollars so that a free black man can freight your supplies somewhere for you. A little supply store and a bank are hardly equal in their impact upon the community, and I am sure the voters in this area will have the good sense to acknowledge that difference on November 4."

"Do you think your position as banker might be a drawback in any way?"

"What do you mean? How could it possibly be a drawback?"

"There are some people who have said they might have trouble trusting you as mayor."

"What people?" he said, his voice rising and his eyes flashing.

"I cannot say *who*," I replied. "But I have talked with some folks who aren't sure they'd altogether like a banker in charge of their town."

"Look, Miss Hollister," he said angrily, "if you want to ask me some questions, that's one thing. But if you're going to come into my office and tell me to my face that I'm not to be trusted, and then put the lies people say about me in your article, I'll have no part of it!" He rose from his chair. "I believe it is time for this interview to come to an end. You can't say I didn't warn you what might happen if you persist in this folly. You tell that fool father and stepmother of yours that for their own good they'd better stop fighting me. I won't be denied what is rightfully mine, and I will not be responsible for people who stand in my way! Good day, Miss Hollister."

I remained seated and returned his stare. That man made it real hard to keep a Christian attitude! But I kept sitting there and didn't get up and leave like he wanted me to. Finally I spoke again, as calmly as I could.

"Please, Mr. Royce," I said, "I was only saying what some people have told me they're thinking."

"During your so-called interviews about the election!"

"That's right," I answered. "And if I'm going to write a fair article, then I ought to know how you would answer those people. Otherwise, if you just make me leave and I have to write the article with only their side of it to go on, then your perspective never gets to be told. I'm trying to give you a decent shake here, Mr. Royce, but you're making it downright hard! Do you want me to tell what *you* think or not? If you want me to leave, I will. But then I have no choice but to write just from the other interviews I get. And I am going to write this article, Mr. Royce, with or without your cooperation!"

He stood looking down at me just a second or two longer, then slowly sat down, like an eagle smoothing his ruffled feathers.

"Go on, Miss Hollister," he said calmly, "what is your next question?"

"Perhaps I should go about this differently," I said. "Why don't you tell me, Mr. Royce, how and why you first came to Miracle Springs, and how you became involved in banking in this community."

On this safe ground, Mr. Royce started up and was soon talking comfortably. I kept taking notes, and asked him more questions about himself, and the rest of my time in his office, while not "pleasant," was calmer than the beginning. When I left fifteen minutes later I had plenty of information to offer a fair look at Royce the candidate—if "fair" is the right word, considering what I knew about Royce that I couldn't say.

I never asked him about the business of calling Mr. Shaw's note due. I knew I could never mention it in the article. And for the time being I'd rather he didn't know I knew about it.

Talk Heats Up

CHAPTER FIVE

I didn't need worry about trying to keep it a secret that I knew of the Shaws' problem.

Within a few days *everyone* knew. And most everyone was plenty riled. If the election had been held right then, Franklin Royce wouldn't have gotten a single vote!

Word had just begun to circulate back through the community that Almeda was going to run after all . . . *and* that she was in a family way. Those two things alone had people talking, and the "Hollister for Mayor" sign back up in the Freight Company window kept it all fresh in people's minds. But when the news got around about Mr. Shaw getting evicted by the bank, Franklin Royce wasn't exactly the most popular man in Miracle Springs that week!

Pa kept saying he couldn't figure out why Mr. Royce did it. "Gotta be the stupidest thing I can think of doing," he said, "just before the election. Why, Tad could run against him now! Anybody in the whole town could beat him hands down."

Almeda was both furious and delighted. This foolish move by the banker suddenly made it seem as if she had a good chance of winning the election. But on the other hand, what good would that do Patrick and Chloe Shaw? Even her being the town's mayor wouldn't get them their house and land back.

Finally Almeda decided to make the Shaws an issue in her campaign, to try to use it to make people think twice about voting for Mr. Royce, and at the same time to coerce the banker into giving the Shaws another chance if they could get caught up and current again with their payments to the bank. "I would gladly sacrifice the election," she said one night at the supper table, "if Royce would negotiate some equitable terms with Patrick."

"Might be that you can do both, Almeda," said Pa, "win *and* make him back down."

"I'm going to do everything I can to try," she replied. "But the first order of business has to be somehow getting the Shaws out of their dilemma."

Almeda planned to give her first campaign speech the very next Sunday after church, right on the main street of town in front of Parrish Mine and Freight. Pa and Marcus Weber got busy building a three-foot-high platform for her to stand on, and the rest of us fanned out all over the community telling everybody to come, that we needed their support. She had some important things to say.

"And, Corrie, Zack, all of you," she said, "make sure the women know how important it is for them to come, even if they can't vote. If they're there on Sunday, and they hear what I say, their husbands will hear every word eventually! Women, children, dogs, horses . . . we just need a good crowd! We've got to show people that we are serious and that the opposition to Royce is real. That's the only way they'll give earnest consideration to voting for me."

By Friday, the whole community was buzzing! One of the town's most well-liked men was on the verge of getting run off his place. A pregnant woman who couldn't even vote herself was running for mayor against the town's powerful banker, and a campaign speech was scheduled in two days. Folks were talking of nothing else!

What a "human interest" item all *this* would make! I began to wonder if the article I was writing would be any good at all, leaving out all the things people were talking about. But I was almost done with it, so it was too late to start over. I thought maybe I should write a second one to come about a week after the first. I'd have to see what Mr. Kemble said.

Before I had a chance to worry about that, it began to come clear to Pa why Mr. Royce had taken the action against Mr. Shaw about his loan.

"He's a schemer all right," Pa grumbled. "He's making an example of Pat, showing folks what he'll do if things aren't to his liking."

"And demonstrating that he isn't afraid, even of what people think of him," added Almeda with a frustrated sigh. "I really don't know how to stop him, Drummond. Right now everyone's mad at him and saying they'll never accept him as mayor. But when it comes down to their decision, and their *own* homes and land that he holds the mortgages on, I'm afraid they'll worry less about how much they like Franklin Royce and more about their own security. And I can't say that I blame them. I don't want people voting for me if they're going to be hurt by it."

"He can't foreclose on everybody," said Pa. "He'd be a fool. He'd be cutting his own throat. His bank would be out of business."

"But don't you see, he doesn't have to follow through with his threats. Just the fear that he *might* will be enough. People won't run the risk. They'll give in to him. That's why he called

Patrick's note due when he did. At first it looked like a foolish campaign move. But in reality it conveyed just the message to this community Franklin wanted it to—*I hold the power and the purse strings in this town, and I am not afraid to use them. I don't care if you like me. I don't even care if you all hate me. But just don't cross me or you'll end up in the same dilemma as Patrick Shaw.*"

"In other words," growled Pa angrily, "vote for me . . . or else!"

"I think that's the basic message he hopes the men of this community will glean from the Shaws' trouble. He doesn't care a bit about all this anger circulating around right now, as long as once it dies down he's succeeded in getting that message across."

Almeda sighed. She knew she had taken on a tough opponent who apparently held all the cards. Her initial enthusiasm was fading some, I could tell, and I knew from her washed-out complexion that she didn't feel well either.

"Well you just give 'em your best in that speech on Sunday," said Pa, trying to bolster up her spirits. "Maybe we can beat that rascal yet!"

Almeda smiled back at him, but it was a pale, wan smile. She rose slowly to her feet and walked to the door and outside. She needed to be alone a lot during those days. Pa knew it and let her go without any more talk between them.

Campaign Speechmaking
CHAPTER SIX

*O*n Sunday morning church was packed, and folks were waiting for what was going to happen that afternoon.

A little after one o'clock, we all rode up to the front of Parrish Mine and Freight in the wagon. A few people were milling around already, and soon others began to arrive for the speech, which was scheduled for 1:30.

More people turned out than we had imagined possible! Not only were there dogs and horses and every woman for miles around and all their children, but a lot of men turned out too. Almeda was noticeably excited. By the time she was ready to stand up, the whole street was filled in front of the freight company office, all the way across to the stores on the other side, and stretching down the street almost to the Royce Miners' Bank. There must have been four or five hundred people, maybe more! The one person I *didn't* see was Franklin Royce, although I was certain he knew of the event.

At about twenty minutes before two, Pa jumped up on the platform and held up both of his hands. Gradually the crowd quieted down.

"I know it ain't necessary for me to make introductions," he said in a loud voice. "If any of you don't know who this is standing here with me by now, then I don't figure you got any business here anyway!"

Laughter rippled through the crowd.

"But this being our first campaign, well I figured we ought to do things proper. So here I am making the speech to introduce our candidate who's gonna speak to you all today. And that's just about all I reckon I'm gonna say! So here she is, Miracle Springs' next mayor, and a mighty fine-looking woman if I do say so myself, Mrs. Almeda Parrish Hollister!"

All the women clapped as loud as they could, and most of the men joined in. Pa gave Almeda his hand and helped her up the steps to the platform. Then he jumped down onto the ground. Almeda turned to face the crowd.

"I can't tell you how much it means to me that you've all come here today," she began. "As my husband said, campaigning for public office is not something we are experienced at, and to tell the truth, I'm more than a little nervous standing up here facing so many of you. I don't really know what a political speech is supposed to be like, so I am simply going to tell you what I think of this town, why I love Miracle Springs, and why I want to be its new mayor."

She paused, looked out over the faces, and took a deep breath before continuing. As she did, some of the people sat down on the ground.

"When I came here, as a few of you know who were here at the time, the town of Miracle Springs was a far different place. My late husband and I had just arrived from Boston, and I have to tell you, all of California seemed pretty wild and rambunctious to me—Miracle Springs included. There were more saloons than stores, more gold than bread, more mules than women, and it was every man for himself. They said California was a state back then in 1850, but it wasn't like any state I'd ever seen!"

The listeners laughed and some joking comments could be heard from longtime residents who knew firsthand what she was talking about.

"That's right, Mr. Jones," Almeda called out with a smile. "I heard that. And you are absolutely correct—it was a fun place to be back then! But it was a hard life too, for those who didn't make a strike. And I don't know about the rest of you, but for myself, I will take the Miracle Springs of today to the Miracle Springs of 1850. Yes, times have changed—here as well as in the rest of the state—and throughout the country. It's a new era. Our fellow Californian John Fremont is campaigning through this great land for the abolition of slavery. And we've all been hearing recently about some of this state's leading men, like Leland Stanford and Mark Hopkins, who are earnestly pursuing the railroad linkage of east and west across this great country. California is becoming a state with a future.

"My point, ladies and gentlemen, is that as the country is changing and growing, we citizens of Miracle Springs must change and grow with it. Gold brought many of us here, and it first put California and Miracle Springs on the map, but gold will not ensure our future. When the nuggets turn to dust, and when even the dust begins to dry up, gold will no longer sustain businesses. Gold will not feed hungry stomachs. Gold will not educate. Gold will not keep the bonds of friendship and love deep. Gold will not raise a church. Gold will not attract the kind of families a community needs to put down roots and sustain itself and grow strong that it might endure.

"You are all familiar with towns, once booming and alive with activity, which have now become silent and empty because the gold is gone. Ghost towns—dead today because they failed to look to the future, they failed to establish a community fabric where roots went down deeper than the gold they feverishly sought."

Almeda stopped, thought for a moment or two, then took in a deep breath and started up again.

"Now, in a few weeks you men have to decide how to vote in Miracle Springs' first election for mayor. And I suppose I'm telling you why I think you ought to vote for me—even though I'm a woman!"

A little laughter went around, but mostly some cheers and clapping could be heard from the women present.

"So I'm going to tell you why you should vote for me," Almeda continued. "I love this town. After my first husband died, I was miserable for a time. I seriously considered returning to the east, but in the end decided to stay here. And I cannot say it was an easy time. Some of you men made it very difficult for a woman, alone as I was, to keep a business going."

The smile she threw out as she said it showed that her words were meant in fun, not bitterness.

"Yet, on the other hand, most of you were good to me. You were considerate, you brought me your business. You treated me with courtesy and respect. And we managed to forge a pretty good partnership, you miners and Parrish Mine and Freight. This town became my home. And as the town grew, I loved it more and more. The church and school were built. A minister and schoolteacher joined our community—"

She smiled and pointed to where Rev. Rutledge and Miss Stansberry were seated together in the minister's carriage.

"Families came in growing numbers. Wives joined the miners—some from as far away as Virginia!"

She turned and threw Katie a smile behind her where she stood with Uncle Nick.

"And now I feel it is time for me to give this community back a little of what I feel it has given to me. I love Miracle Springs, and with everything that is in my heart, I desire to see it grow into a community whose strength lies in its people, and in their bonds with one another. I love it too much to see it become a ghost town, abandoned because the gold is gone from its hills and streams. My friends, even if the gold were to disappear tomorrow, you and I are what make this community vital! And that is the future to which I want to dedicate my-self, as your next mayor.

"Now . . . why do I think you men ought to vote for Alm-eda Hollister? The chief reason is this: a Hollister vote is a vote for the future of Miracle Springs. It is a vote for the whole fabric of this community, not just one aspect of it. Money and gold may make men rich. But when they are gone, money and gold also make ghost towns.

"I am committed to the whole of Miracle Springs' future, not just its financial future." She paused, thought for a mo-ment, and when she spoke again her voice had grown softer and more serious.

"What I say next is not easy for me," she went on. "But I suppose perhaps it is necessary in light of the purpose for which we are gathered. From the beginning, I have been in-strumental in helping Miracle Springs become a real town, not just a gold camp. I helped organize the church and the-school, and brought Reverend Rutledge and Miss Stansberry here. I truly believe I am qualified, both by experience and by commitment, to be your mayor. I suppose my greatest draw-back as a candidate is that I am a woman, and that may be the reason many of you feel you should not vote for me. But on the other hand, perhaps that is the greatest asset I have to offer Miracle Springs, too. The fact that I am a woman makes me, I feel, sensitive to some of the deeper and longer-lasting interests of this community, important things that I fear a one-dimensional focus on gold and mining profits cannot adequately see."

I don't know whether she saw him at first, because she kept right on with the conclusion of her speech. But as I looked up I detected some movement at the back of the crowd, and then realized that a figure had emerged from somewhere near the bank and was now walking slowly forward.

"In closing then, my friends of Miracle Springs and surrounding communities," Almeda was saying, "I simply want to ask for your votes on election day. In return, I pledge to you my commitment to do all that lies in my power to ensure a happy and prosperous future for all of us. Thank you very much for your attention and support."

She turned to step down off the platform, amid a lot of clapping—mostly from the women and children and *our* family, and a few enthusiastic men, like Pa and Uncle Nick and Rev. Rutledge. But suddenly the noise died down abruptly. Almeda turned around to see the cause, just as the crowd split down the middle to make way for Franklin Royce, who was striding purposefully toward the platform.

Royce's Rebuttal

Chapter Seven

$\mathscr{S}$ilence fell over the street as everyone waited to see what would happen. Almeda remained where she was, watching him approach.

"Well, Mrs. Hollister," said Royce in a loud but friendly voice, "that was a very moving speech. You wouldn't deny your opponent equal time in front of the voters, would you?"

"Certainly not," replied Almeda, obviously cooled by his appearance, but trying not to show it.

The banker climbed the steps to the small platform, where he joined Almeda. He flashed her a broad grin, and then, as if he was just going on with the conversation said, "But surely you do not mean to suggest that gold and the financial interests which accompany it are of lesser importance to this community than these other things you mention?"

"I did not use such a term, Mr. Royce," said Almeda. "But now that you put it like that, I suppose I *do* believe that money is less important than people, than friendship, than churches and schools and families."

"Come now, Mrs. Hollister," said Royce with a patronizing smile. "You know as well as everyone here that gold drives this community. Without the gold Miracle Springs would not exist."

"Perhaps not. But I believe it *will* exist in the years to come, with or without gold."

"You are a businesswoman, Mrs. Hollister. You know that money is what makes everything work. Without money, you are out of business. Without money, none of these people would have homes or clothes or wagons or horses. I'm all for friendship and schools and children and churches. But a community needs a solid financial base or all the rest will wither away. Money is what makes it go. Money is what it is all based on."

"Money . . . such as that represented by the Royce Miners' Bank?"

Royce smiled, although he did not answer her question directly. "And all that is why I'm not sure I can agree with your statement that a Hollister vote is a vote for the best future of Miracle Springs. In my opinion, the future must rest upon a solid financial base."

"In other words, with a vote for Royce," she said.

The banker smiled broadly. "You said it, Almeda . . . not I." Some of the men chuckled to see him getting the better of her. "Let's be practical, Almeda," he went on. "Everyone here may have done business with you at some time in the past. But I am the one who has financed their homes, their land, their businesses. Why, Almeda, I have even lent money to you to help *your* business through some difficult times! None of these people would even be here today if it weren't for my bank and what I have done for them. And the future will be no different. If Miracle Springs is to have a future, even the kind of future you so glowingly speak of, it will be because of what I am able to give it, both as its banker *and* its mayor."

Everyone was quiet, waiting to see what Almeda would do. Clearly, Mr. Royce meant his words as a direct challenge to everything she had said and hoped to accomplish with her speech.

When she spoke again, her voice contained a challenging tone of its own.

"Is the kind of future you have in mind for Miracle Springs the same kind as you're imposing on Patrick Shaw and his family?" she asked in a cool tone. "That is hardly the kind of future I would judge to be in the best interest of this community, no matter how much your bank may have done for it in the past."

A low murmur of agreement spread through the crowd. Her words had touched off the anger at Royce that had been circulating all week. A couple of men shouted out at him.

"The lady's right, Royce," cried one voice.

"Shaw's a good man," called out another. "You got no call to do what you done!"

Mr. Royce did not seem angered by her question. It almost seemed as though he had been expecting it, and was ready with a reply.

"Surely you must realize, Almeda," he said, "that politics and business don't necessarily mix."

"Well maybe they *should!*" she shot back. "Perhaps the incident with the Shaws tells us what kind of mayor you would be. Is this how you envision looking out for the best interests of the people of Miracle Springs—making them leave the homes they have worked so hard for?"

By now Almeda had the support of the crowd. Although not a single one of the men present would have dared go to Mr. Royce in person and tell him what he thought, in a group, and stirred by Almeda's words, all the anger that had been brewing

in the community through the week spilled over into mum-
blings and shouts of complaint against what Royce had done.

"Listen to them, Franklin," she said. "Every man and
woman here is upset by what you have done. They want to
know why. They want to know if this is what you mean when
you say you have *helped* the community grow! Is this the future
you offer Miracle Springs—a future whose road is strewn with
failed loans and eviction notices? If so, I do not think it is the
kind of future the people of Miracle Springs have in mind!"

By now everyone was getting into the argument, calling
out questions and comments to the banker. From the look
and sound of it, it didn't seem that Royce could have any
possible chance in the election! But as Pa had said earlier, Mr.
Royce wasn't the kind of man who should be underestimated.

He held up his hands to restore quiet. When he could be
heard again, he turned to Almeda. "What I said, Mrs. Hollister," he replied, still in a calm tone, "was that the future of
Miracle Springs must rest upon a solid financial base. Without
a financial base, there can be no future."

He paused, looked into her face for a moment, then continued. "Let me ask you a question," he said. "As a businesswoman, have you ever extended credit to a bad account?"

He waited, but she did not answer.

"I'm sure you have," he said. "And what did you do when
a customer did not pay you? Did you continue to let him take
merchandise from you, knowing in all probability he would
never pay you?"

"There are plenty of people here today who know well
enough that I have given them credit during some pretty
tough times," she answered at last. "When I trust someone, I
do what I can to help them."

"As do I," countered Royce. "I have made loans and extended credit and helped nearly every man here. But in the
face of consistent nonpayment, I doubt very much if you
would blithely let a man go on running up a bill at your ex-
pense. If you operated that way, you would not have survived
in business so long. Well, in the case of the Shaws, I have been
extremely lenient. I have done all that is in my power to keep
it from coming to what has transpired this past week. You ask
Patrick Shaw himself—he's standing right back there."

Royce pointed to the back of the crowd, and heads turned
in that direction. "Ask him. What did I do when he missed his
first payment . . . his second . . . his third? I did nothing. I continued to be patient, hoping somehow that he would be able to
pull himself together and catch up and fulfill his obligations."

Royce paused a moment, seemingly to allow Mr. Shaw to
say something if he wanted. But Shaw only kept looking at
the ground, kicking the dirt around with his boot.

"I would say that I have been extremely patient," Mr.
Royce went on. "I have done nothing that any honest busi-
nessman wouldn't have done. If you were in my position,
Almeda, you would have been forced into the same action."

By now the crowd had begun to quiet down. They may
not have liked it, but most knew Royce's words were true.
They didn't know he was only telling them half the truth—
that he had refused to rescind the note-call even if Mr. Shaw
made up the four months.

Royce turned and squarely faced the crowd. He spoke as
if Almeda were not even present beside him, and gave her no
opportunity to get in another word.

"Let me tell you, my friends, a little about how banking
works. Banking is like any other business. When my esteemed

opponent here—" he indicated Almeda with a wave of his hand, without turning to look at her, "—offers you a gold pan or a saddle for sale, she has had to buy that pan or saddle from someone else. Now as a banker, the only commodity I have to offer is money. She sells mining equipment. I sell money. Now, I have to get that money from somewhere in order to have it to lend. And do you know where I get it?" He paused, but only for a second.

"I get it from the rest of you," he went on. "The money I loaned Patrick Shaw for his house and land came from money that others of you put in my bank. I lend out *your* money to Mr. Shaw, he pays me interest, and then I pay *you* interest, keeping out a small portion as the bank's share. Mr. Shaw didn't borrow money from *me*. In a manner of speaking, he borrowed money from the rest of you! All of you who have borrowed money from the Royce Miners' Bank have really borrowed it from one another. You who receive interest from the bank are in actuality getting that interest from your friends and neighbors."

Everyone was quiet again and was listening carefully.

"If someone doesn't pay the bank what he has agreed to pay, then how can the bank pay the rest of you the interest due you? What I have done is the most painful thing a banker ever has to face. The agonizing inner turmoil it causes a man like me to have to find himself in the odious position of calling a note due, it is so painful as to be beyond words. And yet I have a responsibility to the rest of you. How can I be faithful to the whole community and its needs if I ignore such problems? My bank would soon be out of business, and then where would this community be?"

He waited just a moment to let his question sink in, then answered it himself.

"I will tell you where it would be. When a loan gets behind and goes bad, the real injury is to *you*. As much as I don't like to say it, Patrick Shaw really is indebted to the rest of you, his friends. His failure to make his payments hurts *you* as much as it hurts the bank. He has not paid *you* what he owes. And if that sort of thing is allowed to go unchecked, it puts the bank in a very serious position. Before long, I might have to call another loan due from another one of you, in order to raise the funds to make up for the note which has been defaulted upon. Do you see, my friends? Do you understand the problem? Do you see the dilemma I'm in?

"All the loans I have made are subject to a thirty-day call, just like Mr. Shaw's. In other words, the bank can legally call *any* note due at any time. Now a banker hates to call a loan due, because it is a very painful experience, as painful for a sensitive man like me as it is to a family who must pack up and leave a home where they have invested years. But if a loan is allowed to go bad, then another loan must be called from someone else, to keep the bank healthy. And so it goes. One can never tell when circumstances may force a banker to begin calling many loans due, in order to carry out his wider obligations to the entire community.

"This is why I said earlier that *if* Miracle Springs is to have a future, it must rest upon the solid financial base that I and the Royce Miners' Bank can give it. Without that solid base, I fear many loans may have to be called due, and Miracle Springs could become one of those ghost towns Mrs. Hollister spoke about. As your mayor, I hope and pray I will be able to keep that from happening."

He stepped back and began to descend from the platform, then turned back for one final statement, as if wanting to avoid any possible confusion.

"I want it to be very clear that if I am elected mayor, I will work strenuously toward a strong financial base, to make sure that what has befallen our friend Mr. Shaw, with whom I deeply sympathize, does not happen to any of the rest of you. In other words, I do not see a string of foreclosures in any way as inevitable, so long as the bank, and I personally, are able to remain in a strong position in the community. I clarify this because I did not want any of you to misunderstand my words."

No one did. Franklin Royce had made himself perfectly clear to everyone!

The banker stepped down, passing close to Pa.

"If you know what's good for that wife of yours, Hollister," he said quietly but with a look of menace in his eye, "you'll get her out of this race before election day. If she's going to continue her attacks against me, she'll find two can play that game! And I warn you, the consequences will prove none too pleasant for either of you!"

He walked on. Pa did not say a word.

Mr. Royce strode straight back toward the bank. The crowd of people quietly began to disperse toward their homes. Hardly a man or woman anywhere liked the banker, but everyone was afraid of him. As sorry as they were for the Shaws, no one wanted to find himself in the same position. And as much as they'd have liked to help, no one had the kind of money it would take to do any good.

Almeda followed Royce down off the platform. She looked at Pa with kind of a discouraged sigh.

"Best speech I ever heard!" said Pa.

She tried to laugh, but the look on her face was anything but happy.

"I may as well have been talking into the wind for all the good it will do," she said.

"Everyone loved it," I told her. "You should have seen their faces! And they clapped about everything you said."

"Both of you are determined to cheer me up," she said, laughing now in earnest. "But you saw what happened—Royce has let it be known that if he doesn't win, more foreclosures will follow. Nobody's going to take that chance, no matter what I say, even if they might actually prefer to vote for me."

That evening it was pretty quiet. I could tell Almeda was thinking hard on her decision to go back into the race and wondering if she had done the right thing.

"Why don't I just go to Franklin," she said at last, "and meet with him privately, and tell him that if he will reconsider the terms of the Shaws' note, I will withdraw from the race? Maybe I was wrong to think we could take him on and actually stop him. But at least maybe we could save the Shaws' place."

"Won't work, Almeda," Pa said.

"Why not? He wants to be mayor, and I'll give him the election. He will have won. He'll have beaten me."

Pa gave a little chuckle, although it wasn't really a humorous one. "As much as you like to complain about us men not understanding women, and about how your kind are the only ones who *really* know how things work, I must say, Almeda, you don't understand men near as much as you might think."

"What do you mean, Drummond?"

"This election isn't about being mayor. It might have been at first, but not anymore."

"What's it about, then?"

"It's about manhood, about strength . . . about power."

She cocked her eyebrow at him.

"Don't you see, Almeda? You challenged Royce for the whole town to see. You've had the audacity not just to run against him, but to pass out flyers, to make speeches, and to ignore two or three warnings from him to stop. You're challenging his right to be the most powerful person in these parts. And your being a woman makes it all the more galling to him. He was there this afternoon. He could see as well as everyone else that folks like you better than him. And he hates you for it. It's gone past just winning for him now. Down inside he wants to crush you, punish you for making people doubt him. Winning isn't enough. He's got to make you pay for what you've done. It wouldn't surprise me if he did what he's done to Pat to get back at us, besides telling the rest of the town not to fool with him."

"Then that's all the more reason we've got to find some way to help!"

"I don't see what we can do," said Pa.

"But why wouldn't he be satisfied with me withdrawing? How does it help him to foreclose and take the Shaws' place?"

"Well, for one thing," Pa replied, "something tells me he wants Pat's place. I don't know why, because according to Pat the gold's about played out. But if I know Royce, it's no accident that he set his sights on Pat's note. And that's just the other reason it ain't gonna do no good. He's gonna find some way to get back at you, and he's also gonna make an example of Pat that folks around here aren't likely to forget anytime soon."

"What harm would it do him to simply let it be known, 'If you elect me mayor, I'll let the Shaws keep their place. But let this be a lesson to you not to cross me, or you might find yourself in the same position'?"

"Power, Almeda—I told you already. If he did that, it would be like backing down. You would have arm-twisted him to letting Pat off, and the whole town would know it. Royce would think you made him look weak. Everyone would know that he was capable of backing down, and so they wouldn't take his threats as seriously. No, I tell you, he's not gonna back down about the Shaws, no matter what you or I or anyone else does. The memory of Pat and Chloe and them kids of theirs having to pack up and leave—that'll keep folks in line as far as Royce is concerned for a long time. Everyone'll know he means to follow through with what he says. He may hate it that folks like you better and would vote for you if they could. But he wants them to fear his power even more than he wants them to like him. And now that you've challenged that, he'll be all the more determined to run Pat off his land, *and* hurt you any way he can in the process."

Almeda sighed. "I just can hardly believe any man would be so vindictive as you say—even Franklin Royce."

"Believe it, Almeda. I saw the look in his eye when he got down off that platform this afternoon. I've met men like him before, and I know the kind of stuff they're made of. And it ain't good."

"Do you really think he'll try to hurt me?"

"He won't go out and find a man like Buck Krebbs to send after you, if that's what you mean. He might have done that to me in the past, but he'll use different ways on you. I have the feeling we've only seen the beginning of his campaign tactics. If I know Royce, and I think I do, it's already a lot bigger in his mind than just the election. I think we may have made an enemy, Almeda, and the town might not be big enough to hold both of us."

Pa was right. It didn't take long to see that Mr. Royce did not intend to stop with mere speechmaking.

Three days later, on Wednesday morning, when Almeda and I arrived in town for the day, a man high up on a ladder was painting a sign across the front of the vacant store building two doors down from the bank. In the window was a poster that said "Coming Soon."

By noon the words the man was painting in bright red had become plain. The sign read: *Royce Supplies and Shipping.*

Meanwhile, I had finished the article I'd been writing.

Going around telling folks about Sunday's speech gave me the chance to get some last interviews. Folks were really ready to talk to me now! I had a long conversation with Almeda on Friday, and then spent the rest of that day and most of Saturday writing and rewriting the final copy. By this time there was a stage running on Saturday too, and I sent off the article to Mr. Kemble by the afternoon mail, along with a letter.

Mr. Kemble had said earlier that he'd pay me $1 for an election article, but things had changed now on account of the Fremont article. I told him that since he'd paid Robin O'Flaridy $4 for his small article about Miracle Springs, I figured what I'd written here was worth at least $7. But I would be willing to settle for $4 because I knew he couldn't pay a woman more than a man. But I would not take one penny less than $4. If he didn't want to pay me that much, he could send the pages back and I would print it somewhere else.

At the end of the letter, I asked Mr. Kemble when the article about Mr. Fremont would be appearing. I thought it important that the *Alta* run my version before the *Globe* had a chance to do a story based on the false information and quotes and interviews of Derrick Gregory. Had it already run and somehow I had missed seeing it? I knew that really couldn't be possible since we got the *Alta* in Miracle Springs (though still two days late), and I had been watching for it every day. I couldn't for the life of me figure out why it hadn't run yet. Nearly two weeks had passed, and the election was getting closer and closer, and I wanted the people of California to know the truth about Mr. Fremont.

Six days later, the following Friday, in the same mail pouch that brought the copies of the *Alta* to Miracle Springs, was a packet addressed to me from Mr. Kemble. In it was a check for $4, and a copy of Wednesday's edition containing my story in full. There was no letter, and no answers to any of my questions. But I hardly cared about that right then! There in the middle of the fifth page, running across two columns, were the words in bold black type: "Mayor's Race Matches Businesswoman against Town Banker."

I found a quiet place, then sat down to read over the words I had written.

> Among the many mining towns of northern California, most of the big news in recent years always had to do with gold. But in the growing community of Miracle Springs, no one is talking about gold these days. Instead, people are talking about the town's first election for mayor, which will be held on November 4, concurrent with the national election between John Fremont and James Buchanan.
>
> This election is big news because of the two individuals who are running against each other. As reported in this paper last month, the election matches longtime Miracle Springs banker Franklin Royce against equally longtime businesswoman Almeda Parrish Hollister.

That's right! Businesswoman. Mrs. Hollister, one of the first women in the west to seek office, will not even be able to vote herself. Yet she hopes to sway enough men in the community to upset rival Royce, who must be considered the favorite.

The campaign between the two town leaders is a hot one, with emotions and reaction among the voters running high.

Franklin Royce first arrived in Sacramento from Chicago in early 1850. He was sent west by the banking firm Jackson, Royce, Briggs, and Royce—a company begun by his father and uncle—to explore possibilities for branch offices in the new gold rush state. He opened an office in Sacramento, but later that year took out a $40,000 loan and moved north to the foothills community of Miracle Springs, where he opened the doors of Royce Miners' Bank. When asked why he chose Miracle Springs, Royce replied, "I wanted to become involved in banking closer to the source, where men were actually digging gold out of the streams. That seemed to me to provide the greatest opportunity for me as a banker, as well as open up the greatest potential for helping a young community grow and prosper."

Within two years, Royce had made Miracle Springs his permanent home and had completely withdrawn from his position with Jackson, Royce, Briggs, and Royce of Sacramento and Chicago. Since that time Mr. Royce has played an active role in helping the young community to grow. According to Royce, his bank has financed the building of 80 percent of the community's homes and has been an active supporter of the miners and their interests.

"Who could be better qualified to lead such a diverse community forward than one like myself, who has been such an intrinsic part of helping in its growth up till now?" said Royce.

Mrs. Hollister came to Miracle Springs a few months before her opponent. She was Almeda Parrish then, and she and her husband had come to California from Boston. After a brief stint attempting to find gold himself, Mr. Parrish started the Parrish Mine and Freight Company. Upon his death from tuberculosis in the early winter months of 1851, his wife decided to keep the business going and to remain in Miracle Springs.

She has been there ever since. During those years, Parrish Mine and Freight has been involved with the miners of the region in nearly every phase of supply and delivery, from small gold pans to the ordering and installation of large equipment for some of the major quartz operations in the surrounding foothills.

Two years ago, the businesswoman and widow married Miracle Springs miner Drummond Hollister.

When asked why she felt qualified to become Miracle Springs' mayor, Mrs. Hollister replied, "I realize the new state of California has never had a woman mayor before. However, I feel that changing times are coming, and that women will play a vital role in the future of this state and this great country of ours. As mayor of Miracle Springs I would bring an integrity and forthrightness to the office, and the families of this town would be able to trust that their future was being watched out for by one of their own."

All the women, of course, although unable to vote, expressed strong support for Mrs. Hollister. "I think the idea of a woman mayor shows what a wonderful thing democracy is," commented the local schoolteacher, Miss Harriet Stansberry.

Among the men, opinions were strong on both sides. Several miners and ranchers expressed reservations about a banker as mayor. "I ain't never yet met a banker I had much a hankering to trust further'n I could throw him!" commented one old miner who said he had been in Miracle Springs longer than both candidates put together. The same prospector added, 'Why, if anybody oughta be mayor of this here place, blamed if it don't seem like it oughta be me. I'm the first one in these parts to find gold anyway!"

Others, who did not want to be identified, also said from their dealings with the two candidates, they felt more trusting toward Mrs. Hollister. "She ain't one to short a feller so much as a penny," said one man. "Don't matter what kind of dealings you have with her, she always gives you the best price and a little more than you asked for. But you're never gonna get something for nothing at no bank, that's for sure!"

Many of the men said they had nothing but the highest regard for Mrs. Hollister, but some expressed concern. "She's a nice enough woman, but that don't mean she ought to be mayor. It's a man's job. I just can't see that I want no woman being leader of my town. Somehow it just ain't right. Mayoring's gotta be something a man does."

Among such men, the comment of one local saloon owner seemed to sum up what many thought, "It don't really matter what I think of Mr. Royce or Mrs. Hollister, there's only one man running. And since only men can vote, I figure they'll stick by their kind."

Whether that proves to be true, and the men of Miracle Springs elect as their mayor the only man on the ballot, Franklin Royce, or whether they go against the odds and elect California's first female mayor, Mrs. Almeda Hollister, the fact is that this election is one to watch. It is surely one of the most unusual elections in all California this year. Whether she wins or loses, Mrs. Hollister is a pioneer in a state full of pioneers. And if she should win, not only the rest of the state, but the whole country will be watching.

*W*e all thought Mr. Royce's decision to open Royce's Supplies and Shipping was a pretty underhanded thing to do. By the time his sign was finished, word had gotten around town about it, and a lot of people were upset that he'd try such a deceitful, low-down tactic as attempting to run Almeda out of business.

But we didn't know the half of it yet. Within a week of Almeda's speech, we began to get wind of a rumor circulating about town. Almeda, according to the gossip, had presented herself falsely to the people of Miracle Springs. She had left Boston and come to California to escape the worst tarnish a woman's reputation could have. Some even said she had met and married Mr. Parrish on the ship north from Panama.

But the worst rumors had to do not with Almeda's past, but with her present. They said that the baby she was carrying was not a Hollister at all.

Franklin Royce, of course, never appeared as the author of the rumors surrounding Almeda. He remained too skillfully concealed behind the scenes for anyone to suspect that he was doing anything other than expressing mild curiosity at the tale as it had been told to him by others.

When the whisper first awoke it was merely the hint that the former Mrs. Parrish had not been a Parrish at all in Boston. In its later stages was added the idea that her former name— however well hidden she had kept her past—was one that all Boston knew. Furthermore, it was said that whatever she had done, although no one could say of a certainty what exactly it was, it was enough to have barred her from the society of respected people. She had escaped the East on a steamer, leaving more than one broken heart behind her—some even said a child. On the boat she fell in with the late Mr. Parrish. The evil gossip reached its culmination with the final suggestion having to do with Pa and her present predicament—something about the chickens of her past coming back to roost. Or, more aptly, the roosters.

We went about our business as usual. Not many people came in to the freight office, and neither Almeda nor I thought much about the occasional peculiar looks on the faces of those people we saw. Whether Marcus or Mr. Ashton had heard anything, I don't know. They acted normal. It did seem activity in town was quieter than usual toward the end of that week. But still we remained in the dark about the talk that was spreading from mouth to mouth.

Sunday came, and we all went to church. The service was quiet and somber. Afterward nobody came up and greeted Pa or Almeda, but just walked off silently in the direction of their horses and wagons. It was eerie and uncomfortable, but still we suspected nothing. We all figured it was a result of the scare Mr. Royce had put into everyone the week before. But the fact that some of his best friends had seemed to avoid him and hadn't come over at least to shake his hand got Pa pretty agitated during the ride home.

All that day none of the whispers and lies and gossip reached the ears of the Hollister and Parrish and Belle clan out where we lived on the edge of Miracle Springs Creek.

Early Monday morning, a buggy drove up carrying Rev. Rutledge and Miss Stansberry. They came to the door while we were eating breakfast. Both wore serious expressions.

"We just heard," said the minister.

"Heard what?" said Pa, rising to invite them in with a smile.

"One of the children who came early to school was talking," he went on. "That's how Harriet heard. She put one of the older children in charge, then came right to me. We drove out here immediately. Believe me, Drummond, Almeda . . ." he glanced at them both as he spoke, still very seriously. "Believe me, I don't believe a word of it. What can we do to help?"

Pa glanced around dumbfounded, then let out a good-natured laugh. "Avery," he said. "I don't have the slightest notion what you're talking about!"

"Almeda?" said Rev. Rutledge.

"It's the truth, Avery. What is it that's got the two of you so worked up and so glum?"

"You really don't know," said Miss Stansberry, almost in amazement. "Oh, you poor dear!"

"Drummond, we have to have a serious talk," said Rev. Rutledge. "What we have to discuss has to be talked about alone."

Pa gave me and Zack a nod. "You heard the Reverend," he said. "Go on . . . git." We silently obeyed, but curious beyond belief.

We heard nothing from inside for probably ten minutes. Then the door of the house was thrown open and out exploded Pa, his face red, his eyes flaming. I'd never seen any man, much less Pa, so filled with anger!

"Drummond, please!" called out Almeda, coming through the door after him. "Please . . . wait!"

"There ain't nothing to discuss, nothing to wait for!" Pa shot back as he strode to the barn. "It's clear enough what I gotta do!"

"We don't know it was him."

" 'Course we do, woman! You told me yourself what he said. No one but him knows anything about Boston. It was him, and you know it!"

Pa was inside the barn, already throwing a saddle over his favorite and fastest horse. Almeda followed him inside.

"At least let me go talk to him first," she pleaded.

"Time for talking's over, Almeda. A man's gotta protect his own, and now I reckon it's my turn to do just that."

"Drummond, please . . . don't do something you'll regret!"

"I won't take my gun with me, if that's what you mean." He was cinching up the straps already.

"Drummond," said Almeda, more softly now, putting her hand on his arm and trying to calm him down. "I can live through this. You don't have to defend me to that evil man. The Lord has healed and restored and remade me. And I am at peace in his love, and yours. I don't care what people say, or even what they think. Drummond, don't you see? I know that God loves me just for who I am—past, present, and future. And I know that you love me in just the same way. That's all I need."

Pa seemed to flinch for just a moment in his determination. Then he said, "I understand that, Almeda. And I'm thankful for what God's done. But sometimes a man's got to stand up for truth, and stand up and defend maybe his own reputation, or maybe his wife's. And even if it don't matter to you, it matters to me what the people of this town think. That man's got no right to say dishonoring things about my wife, or about any woman! And I aim to show this town that he can't get away with it without answering to me! I'm sorry, but I just ain't gonna be talked out of this. I gotta do what's right!"

Pa pulled himself up in the saddle, then paused again and glanced around where all the rest of us were watching and listening, in fear and worry, having no idea what was happening.

"Zack, Corrie," Pa said after a couple of seconds, "you two come with me. At least having my own kids around might keep me from killing the scum!"

In an instant Zack and I were throwing saddles on our horses, and in less than two minutes we galloped out of the barn, chasing Pa down the road toward town.

*Z*ack and I never did catch up with Pa. By the time we rode into the middle of town, we were just in time to see him dismounting in front of the bank.

We galloped up, jumped off our horses, and ran inside after him. The bank had only been open a few minutes, so there were several early-morning customers inside. By the time we got through the door, Pa was already in Mr. Royce's office. His voice was loud enough that you could hear it through the whole building. Everyone else's business had ceased, and they stood stock-still with wide open eyes, listening to the argument going on in the next room.

"Look, Royce," Pa was saying, "I never had much liking for you. But I figured maybe that's just the way bankers were. So I kept my distance and held my peace. But now you've gone too far!"

"I don't have any idea what you're talking about," replied the banker, keeping his calm.

"I ain't ashamed to tell you to your face, I think you're a liar!"

"Careful, Mr. Hollister. Those are strong words."

"Not too strong for the likes of a man who's so afraid of losing an election to a woman that he'd drag her reputation through the mud and spread lies about her. Only the lowest kind of man with no sense of shame would do a thing as vile as that!"

"I tell you, Mr. Hollister, I don't know what you're referring to. I confess I have heard some rumors lately that—"

"Heard them?" exploded Pa. "You started them!"

Slowly Zack and I inched our way toward the open door of the office. I was terrified! I think Pa forgot us after telling us to come with him.

"Accusations, especially false ones, can cost a candidate an election, Mr. Hollister. You would do well to guard your tongue, or your wife will suffer even worse consequences on election day than she has already suffered because of her past reputation."

He still sat calmly behind his big desk, almost with a look of humor in his expression. Pa was standing, leaning over the desk at him. If Mr. Royce was afraid, he didn't show it. He looked as if he had expected the confrontation, and was glad other townspeople were hearing it.

"I ain't said a false word yet!" exclaimed Pa. "Do you deny to my face that you've been talking about Almeda and making up this gossip about her life before she got here?"

"I do."

"Then I tell you again, you're a blamed liar!" Pa's voice was loud and his face was still red.

"Look, Mr. Hollister," said the banker. His eyes squinted and his voice lost whatever humor it might have had. "I've taken about all of your ranting accusations I'm going to take. Now unless you want me to send for Sheriff Rafferty and have you locked up for harassment, you had better leave."

"Simon, lock me up?" roared Pa.

"You and I both know there are worse charges that could be brought against you. When I am mayor, I may find myself compelled to have the sheriff look into *your* past more carefully."

"Simon knows all about my past! And you ain't gonna be mayor of *this* town, Royce, you scoundrel. Not while I have anything to say about it! Any lowlife who'd try to hurt a woman to make himself look good ain't the kind of man who's good enough for anything but—"

"Your wife doesn't have a reputation worth protecting, Hollister!" interrupted the banker, finally getting angry himself. He half rose out of his chair. "You know as well as I do that everything that's being said about her is true. If you don't, and you married her thinking she's the unspoiled preacher-woman she pretends to be, then you're a bigger fool than I took you for!"

"Do you dare to tell me to my face that my wife—"

"Your wife is nothing but a harlot, Hollister! Anybody in Boston could tell you—"

But his words were unwisely spoken. Before another sound was out of his mouth, Pa had shoved the banker's desk aside. He took two steps around it, and the next instant his fist went crashing into the white face of Franklin Royce.

Stunned, Royce staggered backward. Losing his balance, he fell over his own chair and toppled backward onto the floor.

Quickly he started to scramble up. But seeing Pa standing over him, fist still clenched, trembling with righteous anger in defense of the woman he loved, apparently made Royce think better of it.

Then Royce noticed the blood flowing from his nose and around the side of his mouth.

"You'll pay for this, Hollister," he seethed through clenched teeth while his hand sought a handkerchief to stop the blood.

"Your threats don't mean nothing to me," said Pa. "You do what you think you can to me, Royce. Do it like a man, face to face—if you got guts enough! But if I hear of you speaking another word against my wife, I tell you, you'll answer to me! And next time I don't aim to be so gentle!"

He turned and strode with huge quick steps out of the office, hardly looking at us, but saying as he passed, "Come on, kids, let's get out of this scoundrel's hole!"

We followed Pa to the door, while the customers and two clerks watched in shocked silence.

Mr. Royce came running to his office door, a handkerchief to his nose and mouth, and shrieked after us, "You're through, Hollister—you hear me? You're through! You'll regret this day as long as you live!"

But Pa didn't even slow down, only slammed the door behind us with a crash.

Repercussions
CHAPTER TWELVE

All Pa said on the way home was, "I'm sorry you kids had to see that . . . but maybe your being there kept me from doing worse."

About halfway back, we met Rev. Rutledge and Miss Stansberry. Pa stopped, and the minister drew in his reins.

"I'm obliged to the two of you for coming and telling us," Pa said. "I'm afraid you wouldn't approve of what I done, Reverend."

"I understand, Drummond," he replied.

"Well, I'm thankful we got you two for friends," Pa added, tipping his hat, and then moving on.

When we got home, Almeda's eyes were red. I knew she'd been crying. Pa kissed her, then put his arms around her and the two of them just stood in each other's embrace for a long time. Nothing more about the incident was said that day.

Almeda considered whether to go into town at all, now that we all understood why folks had been behaving so strangely.

"We gotta face this thing head on," said Pa. "You go into the office—I'll go with you if you like. We gotta go on with our business and show folks we ain't concerned about Royce and his rumors. We'll go around to people one at a time and tell 'em to pay no attention to what they hear, that it's all a pack of lies drummed up to make you look bad before the election."

"You know I couldn't do that," Almeda replied softly, looking Pa directly in the eyes. "But you're right—it's best we go on with our lives as usual. Corrie and I will go into the office."

"You want me to go into town with you for the day?"

"No, I'll be all right. I'll do my best to put on a brave face."

In the four years I'd known Almeda, I'd never seen her quite like this. Her voice was soft and tired, without its usual enthusiasm and confidence. It was easy to see this was really a blow to her, and that she might not get over it so quickly. All day long her eyes remained red, though I never saw her cry again. I guess the tears stayed inside.

By the time we walked into the Parrish Mine and Freight office two hours later, the whole town was stirred up all over again by news of what Pa had done to Mr. Royce. Old widow Robinson had been in the bank at the time and had heard every word. And that was enough to ensure that within an hour, every man, woman, and child for ten miles around knew about it! The widow's reputation for spreading information certainly proved itself true. Franklin Royce himself never appeared for two days after that, so the news had to have come through someone else who was present, and most bets were on Mrs. Robinson. In all likelihood, she was the one Royce had used to plant the rumors about Almeda. He probably told her in hushed tones, making her promise to keep it to herself, no doubt saying that he'd assured the person *he'd* heard it from that he would say nothing to anybody.

Suddenly the first rumor was old news, and began to take a back seat to steadily exaggerating tales of what Pa had done. At first it was just that he had given the banker a good sound thrashing. Then mention was made of sounds of violence, angry threats yelled back and forth, sounds of scuffling and furniture being broken, and even blood, along with vows to get even. All in all, the story as Marcus Weber said he'd heard it was a considerably wilder affair than what Zack and I actually witnessed with our own eyes.

But it did manage to lessen the impact of what had been circulating about Almeda. Even though they feared him, not too many people liked Franklin Royce much. I think the incident was talked about so much because everybody was secretly pleased to see Royce get his due for once.

Yet they were afraid too, for Pa and Almeda. If Franklin Royce promised to get even, they said with serious expressions, he was not one to make empty threats. As for the election, who could tell now? Royce was a dangerous opponent, and *they* sure wouldn't want to have crossed him! They wished someone else could be mayor, but they had to admit, with Royce as an enemy, the prospects didn't look too good for the Hollisters.

With Almeda, the distance and silence and curious looks turned into sympathy. Pa silenced the gossip once and for all, and nobody was inclined to spread the rumors any further and run the risk of Pa finding out. Whether folks believed what they'd heard—and after what Pa did, I think most figured Royce had made it all up—they didn't show it, and talk now centered around Pa.

When Mr. Royce began to be seen around town again, he kept his distance. However, he continued his subtle tactics both to make sure people voted for him, and to pressure Almeda into capitulating. By the end of the week, the sign across the street was done, and there was activity inside the place, as well as some merchandise displayed in the shop windows. Almeda muttered a time or two, "Where can he have gotten that stuff so quickly?" But there seemed to be no question about it—he *had* it, and *was* going to open a business to compete with Parrish Mine and Freight. And obviously his intent was not merely to compete, but to drive her out of business. A second paper soon appeared in the window: "Mining, ranching, farming tools, supplies, and equipment at the least expensive prices north of Sacramento. Shipping and freight services also available."

That same week, whispers of a new kind arose. If Franklin Royce did not become Miracle Springs' next mayor, it was said that he would be forced to review all outstanding loans, and would more than likely be compelled to call a good many of them due. As much as they respected Pa for standing up for his wife's honor, and as little as they cared for Royce, most of the men were agreed that they just couldn't take the chance of having what had happened to Pat Shaw happening to them. They *had* to vote for Royce. They just didn't have any other choice.

To make matters worse, Pa got an official-looking letter from some government office in Sacramento saying that the title to his land was being challenged in court by an anonymous plaintiff, and that investigators would be contacting him shortly for additional information.

"Well, if that don't just about do it!" said Pa, throwing the letter down and storming about the room. "The man's not gonna stop till he's ground us into the dirt and got our land and our business and everything!"

He walked angrily out of the house. Almeda picked up the letter and read it, then showed it to the rest of us.

"I think we'd better pray for your father," she said softly. We all sat down and took hands, while Almeda prayed out loud for Pa, for the claim, for Mr. Royce, and for God's purpose to be accomplished through all these things that were happening to us. "And show us what you want us to do, Lord," she concluded. "Make it plain, and give us the strength and courage to do it—whether we're to give in, or whether we're to stand up and fight for what we think is right. Help us not to act in our own wisdom, but to depend on you to show us what you want."

When Pa walked in a few minutes later, he was calm and quiet. He sat down, rested his chin between his hands, and let out a big sigh. Anger had obviously given way to defeat and frustration.

"We gotta quit, Almeda," he said at length. His voice was soft and discouraged. "I wish I'd never got you into this."

"You didn't get me into a thing, Drummond. I made the decision to run for mayor on my own. I brought this trouble on the rest of you."

"Well, I sure didn't make it no better, flying off against Royce like I done. Though the rascal deserved it!"

"Now we've got to decide what's to be done. With Franklin threatening two claims, ours and Shaw's, there's no telling where it'll end. Not to mention the business in town."

"We gotta give in," said Pa, in as depressed a voice as I'd ever heard from him. "He's got us licked. If we let him have the election, maybe he'll lay off from all this other harm he's trying to bring us."

Fighting Fire with Fire
CHAPTER THIRTEEN

I don't know if all marriages work this way, but I'd noticed that Pa and Almeda were both quicker to defend each other than they were themselves. When Franklin Royce started spreading gossip about Almeda around town, Pa got so filled with anger that he went right into Royce's office and knocked the banker down and bloodied his nose. Pa knew it was *his* duty to defend Almeda's honor, not hers.

And in the same way, Almeda would fight for Pa. When folks were talking about her, Almeda couldn't help the discouragement it caused. But now that Mr. Royce was threatening Pa and was threatening to take away all Pa had worked for and held dear, it was *her* turn to get fighting mad, like a mother bear protecting her family. The banker could threaten her reputation and her business all he wanted, but once he dared threaten the husband she loved—look out! She wasn't about to take that lying down!

"He's not going to lay off, Drummond," she said to Pa's last statement after a few moments' thought. "There are times when to lay down your arms and surrender is the best course of action. Jesus said we must deny ourselves, and do it every day. But there are also times when wrong must be fought with aggressiveness. Jesus did that too. He laid down his life without a word of self-defense, but he also drove the moneychangers out with a whip and strong words. How to know when to do which is the challenge for a Christian. And I can't help thinking that this is a time for the whip and strong words."

"We've already tried it," said Pa, "you with your handbills and your speech, and me with my ranting and raving like an idiot in Royce's bank. All we've done is made him madder and made it worse for everyone around here."

"The Lord will show us what to do. The children and I were just praying while you were outside. We asked him to make it plain what we're to do and to give us the courage to—"

She stopped and her face got serious a moment, then lit up.

"You know, I just had a thought," she said. "A wild, crazy, impossible idea!" She pressed her hands against her forehead and thought hard again. "It's too unbelievable an idea ever to work, but . . . if God is behind it . . . you just never know what can happen!"

"What in tarnation is it?" exclaimed Pa. "Your face looks like you swallowed a lantern. It must be *some* notion that's rattling through that brain of yours!"

She laughed. "It is, believe me. It just might be the highest-stakes poker game you ever played, Drummond Hollister, with the mines and homes of every man in Miracle Springs in the middle of the table—winner take all. And if Franklin Royce doesn't blink first and back down, and if he decides to call our bluff, then it just might cost more people than the Shaws their places."

"Sounds like a mighty dangerous game."

"I'm afraid it is. That's why we have to pray hard for God to show us if this is *his* idea, or just something my own mind cooked up."

"Then let's pray that right now," said Pa, "before it goes any further." He got down on his knees. "Come on, kids," he said to all the rest of us. "We got some serious praying to do, and it's gonna take all seven of us. We've gotta do what the Book says and ask the Lord above for wisdom, cause if we do wrong, a lot of folks are gonna be hurt. We gotta be sure we're doing what the Lord wants."

We obeyed, and Pa started to pray. We'd all heard him pray before, but somehow this time there was a new power in his voice that seemed to come from deep down in his heart. When we all got up a few minutes later, I think every one in the room had the sense that God had spoken both *to* Pa, and maybe *through* him to the rest of us. I know what *I* felt inside, and judging from the looks on Pa's and Almeda's faces, I think they too thought the answer was to go ahead.

"Well, don't keep us in suspense, woman," said Pa with a smile. "What's this dangerous new plan you're thinking of?"

"Before we could even know if it had a chance to succeed," she said, "it would take a trip to Sacramento. And with the election coming up so fast, there might not be time. But here's what I'm thinking."

She paused and took a breath.

"Back when we started, and Franklin was doing everything he could to threaten us, he made a comment that I haven't forgotten. He said, 'Two can play this game as well as one.' He was, of course, referring to my flyer and Corrie's interviewing and what he considered our going on the attack against him. But the moment we started praying about what to do, his words came back to me, and I suddenly found myself wondering what is to prevent us from applying the same principle. If he's going to try to undercut us by taking away business from Parrish Mine and Freight, and if he's going to start hurting our friends and neighbors by calling up their loans, then why don't we use the exact same tactic, but in the opposite way? We will take business from *him*, and will try to *help* people at exactly the point where he's trying to hurt them and pressure them into supporting him!"

"Fight fire with fire, eh?" said Pa grinning.

"Exactly! There are times to back down and admit defeat. But I don't think this is one of them. Not yet at least."

"But you shouldn't travel, not in your condition," said Pa. "Whatever's to be done in Sacramento, I can do."

"No, I have to be the one to go," insisted Almeda. "I'll need to see my friend Carl Denver and get his advice. I don't know whether there's anything his company can do, but he might know someone else in the city who can help."

"I'll at least go with you, to make sure you're all right."

"I'll be fine. Besides, you ought to stay here," said Almeda, pointing to the letter that still lay on the table where she had laid it.

The look on Pa's face said he wasn't convinced.

"I'll be fine," she repeated. "I'm a strong woman. Corrie," she said turning to me, "can you handle things at the office?"

I nodded.

"You shouldn't go alone. That I *won't* let you do," said Pa. "Zack," he said, turning his head, "you want to ride to Sacramento with your stepmother, keep her company, and protect her at the same time?"

"You bet, Pa!" Zack replied brightly.

"I'm going to let you take my rifle," Pa added. "But un-less there's trouble, you keep it packed in the saddle case. No foolin' around with it."

"Yes, sir."

"Do you really think that's necessary, Drummond?" asked Almeda.

"Maybe not. But I don't want to take no chances with the two of you out there alone. I don't trust Royce. It ain't been that many years ago he was hiring no-goods like Buck Krebbs to sneak around and set fire to houses. I'd feel safer if I knew Zack had the gun."

"Can I go too, Pa?" asked Tad.

"You couldn't keep up, you pipsqueak!" laughed Zack.

"I could so!" insisted Tad. "I can ride just as fast as you or Little Wolf!"

"That'll be the day! I could ride from here to Little Wolf's and back twice before you'd have your horse out of the barn."

"That ain't so! Why I could—"

"Hey, the two of you—cut it out!" interrupted Pa. "Time's a wastin', you gotta hit the road. Tad," he said, "I gotta have you here with me. If Zack's gonna be protecting your ma, then I'll need your help here watching over the claim. You'll be my number-one man, and I can't have the both of you gone."

Almeda rose, Zack ran outside to the barn, and the rest of us did what we could to help them get ready. In less than an hour, we were watching the dust settle from Almeda's buggy and Zack's horse after they'd rounded the bend in the road and disappeared from sight.

Those next days waiting for Zack and Almeda to get back were dreadful, wondering all the time what was going to come of it.

How wonderful it would be if there was a railroad to Sacramento! They were laying down track for new train lines between the big cities, and the talk of a train connecting the two oceans was enough to make your head swim. I could hardly imagine it! Wagon trains took months to cross the country. Overland stagecoaches, along the southern route where there wasn't as much snow, usually took between thirty and forty days. And stories were told of madcap horsemen who rode their horses to their deaths to make it from St. Louis to San Francisco in fifteen to twenty days. I'd thought about trying to find such a man to interview for an article sometime, to find out if the stories were true about dashing across the plains at a hundred miles a day. But I could barely imagine going across the country in a comfortable train car in only eight or ten days.

Well, they didn't have a train to ride on. But they had good horses, and Zack and Almeda returned faster than Pa had expected. They left on Saturday, and about midday of the following Wednesday Zack and Almeda rode in.

It was obvious from the lather on the horses that they'd been riding hard. Their clothes and faces were covered with dust, and they both looked exhausted. But the instant Almeda saw Pa, she flashed a big smile.

"I got it!" she said excitedly, patting the saddlebags next to her on the buggy seat. "Go get Pat and we'll tell him the news!"

Pa helped her down from the buggy, then gave her a big hug and kiss. "You're a mess, woman!" he laughed, standing back to look over her dirty face.

"Don't push your luck, Drummond Hollister," she replied. "You know how a woman can get riled when she's tired!"

"Well, you heard your ma," said Pa, turning around to the rest of us. "Who wants to ride over the hill and fetch Mr. Shaw here?"

"I will, Pa," I said. "Come on, Tad. Wanna go with me?"

But he was already scampering toward the barn to start saddling his pony. One thing about Tad—he never had to be asked twice!

We took the quickest way to Shaws, the back trail around the mountain. All the way back Mr. Shaw kept quizzing us about what was up, and I said I didn't know all the details, which I didn't, but that Pa and Almeda had some exciting news for him, and they'd tell him everything as soon as we got back to our place.

By the time we arrived back at the house, Almeda had gotten herself cleaned up and had changed clothes. Her eyes looked tired, but the smile still shone from her face.

"Come in . . . come in, Pat," said Pa, shaking Mr. Shaw's hand. "Sit down. Want a cup of coffee?"

"Yeah, thanks, Drum," he replied. "But what's this about anyway?"

"We'll tell you everything, Pat. Just have a seat, and I'll get you that coffee."

Bewildered, Mr. Shaw obeyed.

Pa returned in a minute, handed Mr. Shaw a steaming blue tin cup, then sat down himself. Almeda joined him.

"This has been Almeda's idea from the start," Pa said, "so I reckon I'll let her tell you about the scheme she hatched to try to foil ol' Royce." He cast her a glance, then sat back and took a sip from his own cup.

"It all began last week," Almeda began, "when we were praying about what to do about the election. We were asking the Lord whether to quit and give in, or whether to fight on somehow, even though it seemed, as you men would say, that Franklin held all the right cards. Your note had been called due, we'd just received word that the title to our land was being questioned, and word was going around town that a vote against Franklin Royce would result in the same kinds of things happening to others. We just didn't see what could be done. But then I had an idea! And I think it was God speaking providentially to us. I certainly pray it was, but I suppose time will tell. I have no idea if it will work. And if it goes against us, it could mean doom for everybody."

"I don't understand a word of what you're talking about," said Mr. Shaw. "From where I sit, it don't appear there's nobody in any danger except you folks and us."

"Just hear her out, Pat," said Pa. "Go on, Almeda, quit beating around the bush. Pat's dying of curiosity!"

Almeda smiled. "I just returned from Sacramento," she said. "I rode down there with Zack, and on Monday morning I went to see a man I've known for several years, Carl Denver. He is one of three vice-presidents of the banking and

investment firm Finchwood Ltd. I think they're connected
somehow to a bank in London, but I don't know for sure. My
late husband knew Carl, and when we first came west, Carl
helped my husband secure a small loan to open our business
in Miracle Springs. That loan was paid off long ago, but Carl
and I have kept in touch through the years, and I've borrowed
from them a time or two and have done some freight business
with his firm as well. And now Carl's risen to a fairly promi-
nent position.

"Well, I explained our situation to him. He said he'd read
about the mayor's race in the *Alta*, and I told him the article
was written by my stepdaughter."

She looked over in my direction. I couldn't help but be
pleased that somebody Almeda knew had seen it!

"When I told him some of the things that have happened,
he became positively livid. 'Anything I can do to help,' he said.
'Anything!' But when I mentioned the sum of eighteen thousand dollars, his enthusiasm cooled. 'That's a great deal of
money, Almeda,' he said. I knew that only too well! I'd never
borrowed more than five or six thousand from him before. I
told him I'd secure it with my house and the business and what
stock-in-trade I have, although that wouldn't amount to more
than ten or twelve thousand. I knew it would be going out on
a limb for him, but I assured him that the other property involved—that's yours, Mr. Shaw—was solid, and that we could
add to the collateral amount later to more than cover the full
amount of the loan. He said he'd have to discuss the matter
with the higher-ups of Finchwood, but that he'd do everything
he could on my behalf, and to come back about noon."

"So Zack and I left and I showed him around some of
Sacramento. We had a good time together, didn't we, Zack?"

Zack nodded.

"We returned to Carl's office just before twelve. From the big smile across his face, I could tell he had good news!

" 'You'll never believe this!' he exclaimed. 'I don't believe it myself. But we hit Mr. Finch on just the right day!'

" 'What do you mean?' I asked.

" 'He knows Royce,' Carl answered. 'And in plain English, Almeda—he hates him! Seems several years ago, when different companies were new to California and were trying to get firmly established, Jackson, Royce, Briggs, and Royce pulled some underhanded things against Finchwood. Nearly put them out of business, the way I understand it. And ever since, the rivalry between the two has been fierce . . . and bitter. Just last week, Mr. Finch told me, the old man of the outfit, Briggs, stole one of Finchwood's largest clients away from them. And that's why Finch is roaring mad. I told him that this Royce you're dealing with isn't with his father's firm any longer, but Finch said he didn't care. "A Royce is a Royce!" he said. "And besides, I still owe that young weasel of a Royce a thing or two from '51!" Anyway, I went on to explain your whole predicament to him, and almost before I was done, he said, "Look, Carl, you bring that lady-friend of yours in to meet me. I want to shake hands with the woman with guts enough to square off in an election against that snake. And then you tell her we'll back her up. We don't need her collateral either. I trust her from what I know of her, and your word vouching for her is good enough for me. I'd love to see her put that pretentious imposter out of business, though I don't suppose we could be *that* fortunate!" ' "

Almeda took a breath and smiled.

"I still ain't sure if I see how my property has anything to do with your banking friends," said Mr. Shaw.

"I'm just about to get to that," said Almeda. "Well, Carl took me right into Mr. Finch's office. The president of the company treated me like royalty—got a chair for me, offered me something to drink, and then shook my hand and said what an honor it was for him to meet me! Can you imagine that! An honor for *him* to meet *me*!

"We talked for quite a while. He said he'd investigated the northlands up around here a time or two, and had even thought of expanding and investing in this direction but nothing had ever come of it. The more we talked, the more interested he became, he even scratched his head once and said he thought he'd heard of the new strike at Miracle Springs. 'Had something to do with a kid getting caught in a mine and being pulled out by his brother, didn't it?' I said that indeed it did, and that those two boys were now fine young men and that I was privileged to call them my sons."

Tad was beaming as she spoke.

"He said that if worse came to worst, and he wound up holding mortgages on half a dozen pieces of property, he'd consider it a good investment, and worth every penny to put a corrupt man like Royce out of business."

Finally Almeda looked straight into Mr. Shaw's face. "The long and short of it, Patrick," she said, "is that I brought the solution to your problems with the Royce Miners' Bank home with me from Sacramento right in these saddlebags!"

She picked up the leather pouches that had been sitting beside her, stood up, and turned them upside down. Bundles of paper money poured out onto Mr. Shaw's lap.

All of us gasped. Almeda laughed at everyone's reaction as the fortune in greenbacks spilled onto the chair and floor.

"Thunderation, woman!" roared Pa. "You came all the way from the city with *that* in your bags? What if you'd been stuck up? *Tarnation,* that's a pile of money!"

"I had your son to protect me," Almeda replied. "How could I be afraid? And Zack and I prayed for the Lord's presence to go beside us. We read Psalm 91 together, and we took our Father at his word."

All this time poor Patrick Shaw just sat where he was, in speechless silence, gazing down at more money than he'd ever seen in his life.

"It's to pay off your loan, Pat," said Pa at length. "How many days you got left on the call?"

" 'Bout nine. Chloe's already started to pack up our things."

"Well you tell her to *un*pack them," said Almeda firmly, "and you ride straight into town and march into Royce's bank and put this money down on his desk, and you say to him, 'Mr. Royce, here's your money, just like your notice-of-call said. Now if you don't mind, I'd like a receipt and the clear title to my property.' "

Still dumbfounded and bewildered, Mr. Shaw managed to stammer out the words, "But I can't take this . . . this ain't my money."

"Don't worry, Mr. Shaw," said Almeda. "We'll make everything legal and tidy and you don't have to be concerned about us. We're not *giving* you this money, we're *loaning* it to you. I borrowed it from Mr. Finch at 4.5 percent interest. We will make you the loan at the same rate. You pay off the Royce bank, and next month begin making payments to us instead. We will then pay back Finchwood Ltd. as you pay us. And since the interest rate is less, your payments every month will be less than Franklin was charging you. You'll be out from under his yoke, you'll have your land back, and as long as you keep the payments up from now on, everything will be fine."

"I—I don't know how to thank you," said Mr. Shaw.

"No thanks is needed, Pat," said Pa. "You'd have done the same thing to help us if you were in a position to."

"It's an investment for all of us," added Almeda. "For us and for Mr. Finch, for the future of Miracle Springs and its people, and against the scare tactics of Franklin Royce."

"Well, I reckon I can understand that. But I can't see how it'll help anyone else around. They're still gonna be too afraid to vote against him for mayor. And Royce is liable to be so mad he'll start calling other folks' loans due, and then we'll just be making it worse for everybody."

"You've put your finger right on the risky part of our plan," said Almeda. "Before I left for the south I told Drummond it was going to be like a giant poker game. And here's where we have to hope our bluff works."

"How's paying off my note gonna bluff him?"

"Because you're gonna tell the other men around just what you've done," said Pa. "You're gonna tell them you paid Royce off with money you borrowed, and that there's more where that came from."

"But you can't tell them where we came by it," added Almeda. "Just say that you borrowed it. And then you tell them that we'll back anybody else up whose loan gets called too."

"You mean it?" exclaimed Mr. Shaw in disbelief.

"We mean to try," answered Pa. "You just spread the word around town that nobody's got to be afraid of voting for Almeda on account of what Royce might do with their loans. You tell 'em that *you're* gonna vote for her—that is, you *are* gonna vote for Almeda, ain't you, Pat?"

"You're dang sure I am! After what you've done, how could I not? It's not every man who's got friends like you! You two are just the kind of mayoring this town needs, and I aim to tell everyone I can too!"

"Well, you tell 'em to vote for Almeda and that Royce's not likely to do a thing to 'em. If he tries and starts threatening other folks like he did you, then you tell 'em to come see us."

"I still don't see how you can do such a thing."

"What my husband has been trying to say is that we'll back up our promise as far as we can," said Almeda, "and we're praying it's far enough. Mr. Finch said he would support us up to fifty thousand dollars. That should enable us to protect three or four others from being evicted by Royce. If he persists beyond that, then we could be in trouble. That's when we have to hope he won't call our bluff."

"Well, I'll do what you say."

"Just remember—you keep quiet about all this we talked about," said Pa. "Pay off your loan and start talking up *Hollister for Mayor*. Then we'll leave our friend Royce to stew over it."

*I*f we thought Almeda's handbill caused a commotion, or Pa's marching in and smacking Mr. Royce in the face while the widow Robinson got an earful in the other room, that was *nothing* compared to the uproar caused when Mr. Shaw walked into the Royce Miners' Bank that same afternoon, calmly asked to see Mr. Royce, and then dumped eighteen thousand dollars in green United States bills on the desk in front of him, asking for his change, a receipt, and the cancelled mortgage note and clear deed of trust for his property.

The exclamations from the bystanders, and the look on Mr. Royce's face, according to Mr. Shaw telling us about it later, was a sight to behold.

"His greedy eyes got so big seeing all that money in front of him," he said, "for an instant I thought he was gonna dive right on top of the desk after it! But then the next second he suddenly seemed to remember this money meant he wouldn't be able to get his hands on my land *and* wouldn't be getting that 6.25 percent interest no more.

" 'What kind of a trick is this, Shaw?' he said.

" 'Ain't no trick,' I answered him. 'You called my note due, and there's the payment, just like you asked—nine days early.'

" 'Where'd you get it, Shaw?' he asked.

" 'Nothing in your notice of call said I had to tell you everything I do. You said I had to pay you, and I done it.'

" 'I know you don't have a dime to your name,' he growled. And watching him when I put that money in front of him made me realize that he wasn't after the money at all, but that he wanted my place. 'What did you do, hold up a stage? Or is it counterfeit?'

"By now I was enjoying myself, and I decided to pull a little bluff of my own. 'Mr. Royce,' I said, 'that is good U.S. legal currency. I come by it perfectly legal. I'm paying you off in full with it. Now, if you don't write me a receipt and give my note back showing it's paid in full, with the extra from the eighteen thousand I got coming back, then I'll just be on my way over to the sheriff's office!'

"Well, he blustered a while more, but finally he took the cash and put it in his safe, and got out the papers and signed everything over to me. But he didn't like it, I could tell. There he was with eighteen thousand dollars, and a look on his face like I'd gotten the best of him. And he gave me back the extra—there's $735 back from your $18,000!"

He plunked the money down on the table.

"Keep it, Pat," said Pa. "You use that to clear up your other bills, and if you still got extra, then it'll help make the first few payments."

"Then you come by the office tomorrow," added Almeda, "and we'll draw up a note and some terms. At 4.5 percent, it shouldn't be more than $135 or $140 a month."

"I can't tell you how obliged I am to you!"

"You just get folks over being afraid of voting for us!" said Almeda.

"Oh, I've already been doing that! Once that money fell out onto the desk in Royce's bank, it was like I'd stirred up a hornet's nest! I no more'n walked out the door of the bank, and it seemed the whole town knew already. All the men came pouring out from the stores and their houses, cheering me and shaking my hand and hitting me on the back. Why, you'd have thought I struck a new vein under the mountain! And of course the question they was all asking was, 'Where'd the loot come from, Pat? Where'd you get that kind o' cash?' But I just kinda kept to myself, smiling like I knew a big secret, and said, 'Let's just put it this way, boys. Wherever I got it from, there's more where that came from. And so you don't need to be one bit afraid of what's gonna happen if you vote for Mrs. Hollister for mayor. Matter of fact, boys,' I added, and I let my voice get real soft like I was letting them in on a big secret, 'matter of fact, it's come to my attention that our old friend Royce is charging us all close to 2 percent *more* interest than the going rate down in Sacramento. Unless he's a dang sight dumber than I think, he ain't gonna call your loans due. He's been making a killing on us all these years, and he ain't about to upset his money-cart now.'"

"What did they say to that?" asked Almeda. Pa was laughing so hard from listening to Mr. Shaw that he couldn't say anything!

"They were plenty riled, I can tell you that. And once I told them that I had it on the word of a man I trusted that they'd be protected in the same way if Royce called their loans due, they all walked off saying they weren't gonna vote for no cheat like him for mayor!"

"You done good, Pat," Pa said finally.

"Did you tell anyone that it was us who was behind it?" asked Almeda.

"Rolf Douglas came up to me afterward, kinda quiet. Said he was two months behind with Royce and was afraid he was gonna be next. I told him to go see you, in your office, Mrs. Hollister. I think you can likely expect a call from him real soon."

"Rolf ain't no Widow Robinson," said Pa. "But I don't doubt that word'll manage to spread around."

"Maybe I shouldn't have told him," said Mr. Shaw, worried.

"No, no, Patrick, it's just fine," said Almeda. "Word had to get around. Just so long as folks don't know *how* we were able to do what we have done—at least not for a while. We want to keep Franklin off guard and guessing."

*W*ord got around, all right—in a hurry!

Two days later we got a call from Franklin Royce that was anything but friendly. Pa must have sensed there was fire coming out of the banker's eyes while he was still a long way off. The minute he saw the familiar black buggy, he said to Almeda, "I'll handle this," and walked a little way down the road away from the house.

"I'm here to talk to you and your wife, Hollister," said Mr. Royce, hotly reining his horse up in front of Pa but remaining seated in his carriage. As he spoke he glanced over to where Almeda and I were standing near the door. His eyes threw daggers at us.

"What you got to say, Royce," replied Pa, "you can say to me. I'm not about to put up with any more of your abuse or threats to my wife or daughter. If you haven't learned your lesson from what happened in your bank last week, then maybe I'll have to knock some more sense into that head of yours."

"You dare lay a hand on me, Hollister, and I'll have you up on charges before the day's out!"

"I don't want to hurt you," said Pa. "But if you dare to threaten anyone in my family again, I won't stop with bloodying your nose. Now go on . . . say your piece."

"I'd like to know what the two of you think you're trying to do, paying off Patrick Shaw's note like that?"

"We made him a loan. I don't see anything so unusual in that."

"You're mixing in my affairs, that's what's unusual about it!"

"Ain't no law against loaning money to a friend."

"You don't have that kind of cash!"

Pa shrugged.

"I want to know where you got it!"

"There also ain't no law that gives a banker the right to meddle in someone else's private affairs," Pa shot back. "Where Pat Shaw got the money to pay you off is no more your concern than where we might have gotten it to loan him—that is *if* we had anything to do with all this you're talking about."

"You know good and well you have everything to do with it, you dirty—"

"You watch your tongue!" shouted Pa, taking two steps toward Royce's buggy. "There are ladies present. And if I hear one more filthy word from your mouth, I'll slam it shut so hard you won't speak *any* words for a week!"

Cowed but not humbled, Royce moderated his tone.

"Look, Hollister," he said, "I know well enough that you are behind that money of Shaw's. It's all over town. You know it and I know it and everybody knows it! Now I'm here to ask you—the two of you—" he added, looking over at Almeda, "businessman to businessman, having nothing to do with the election, I'm asking you what are you trying to do by meddling in *my* affairs! Banking and making loans is my business, and you have no call to step into the middle of my dealings with *my* customers! I want to know what your intentions are."

"I figure our intentions are our own business," replied Pa coolly.

"Not when they interfere with *my* business!" Royce shot back. "And word around town is that you intend to continue sticking your nose into my negotiations with people who owe my bank money. So I ask you again, Hollister, what are your intentions?"

"Our intentions are to do what's right," answered Pa.

"Paying off other men's loans, even when they are in legal default?"

"I ain't admitted to doing any such thing."

"Cut the hog swill, Hollister!"

"You want to know my intentions," Pa said. "Then I'll tell you straight: it's my feeling that a man's duty-bound to stand by his neighbors, whatever that means. And that's what I intend to do. I'll tell you, Royce, I'm not really all that concerned about you or your banking business, because from where I stand it seems to me you're looking out for nobody but yourself. Now you can do what you want to me. You can say what you want. You can spread what lies you want. You can sic some investigator on me to try to run me off my land. You can beat my wife in this election. And maybe in the end you *will* run me out of Miracle Springs and will someday own every stitch of land from here to Sacramento. But nothing you do will make me stop standing up for what's right, and for trying to help my friends and neighbors so long as there's anything I can do for them. Now—is that plain-spoken enough for you?"

"So you intend to continue backing up the loans of others around here even if they should be called due, as people are saying?" repeated Royce.

"I said I aim to do what's right."

"What are you trying to do, Hollister, open a bank of your own?"

Pa shrugged. "I got nothing more to say to you."

"You can't do it, Hollister. You'll never pull it off. You can't possibly have enough cash to stand up to me."

Almeda began walking toward the two men.

"Franklin," she said approaching them, "do you remember just after I entered the mayor's race, you said to me, 'Two can play this game?' You were, of course, insinuating that you could be just as underhanded toward me as you thought I was being to you by the publication of my flyer. I think anyone with much sense would say that this last month demonstrates that you have few equals when it comes to underhanded tactics."

"How dare you suggest—" the banker began, but Almeda cut him off immediately.

"Let me finish, Franklin!" she said. "You have spread rumors about me throughout the community. You threatened my daughter and my husband in different ways. And now you are opening a store just down from mine intended, I presume, to drive me out of business. All we have done is help a friend. That hardly compares with your ruthless and self-serving behavior. And if it takes our going into the lending business to keep you from hurting any more of the families in this town, then so be it. Your own words condemn you, Franklin. Two *can* play this game! And if you feel compelled to enter the supplies and freight business, perhaps we will feel compelled to open a second bank in Miracle Springs, so that people can have a choice in where they go for financial help."

"That is utterly ridiculous!" laughed Royce with disdain. "The two of you—a miner and his shopkeeper of a wife—

financing a bank! I've never heard of anything so absurd! It takes thousands, more capital than you'll ever have in your lives! The very notion makes me laugh!"

"You are very cocky, Franklin," she said. "It may well prove your undoing."

"Ha, ha, ha!" laughed Royce loudly.

"It isn't only capital a business needs. Besides money, it takes integrity and a reputation that people can trust. I would say that you may be in short supply of those latter assets, Franklin, however large may be the fortune behind your enterprises."

"A bank takes money, and nothing else. I don't believe a word of all this! You may have stashed away a nest egg to help that no-good Shaw, but you won't be so lucky next time."

"We were hoping there wouldn't have to be a next time, that you would see it will do you no good to call the notes you hold due."

"Don't be naive, Almeda. I'm a banker, and money is my business. And it's not *yours*! So stay out of it!"

"If you call Rolf Douglas' note, or anyone else's, Royce, you're going to find yourself straight up against us again," said Pa, speaking once more. His voice rang with authority.

"I don't believe you, Hollister. I've checked your finances, and I know your bank account. You don't have that kind of money."

"Then go ahead and do your worst, Royce," said Pa.

"You're bluffing, Hollister. I can call any of a dozen notes due, and there's no possible way you can back them up."

Pa stared straight into Mr. Royce's face, and for a moment they stood eye to eye, as if each were daring the other to call the bluff. When Pa spoke, his words were cold and hard as steel.

"Try me, Royce," he said, still staring into the banker's eyes. "You just try me, if you want to take the chance. But you may find I'm not as easy an adversary as you think. People in these parts know I'm a man of my word, and they can trust me. I don't think you'd be wise to go up against me."

"What my husband is trying to tell you, Franklin," said Almeda, "is that you can call notes due and try to foreclose all you want. We've let it be known that if people find themselves in trouble with you, they can come see us. You may call those dozen loans due, but once they are paid off, what are you left with? A vault full of cash. Without loans, a bank cannot make a profit. You'll wind up with no loans, no land, no property, and before long the Royce Miners' Bank will be out of business, Franklin."

"That's too ridiculous to deserve a reply!"

"Do you think the people of this town will think it ridiculous when they learn that the 6.25 percent interest you have been charging them is almost two full percentage points *higher* than the current rate in San Francisco and Sacramento?"

"Rates are higher further away from financial centers."

"Your rates are two points higher than what *we* intend to charge people on *our* loans."

"You would dare undercut me?"

"No, we merely intend to charge our borrowers the fair and current rate."

"I don't believe you!"

"If you don't have better manners toward women yet, Royce," interrupted Pa angrily, "than to call them liars to their face, I suggest you go see Pat Shaw and take a look at the note we drew up for him. Four and a half percent, just like my wife said! You can squawk all you want about it, but when folks find out you've been taking advantage of them, they won't take too kindly to it. They're gonna be lining up at your door begging you to call their notes due so they can borrow from us instead!"

He paused just long enough to take a breath. Then his eyes bore into Franklin Royce one final time.

"So like I said, Royce," he added, "you go ahead and do your worst. You think I'm bluffing, then you try me! You'd be doing this community a favor by calling every loan you hold due, and letting the good folks of Miracle Springs pay you off and start borrowing from somebody else at a fair rate. Then you can see what it's like trying to make a living competing with my wife in the freight and supplies business!"

Mr. Royce returned Pa's stare as long as he dared, which wasn't long, then without another word, flicked his whip, turned his horse around, and flew off down the road back toward town.

Pa and Almeda watched him go. Then she slipped her hand through his arm, and they turned and walked slowly back to the house. They seemed at peace with what they had done, because they knew it was right, but they couldn't help being anxious about the results. If Royce *did* start calling notes due, there wasn't much they could do to stop him beyond helping a handful of other men, and that would only make it worse for everybody else. If they did bail out Rolf Douglas and whoever followed him, once they reached the fifty-thousand-dollar limit that Mr. Finch had promised, they would have no more help to give. And then, once word got out that the Hollister-Parrish "bank" had run dry, Mr. Royce would get his chance to foreclose on everybody in sight, run Parrish Mine and Freight out of business, gobble up all the

land for miles around, get elected mayor, and gain control of
the whole area.

Everything Pa and Almeda had said was true, and they
meant every bit of it. But there was a lot of bluff in their words
too. Now there was nothing left to do but wait and see how
Mr. Royce decided to play his cards.

"Well, Corrie," said Pa with a half smile as they came
toward me, "I reckon we've done it now. Your next article
may be about the end of Miracle Springs and the beginning
of Royceville!"

Almeda and I laughed. But all three of us knew Pa's joke
was a real possibility, too real to be very funny.

*T*he election was less than two weeks away.

The moment Franklin Royce disappeared down the road in his black buggy and we went back inside the house, a last-minute let-down seemed to come over Almeda.

There was nothing more to be done. She wasn't going to give any more speeches or write any more flyers. And as far as visiting and talking with folks was concerned, she said everything had already been stirred up plenty. The people had more than enough to talk about for one year, she said, and Franklin Royce had enough fuel to keep his hatred burning for a long time. It was best just to wait for events to unfold.

Almost immediately, her whole system seemed to collapse. Even as they walked away from the conversation with Mr. Royce, her face was pale and her smile forced.

The minute they were inside, she sat down heavily and breathed out a long and weary sigh. Tiny beads of perspiration dotted her white forehead. Pa saw instantly that she wasn't feeling well at all. She didn't even argue when he took her hand, helped her back to her feet, and led her into the other room to their bed. She lay down, and Pa brought her a drink of water. He wiped her face for a minute with a cool, damp cloth, and before long she was sound asleep.

Almeda remained in bed the rest of that Friday and all day Saturday, only getting up to go to the outhouse. Pa tended her like a mother with a baby. When Katie or Emily or I would try to take Ma something or sit beside her or help her on one of her many walks outside, Pa would say, "No, she's my wife. Nobody loves her as much as me, and nobody is gonna take care of her but me. Besides," he added with a wink, "I got her into this here fix, so I oughta be the one who helps her through it!"

The rest of us fixed the meals and cleaned up the house, but Pa took care of Almeda. He even sat beside her while she was sleeping, held her hand when she got sick, and read to her now and then, either from a book or from the Bible. If the rest of the town could only have seen him, some of the men might have made fun of him for doting on her. But no woman would have thought it was anything short of wonderful to have a husband love and care for her so tenderly as Pa did Almeda.

In the midst of all the turmoil over the election and loans and money and rumors and legal questions about Pa's claim and the future of Parrish Freight, it had been easy to forget that Almeda was in the family way. Except when she'd get sick for half an hour or hour every few days, she didn't seem any different, and she wasn't showing any plumpness around her middle.

But Pa started to get concerned about her condition on Saturday afternoon when she still lay in bed, looking pale and feeling terrible. He sent Zack and Tad off on their horses to fetch Doc Shoemaker.

When the Doc came an hour or so later, he went immediately into the sick room with Pa. After examining Almeda he shook his head, puzzled.

"Everything seems fine," he said, "but she's weak, and mighty sick. I don't quite know how to account for it. Came on her sudden, you say?"

"Yep," answered Pa. "She was fine and full of pep for a day or so after she got back, and then she started to tire out pretty bad."

"Back from where?"

"Sacramento."

"Sacramento? How'd she get there?"

"In her buggy, how else?"

"She bounced around on a buggy seat for that whole trip and back?"

"I reckon so," said Pa reluctantly. By now he realized Doc Shoemaker was mighty upset.

"Drummond Hollister, you idiot! What in blazes did you let her do that for?"

"She didn't exactly ask," said Pa. "She just said she was going. I asked if she wanted me to go with her, and she said no, that I oughta stay here, and I didn't think any more about it. She just went, that's all."

"This lady's between three and four months pregnant! She can't be doing things like that. I'm surprised she hasn't already lost the child from the exertion of a journey like that. She still may."

All the color drained from Pa's face. I had never seen him so scared. "I—I didn't think of all that," he stammered. "She's the kind of woman who's used to doing what she likes, and I don't usually stand in her way."

"Well, you're her husband and the father of the baby she's carrying. So you'd just better start telling her to take it easy. If she doesn't like it, then you put your foot down, do you hear me? Otherwise you might lose both a baby *and* a wife!"

"Is she really in danger, Doc?" Pa's voice shook.

"I don't know. I hope not. But she needs rest—and you make sure she gets it!"

A Few More Cards Get Played

CHAPTER EIGHTEEN

Almeda was up and out of bed some by Monday. Most of the color had come back into her cheeks and she was smiling again.

Pa made her stay in bed most of the day, and the minute she even had a fleeting thought about going into town or doing any last-minute campaigning, he wouldn't hear of it for a second!

"Corrie can manage the office fine without you," he said. "And whatever campaigning's to be done—which I don't figure is much—I'll do myself. There's not much we can do anyway, and the best thing for you is more rest. I don't aim to take any more chances!"

"Why, Drummond Hollister," she said, "I declare, if I didn't know better I'd take you for one of those slave-driving husbands who thinks his every word is supposed to be absolute law!" Her voice was still a little weak, but it was good to hear her joking again.

"Well, maybe it's time I started exerting my authority a mite more over an unruly wife who sometimes doesn't know what's for her own good," Pa gibed back. But joking or not, he still was determined to make her stay home and stay in bed as much as he could.

I went into town to the office, but I quickly discovered that while Almeda had been sick and we had been thinking only about her, the rest of the town had been talking about something else. And although the election was only eight days away, the elections to vote for mayor or United States President were not on people's minds.

I came back home on Raspberry about half an hour before noon. "Pa," I said, "I don't know what to do. The office has been full of people all morning."

"Don't ask me," he answered, "you and Almeda know the business, not me."

"It's not the business they're coming in about, Pa. It's about money and the worries about Royce."

"Who's been coming in?" he asked.

"Several of the men—asking to see Almeda . . . or you, when I told them she was sick. Mr. Douglas was one of the first."

"Rolf?"

"Yes, and he didn't look too happy."

A worried look crossed Pa's face. "Royce musta called his note due," he muttered. There was no anger in his voice, only a deep concern. Mr. Royce had apparently decided to play another card and call Pa's bluff.

Pa let out a deep sigh. "Reckon I'd best head into the office and see what's up," he said, "though I'm not sure I want to. What's going on now?" he added, turning to me. "What's Ashton doing?"

"I told him I was coming home to talk to you and to tell anyone who asked that I'd be back after a spell."

"Okay . . . I'll go saddle up the horse in a minute, and we'll ride back in."

He went into the bedroom to talk to Almeda a minute, then said to Emily and Becky, "You girls take care of your mother if she needs anything. And if she tries to get up and about too much, you tell her I told you to make her lie down again."

"Yes, Pa," said Emily. "Don't worry about her at all. We'll see that she keeps resting."

"Good. Corrie, we'd best be off." He went out to the barn while I went in to visit with Almeda for a few minutes. She was feeling a lot better, but she seemed quiet and thoughtful and a little sad. I suppose she was anxious about the men in town, and maybe about the election.

When Pa and I rode into town, we saw a small group of men standing around the door of Parrish Mine and Freight. A few were leaning against the building, and a couple sat on the edge of the wooden walkway, chatting aimlessly and waiting for Pa. When we rode up, they stood and turned in our direction. Worry filled all their faces. Rolf Douglas was at the head of the line right next to the door.

"He done it, Drum," said Mr. Douglas as we rode up, holding the paper he held in his hand up toward us.

"Thirty days?" said Pa, dismounting.

"Yep. I already been to see him to ask whether he would reconsider if I got back up with the two months I'm behind. But he said nope, got to have the cash or be out in thirty days."

"Well, come on in," said Pa, opening the door and leading the way into the office. "We'll see if we can't work something to help you out."

"What about the rest of us, Drum?" someone else called out. "We've got loans with Royce too."

"Any one of us could be next," called out another.

"Hold your horses, all of you," said Pa. "Right now Rolf here's the one with immediate problems with Royce. Let me get him taken care of first. Then we'll talk about what's to be done next."

He and Mr. Douglas went into Almeda's office. Ten minutes later they emerged and walked back outside. Mr. Douglas's expression was completely changed, and even Pa had the beginnings of a smile on his face. In that short time, the assembly of men outside had grown to ten or twelve.

Pa gave Mr. Douglas a slap on the back, then the two men shook hands. "You come back and see me in three weeks, Rolf," Pa said. "That'll give you eight or ten days before the money's due to Royce. We'll finish up our arrangement then."

Mr. Douglas thanked him, and by then all the other men were clamoring around, asking questions, wanting to know how things stood with them if they suddenly found themselves in the same predicament.

I don't know whether Pa was aware of it or not, but I thought I could see the outline of a familiar face in the bank window down the street. Word of the goings-on outside the Parrish Freight office would get back to Royce's ears soon enough.

"Listen to me, all the rest of you," Pa said. "We can't help you out until Royce tries to foreclose on you. Even the Hollister-Parrish bank's got limits, you know!"

He laughed, and all the men joined in.

"But we'll help you out when your time of need comes, you can depend on that. So long as we're able, whatever we got is yours. The minute Royce sends you a paper, you come see me and we'll sit down and talk. Until then, all of you just hang tight and go on with your business."

"Thanks, Drum . . . we're obliged to ya. We all owe you an' your missus, and we won't forget it!" called out several of the men as they began to disperse down the street."

"Just remember," Pa called out, "you men vote according to your consciences a week from tomorrow. I ain't gonna mention no names, but you just remember that as long as you got friends you can trust, no one is gonna be able to hurt you no matter what they may threaten to do."

He didn't have to mention any names. Every one of the men understood perfectly what Pa meant.

And as the week progressed and the days wound down toward the election, this statement of Pa's spread around town and became a final campaign pledge that stuck clearly in people's minds.

Judging from his action, it was obvious that Franklin Royce had heard Pa's statement about friends you could trust too.

By the middle of the week, Almeda was back to a normal schedule and was going into town for at least a good part of the day. But she was unusually quiet, and it seemed as if something weighed on her mind. I didn't know if it had to do with the election or the Royce trouble or anxiety about the baby.

After all that had gone on with the build-up to the election, the last week was completely quiet—no speeches, no rumors, no new banners. No one saw Mr. Royce. Almeda kept to herself. There were no more threats of foreclosure. Business went on as usual, and Tuesday, November 4, steadily approached. The most exciting thing that happened had nothing whatever to do with the election. That was the news that Aunt Katie was expecting again. The two new cousins were both scheduled to arrive sometime in the early spring of 1857.

Time had slipped by so fast that I didn't have the opportunity to get a second article written about the election. But almost before I had a chance to think through the possibility of a post-election story, which I wasn't sure I wanted to do if Mr. Royce won, all of a sudden a realization struck me. I still hadn't seen my Fremont article in the *Alta*!

What could have happened? Did I miss it? I'd been so preoccupied with everything that was going on, I hadn't read through every single issue. Had it come and I hadn't seen it?

I couldn't believe that was the case. Mr. Kemble always sent me a copy of my articles separately. He had done so with every one he had ever printed. Then why hadn't *this* article been printed? It was the most important thing I had ever written, and it was almost too late!

I rushed home that day and frantically searched through the stack of *Altas* from the last three weeks. It was not there. My article had still not been printed!

All that evening I stewed about it, wondering what I ought to do. By the next morning nothing had been resolved in my mind. So when we got ready to go into town, I asked Almeda if I could ride with her in the buggy instead of taking Raspberry like I usually did.

I began by telling her about the article's not appearing, and about Mr. Kemble.

"After a while," I said, "I started to get so tired of him looking down on me because I was young, and because I was a girl, that I became determined to show him that I could write as well as anyone else. But sometimes I must have sounded mighty headstrong, like I wouldn't accept anything but my own way. Do you know what I mean?" I asked.

Almeda nodded.

"I know there are times you've got to fight for something you believe in. You've taught me that. But then again, Mr. Kemble *is* the editor, and he *does* have years' more experience than I do, and I *am* young. Sometimes I wonder if I'm presuming too much to think I'm so smart and such a great writer that I can just tell him what I want."

I glanced at Almeda. She was obviously thinking a lot about what I was saying, but still she let me keep talking.

"And not only am I young and inexperienced, I *am* a girl—"

"Not anymore, Corrie," Almeda interrupted. "You're a woman now."

I smiled. "What I mean," I said, "is that I'm not a man. . . . I'm a girl, a lady, a woman—a female. I wish Mr. Kemble could look at something I write and *not* think of it as written by a woman. But there's a division between men and women that affects everything—it affects how people look at you and what they expect from you and how they treat you. And as much as I find myself wishing it *wasn't* that way, there's no getting around that it *is*. There *is* a difference between men and women, and maybe it *is* a man's world, especially here in the West. I don't know any other women newspaper writers. There aren't any other women in business around here but you."

I stopped, struggling to find words to express things I was feeling. "Maybe Mr. Kemble is right when he says that it's a man's world, and that a woman like me can't expect to get the same pay or have it as easy as I might like it. Maybe it *is* a man's world, and I've been wrong to think things are unfair because Robin O'Flaridy can get paid more than I do for the same article. Maybe that's just the way it is, and it's something I have to accept."

"How did your article's not being in the paper lead you to think about all that?" asked Almeda.

"I don't know. It's just hard to know how to fit being a woman into a man's world."

"Very hard!" agreed Almeda. "Believe me, Corrie, I have struggled with that exact question almost from the moment I arrived in California."

"My first reaction was anger," I continued. "I wanted to march right into Mr. Kemble's office and say, 'Why haven't you published my article?' A time or two I've been really headstrong and determined with him. Part of me still says that's the right approach. That's how a man would probably do it." I paused for a moment.

"But another side of me started thinking in this whole new way," I went on, "wondering if the way I've handled it in the past wasn't right."

"It's the Spirit of God putting these thoughts in your heart, Corrie," said Almeda. "You're maturing as a daughter of God. He's never going to let you remain just where you are. He's always going to be pulling and stretching you and encouraging you to grow into new regions of wisdom and dedication to him. And so he'll continually be putting within you new thoughts like this, so that you'll think and pray in new directions. He wants you to know both him and yourself more and more intimately."

"If it's God's Spirit speaking to me inside, then what's he trying to tell me?" I asked.

She laughed. "Ah, Corrie, *that* is always the difficult question! It's often very hard to know. Separating the voice of God's Spirit from our own thoughts is one of the Christian's greatest challenges."

The look on her face changed to one of reflection. "It's funny you should bring this up," she said after a minute. "I've been facing a real quandary myself. Different from yours, I suppose, but very similar at the same time."

"You mean about knowing if it's God saying something to you?"

"Partly. But more specifically, the issue of being a woman, and how to balance the two sides that sometimes struggle against one another inside."

"That's just it!" I said. "I feel that there's two parts of me, and I'm not sure which part I'm supposed to listen to and be like. One part wants to do things and be bold and not be looked down on for being a woman. That part of me resents hearing that it's a 'man's world' and that a woman's *place* is supposed to be somewhere different, somewhere less important, doing and thinking things that men wouldn't do. That part of me wants to think that I'm just as important as a man—not because women are *more* important, but just because I'm a human being too. Do you know what I mean?"

"Oh, I know exactly what you mean, Corrie!" answered Almeda. "Don't you think I've wrestled with that same question five hundred times since my first husband died? I've spent years trying to run a business in this 'man's world'! I always had to prove myself, to show them that I could run Parrish Mine and Freight as well as any man. Oh, yes, Corrie, I've struggled and prayed and cried over these questions you're asking!"

"Then you must feel the other half of what I've been feeling too," I went on.

"Which is?"

"Well, maybe it's not altogether right to expect to be treated the same as a man. Maybe it *is* a man's world, and I've got to accept my place in it. Even if Mr. Kemble says or does something I don't like, or even something I don't think is fair, maybe I have to learn to accept it. After all, he *is* the man, he *is* the editor, and maybe he has the right to do what he thinks best, whether I like it or not. After all, it isn't *my* newspaper. So who do I think I am to think that I have a right to expect Mr. Kemble to do what I want?"

Almeda drew up on the reins and looked at me intently. "Corrie," she said, "it seems there are two principles at work here. Maybe you're feeling the need to accept Mr. Kemble's judgment about the paper and your articles. But it's not just because he's a *man*—it's also because he's in a position of authority, and deserves your respect even when you disagree with him."

I nodded. "I guess so."

"But there's more to it than just the question of who makes the final decisions about your stories, isn't there?"

"Yes. I guess the last couple of years, since I started trying to write more seriously, I've been wanting the people I meet—first Mr. Singleton, then Mr. Kemble, and then even Robin O'Flaridy or Derrick Gregory—to treat me like an equal and not look down on me just because I'm not a man. But maybe I'm not supposed to be an equal. Maybe that isn't the way God wanted it to be. I don't like the thought that I'm not as important in the world as a man. But I've been wondering if that's the way it is."

"Corrie . . . Corrie," sighed Almeda, "you've really hit on the hardest thing of all about being a woman, especially out here in the West where we sometimes have to fend for ourselves and be tough."

"You mean accepting the fact that we're not equal to men, and that what we do and think isn't as important?"

"Oh no—not that. We *are* just as important. The question isn't about equality, Corrie, because in God's eyes, men, women, children—*all* human beings—are equal and precious.

The soul of the poorest black woman is just as important to God as the soul of the richest white man. The President of the United States, in God's eyes, is no more important than a child dying of starvation somewhere in deepest India or Africa. No—men are all equal, and by *men* I mean all of mankind—men *and* women. You are just as important as Mr. Kemble or anyone else, and your thoughts are just as valid. Never think that you're not as *good* as someone else—as a man. On the other hand, never think that someone else isn't as good as you! Equality works in all directions."

"Then what's that hardest thing about being a woman?" I asked.

"I said you were wrong about us not being *equal*. But you were right when you said we were *different*! And that's what is so hard about being a woman—trying to find how we're supposed to be equal and different at the same time. That is the struggle, Corrie."

"It's a struggle, all right. Half of me wants to tell Mr. Kemble off, and the other half wonders if I've got any right to."

"That's where women make a big mistake, Corrie. We want to be treated equally, but we forget that we really *are* different. We're supposed to be. God didn't make men and women to be the same. He made us equal but different. And so we're supposed to fulfill different roles. And the minute we try to start turning our equality with men into *sameness* with men, we lose sight of what it truly means to be a *woman*. I think we become less of a woman, in the way God intended womanhood when he created it, when we try to compete with men and do everything men do."

"Do you mean maybe I *shouldn't* be trying to be a reporter, because it is something mostly men do?"

"No, it's not that at all, Corrie. I think it's all right to *do* many of the same things men do. There aren't certain limits or restrictions God places around women. But even though we may be involved in many of the same pursuits, we're still women, not men. There's still a difference. There is still a leadership role which God has given to men, and a follower's role God has given to women. That's part of the difference I spoke of. Equal but different. Man is to be the head, the spokesman, the leader. A woman is to fit into that arrangement, not try to compete with it."

"You mean, like Mr. Kemble being the editor of the paper, and so I have to realize the importance of his position?"

"Something like that."

"And even if it weren't for his being editor and me just being a raw young writer, him being a man and me being a young woman makes it that way, too."

"I suppose in a way, although I wouldn't want to assume that any man, just because he is a man, has the right to control your life and your decisions. I believe that God has set certain men—a husband, for example, or an employer—into positions of leadership. As women, we need to acknowledge that God-given leadership. But I have to admit that I don't always know how it works out in practice. Lately I've been struggling with it a lot myself."

"Is that how it is in a marriage too?" I asked. "Like between you and Pa?"

She didn't answer immediately, but looked down and sighed deeply. I glanced away for a moment. When I looked back toward her, to my astonishment I saw that Almeda was crying.

*W*hat's the matter, Almeda?" I asked. My first thought was that something I'd said had hurt her feelings.

"I'm sorry, Corrie," she said, looking over at me. I'd never seen such an expression on her face. To me, Almeda had always been so strong, so in control, so much older and more mature than I. For three or four years she had been the one I had looked to for help and advice. I guess before that moment it had never crossed my mind that *she* had inner struggles too. But that look on her face, with tears silently running down her cheeks, was a look of confusion and uncertainty and pain—a look I had never expected to see from Almeda!

I reached over and took her hand.

The gesture made her cry even more for a minute, but I kept my hand on hers, and she held on to mine tightly. Finally she reached inside her pocket for a handkerchief, then blew her nose and tried to take a deep breath.

"I've been struggling with this for several days," she finally said, "ever since coming back from Sacramento and getting sick. I suppose I've needed someone to talk to. But I haven't even been able to bring it up to your father yet, because I haven't known how to put into words all that I was feeling."

"What is it?" I said. "Is there something wrong between you and Pa?"

"Oh, no. Nothing like that. Although it certainly has to do with your father." She paused, took another breath, then took my hand in both of hers again.

"I've always been a pretty independent sort of woman, Corrie," she said. "Just the other day, when I was sick, I heard your father saying to the doctor that I was the kind of woman who was used to doing what I liked. When the thought of going to Sacramento came to my head, just like your father said, I didn't ask him, I just said I was going and that was that—I went. Perhaps getting sick, and hearing those words of Drummond's, and realizing that my impetuousness could have cost our baby's life—all that set me to thinking about some things I hadn't ever thought of in quite the same light before. And last week, as I lay in bed recovering, I spent a lot of time in prayer. And I must tell you, I'm having to take a new look at some things in myself. It's not an altogether pleasant experience!"

She paused for a moment, dabbed at her eyes, then went on.

"Ever since I was a child I've had a determined streak. And that's not necessarily a bad thing. My past was anything but a spiritual one. I did not begin walking with God until I was in my midtwenties, and before that I was a much different person than the one you have known. I did much that I am not proud of. And when I discovered who my heavenly Father was, and realized that he loved me and desired something more for me than what I was, I set my heart and mind to give myself to him completely. As a Christian, my inner determination has been a good thing. I have wanted to settle for nothing less than God's fullest and best for me. I have determined to give my all to him, in every aspect of my being, to let him remake me into what *he* wants me to be, rather than just settling for what I have always been. And thus, I really am a different person than I was fifteen years ago. He *has* created in me a new heart, a new mind. And I am thankful that he gave me the determination to seek him with my whole being. Some people do not have that hunger, that earnest desire to give their all to God. But he gave me that hunger, and I am glad.

"After Mr. Parrish died, I'd have never made it in business in Miracle Springs without being what your Pa calls 'a mighty determined lady.' I had to fight for what I wanted to do, and prove myself to people, mostly to the men of this community. It's just like what we have talked about before, Corrie—fighting for what you believe in. God puts that fight, that determination into women's hearts too, not just men's. He fills women with dreams and desires and ambitions and things they want to do and achieve, and I really believe that God wants determined daughters as well as determined sons, willing to believe in things strongly enough to go after them. Like your writing. I think God is filling you not only with the desire to write, but the determination to fight for it, even when it might mean occasionally standing up to Mr. Kemble and speaking your mind.

"But on the other hand, there's a danger women face that men don't. Sometimes a single woman, who has only herself to depend on, can get too independent and lose sight of what it means to live in partnership with someone else. After I lost my first husband, I got accustomed to doing things for myself, in my own way, without asking anyone's permission or what anyone thought. I had to, I suppose.

"But when your father and I were married, I continued thinking pretty much the same way, even though I was a wife again. I didn't really stop to consider that maybe now I had to alter my outlook. I still thought of my life as *mine* to live as I saw fit. Once when we were talking about your future, I told you that I was the kind of woman who believed in exploring all the possibilities for yourself that you could. When your father suggested shutting down Parrish Freight for a while, so that I could be a more traditional wife and mother, I nearly hit the roof. I wasn't about to have any of that, and I told him so!

"The trip to Sacramento and getting sick last week suddenly made it clear to me that I have carried that independence into my marriage with your father. I haven't stopped to consider things, or to ask him about what I do, or to defer to him in any way as my husband, I've just gone on ahead and done what I wanted to do. And the instant I realized it—I have to tell you, Corrie, it was very painful. I love your father so much. Realizing that I haven't been to him what God would have me be fills me with such remorse and sadness and—"

She stopped and looked away. I could feel her hand trembling in mine. I knew she was weeping again. After two or three minutes of silence, she continued.

"Your father has been so good to me," she said. "He has never pressured me, never said a word. He has let me be myself, and even be independent. Yet now I see that I have done some things that perhaps he wouldn't have wanted me to.

"Why, this whole thing of running for mayor—I never *asked* him about it, Corrie. We prayed about it when I decided to get back in the race, but I never really sought your father's counsel as a man of wisdom. The initial decision for me to run was a decision I made. I never even sought his advice as my husband and as the leader of this family. I genuinely thought

I was being led of God, and perhaps to a degree I was. But the point is, I never consulted your father in any way or allowed him to help me arrive at a decision. You were there that evening last July—I simply walked in and announced that I had decided to run against Royce."

Again she stopped, tears standing in her red eyes. "Don't you see, Corrie—I haven't been fair to your father at all! My determined nature just lost sight of the fact that we're not supposed to act independent of men, but *with* them, and following them, and allowing them to help guide us. God made women to live *with* men, not to act independently of them— especially in a marriage. And I haven't done that with your father, the man I love more than anyone else in the world!

"Probably God was trying to get my attention even before last week. From the very start of the election, all the mischief and deceit Franklin has been up to—maybe that has been the Lord's way of telling me some of my priorities haven't been as he would have them. When he started spreading those rumors about me, even then God was stirring me up, though I didn't know what he was trying to say."

"But what could all those lies about you have to do with what God wanted to say to you?" I asked.

A faraway look passed across Almeda's face. "Yes, a good portion of what people were saying was false, Corrie," she said softly. "But not everything. I lived for many years outside God's plan for me, and I had much to repent of. He had many things in my character to change. Perhaps I will have the opportunity to tell you about it one day. I would like that. Your father knows everything. I have held no secrets from him. And it is to his great credit that he married me knowing what he knew. I love him all the more for it.

"And so when Franklin began stirring up the waters of my past, God began to probe the deep recesses of my heart as well. And now I find myself wondering if this whole election came up, not so that I could become mayor of Miracle Springs, but so that I would finally face some things in my own heart that I had never let go of, so that I would put them on God's altar once and for all."

"But surely you can't want Mr. Royce to be mayor!" I said in astonishment.

"Wouldn't it be better for me to withdraw from the election, even if it means giving the mayor's post to him, than to go ahead with something that is outside of God's will for me?"

"I suppose so," I answered hesitantly. "But I just can't stand the thought of Mr. Royce getting his own way and gaining control of this town."

"I can't either," she replied. "But he is not a Christian, and I am. Therefore I am under orders to a higher power. To *two* higher powers—the Lord God our Father, and to my husband Drummond Hollister. And maybe it's time I started to ask the two of them what I am supposed to do, instead of deciding for myself."

"I just can't abide the thought of Mr. Royce being mayor."

"Look at me, Corrie," she said tenderly, placing her hand gently on her stomach. "The baby that is your father's and mine is beginning to grow. Before long I will be getting fat with your own new little brother or sister. Do I look like a politician . . . a mayor?"

"I see what you mean," I said.

"Do you remember what you said when we first started talking, about the two parts struggling inside you?"

I nodded.

"It's the same thing I've been wrestling with. It's hard. It's painful. That's why I've been praying, and crying. I *want* to be mayor. But at the same time, my first calling is to be a woman—to be your father's wife, to be a mother to his children, and this new child I am carrying. Balancing the two is very difficult! That's why I don't know what to tell you to do about your article and Mr. Kemble. Because I don't even know what I'm supposed to do in my *own* dilemma."

We both were silent for several minutes. "What will you do?" I asked finally.

"I don't know," Almeda answered. "But the one thing I *do* have to do is talk with your father—and pray with him. This is one decision I am not going to make without him!"

She looked at me and smiled, wiping off the last of the tears on her face with her handkerchief.

"Thank you for listening, Corrie," she said. "You are a dear friend, besides being the best daughter a woman could have. Pray for me, will you?"

"I always do," I replied. I leaned toward her and gave her a tight hug. We held one another for several moments.

"O, Lord," I prayed aloud, "help the two of us to be the women you want us to be. I pray that you'll show Almeda and Pa just what you want them to do. And help me to know what you want me to do, too."

"Amen!" Almeda whispered softly.

When we released each other, both of us had tears in our eyes. They were not tears of sadness, but of joy.

All day Thursday after Almeda and I had our long talk, neither of us could concentrate on work. About three in the afternoon, Almeda suggested we go on home.

We hadn't been back more than forty or fifty minutes when Alkali Jones rode up as fast as his stubborn mule Corrie's Beast could carry him—which wasn't very fast!

Pa was just walking down from the mine to wash up and have a cup of coffee. We'd been inside the house, but hadn't yet seen Pa since getting home. Mr. Jones spoke to all of us at once as he climbed down off the Beast.

"Ye left Miracle too blamed early!" he said to me and Almeda. "Weren't five minutes after ye was gone, ol' Royce come out o' his bank, an' starts talkin' to a few men who was hangin' around the Gold Nugget. Told 'em he was gonna be givin' kinda like a speech tomorrow mornin', though not exactly campaignin'. But he said whatever men owed his bank money oughta be sure an' be there. He said he'd like to notify 'em all by letter, but there weren't enough time, so would the men spread the word around town."

"And what else?" asked Pa.

"That's it," said Mr. Jones. "He's gonna be sayin' something he says is mighty important an' folks oughta be there."

Pa looked at Almeda. "Well, I reckon this could be it," he
said. "Looks like he's gonna call our bluff and foreclose on the
whole town at once."

"He wouldn't dare," said Almeda.

"As long as you've known Franklin Royce," said Pa, "you
still think he'd be afraid to do anything? Nope, that's what
he's gonna to do all right. One last threat to finalize his election on Tuesday."

"I just can't believe he'd have the gall."

"He'll do anything to win."

Everybody was silent a minute.

"Well, I can't be there," said Almeda finally. "I wouldn't
be able to tolerate that conniving voice of his addressing the
men of this town. I'm afraid I would scream!"

"I'm not gonna be there, that's for sure!" added Pa. "I'd be
afraid I'd clobber him, and then Simon'd have to throw me in
the pokey. Alkali, you want to go and hear what the snake has
to say? You'd be doing us a favor."

"You bet. Maybe I'll clobber the varmint fer ye! Hee, hee,
hee! I don't owe him nuthin'. He cain't do a thing to me!"

"No, you just stand there and listen. Won't be doing our
cause no good for *anybody* to clobber him, as much as I'd
like to!"

They went into the house and had some coffee and talked
a while longer, and then went back to the mine where Pa
worked for another couple of hours.

That evening was pretty quiet. It felt as if a cloud had
blown over the house and stopped, a big black thundercloud.
I think Pa and Almeda were afraid that whatever Royce did
in the morning would send a dozen or more men running to
them for help with their loans, and then the cat would be out

of the bag that they didn't have enough money to help them all. They didn't actually have any money at all! Once they were forced to admit that fact, like Pa said, the jig was up. Royce would then have everyone over a barrel and could do whatever he liked.

The next morning we all tried to keep busy around the house, but it was no use. We were on pins and needles waiting for some news from town. I think Pa was halfway afraid that he'd suddenly see ten or twenty men riding up, all clamoring for help with their loans, and when he had to level with them and say there was no way they could back them all up, that they'd turn on him and lynch him from the nearest tree!

The morning dragged on. Two or three times I could tell from Pa's fidgeting that he was thinking of riding into town himself to see what was up. But he stuck with his resolve, and attempted to busy himself in the barn or around the outside of the house.

The first indication we had that word was on the way wasn't the sight of dust approaching or the sound of galloping hoofbeats rounding the bend. Instead it was the high-pitched voice of Mr. Jones shouting at his mule as he whipped it along. Long before he came into view, his voice echoed his coming.

"Git up, ye dad-blamed ornery varmint!" he yelled. "Ye're nuthin' but a good-fer-nuthin' heap o' worn-out bones! If ye don't git movin' any faster, I'm gonna drive ye up the peak o' Bald Mountain an' leave ye there fer the bears an' wolves—ye dad-burned cuss! Why, I shoulda left ye in that drift o' snow last winter! Ye're slower than a rattlesnake in a freeze!"

By the time he rounded the bend and came in sight, Pa was already running toward him, and the rest of us were waiting outside the house for news.

Seeing Pa and the rest of us, Alkali's jabbering changed and his face brightened immediately.

"Ya done it!" he shouted out. "Ya done it, ye wily rogue!"

"Done what?" said Pa. "Who's done what?"

"*You* done it!" repeated Mr. Jones. "Ya made the rascal blink, that's what! Hee, hee, hee!"

"Alkali, I don't have a notion what you're babbling on about!"

"He backed down, I tell ye! Your bluff worked!"

"What did he say, Mr. Jones?" said Almeda, "Are you telling us he *didn't* call all the men's notes due like we feared?"

"He didn't do nuthin' o' the sort, ma'am. Why, he plumb was trippin' over his own tongue tryin' to be nice, 'cause he ain't used enough to it."

"What did he say, Alkali? Come on—out with it!" said Pa.

"Well, the varmint got up on top of a table so everybody could hear him. There was likely thirty, forty men gathered around, all of 'em that owes the rascal money. An' they was all worried an' frettin', and your name came up amongst 'em afore Royce even got started, and they was sayin' as how they'd have to be over t' see you next.

"But then Royce climbed up there, all full of smiles, and said he'd been thinkin' a heap 'bout the town an' its people and about his obligation as the banker an' the future mayor. An' he said he had come t' the realization that ye gotta have friends ye can trust when times get rough—"

"He stole that from you, Pa," I interrupted.

Pa just nodded, and Mr. Jones kept going.

"An' he said that as Miracle Springs' banker, he was proud of bein' a man folks could trust. An' then came the part that jist surprised the socks clean off everybody listenin'.

He said that he'd been thinkin' an' was realizin' maybe he'd been a mite too hard on folks hereabouts. An' so he said he was gonna do some re-figurin' of his bank's finances and had decided fer the time bein' t' call no more loans due. An' he wanted t' git folks together 'cause he knew there'd been some worry around town and he wanted t' put folks' minds at ease.

"An' then blamed if he didn't hold up a piece a paper, an' he said that it was the call notice on Rolf Douglas' note. An' he said he'd reconsidered it too, an' then all of a sudden he ripped that paper in half right afore our eyes! An' then he said he wanted them all to remember that he was their friend, an' a man they could trust."

"That was all?" asked Pa, stunned by the incredible news.

"The men was jist standin' there with their mouths hangin' open, an' no one knew whether t' clap fer him or what t' do, they was all so shocked. An' then he said he hoped they'd remember him on election day. But if ye ask me, gatherin' from the gist of what I heard as the men was leavin', I figure the only person they's gonna be rememberin' next Tuesday is this here missus of yours, Drum, now that they don't figure they need to be afeared of Royce!"

He stopped and looked around at all our silent amazed faces.

"Hee, hee, hee!" he cackled. "Ye all look like a parcel of blamed ghosts! Don't ye hear what I'm tellin' ye? Mrs. Hollister, ma'am, I think you jist about got this here election in the dad-burned bag!"

Pa finally broke out in a big grin, then shook Alkali Jones' hand, and threw his arm around Almeda.

"Well, maybe we have done it after all, Mrs. Hollister!" he exclaimed. "I just don't believe it."

But Almeda wasn't smiling. One glance over in my direction told me this latest news was like a knife piercing her heart. Knowing that suddenly she had a chance after all was going to make what she had to do all the more difficult.

All the rest of that Friday, Almeda was quiet and kept to herself, while everyone else was happy. Around the house Pa was all smiles, laughing and joking. I'd hardly ever seen him like that! To know they had gone up against a skunk like Royce and won was more than he'd expected. We still didn't know what effect it would have on the trouble he was trying to cause about *our* claim. But at least the men with overdue loan payments appeared out of danger.

Uncle Nick and Katie came down to the house, and the minute they walked in, Pa took Katie's hand, even in her condition, and did a little jig, and then said to her and Uncle Nick, "The two of you watch how you talk around here from now on—this is the home of the soon-to-be mayor of Miracle Springs!" And that set off the celebrating all over again!

Even more than being glad about Royce's backing down about the loans, Pa was jovial because he figured Almeda was a cinch to win the election on Tuesday! Pa was so excited he could hardly stand it. They were going to beat Royce in two ways!

Despite Royce's last-minute ploy with his speech, tearing up Mr. Douglas' call notice and trying to convince folks he was their friend, the word around town was that most of the men were going to go with the person their gut had told them all along they could trust. The words *Mayor Hollister* went down a lot smoother than *Mayor Royce*.

Uncle Nick was in town a couple of hours after the banker's speech, and when he came back he confirmed exactly what Mr. Jones had said. People were relieved at what Royce had done. But a lot of them said they hadn't been that worried anyway because they knew Drum would help them out. And now more than ever they knew who they were going to vote for, and it wasn't the man with all the money in the fine suit of clothes from New York.

"Everybody's sayin' the same thing, Drum," said Uncle Nick, "and what Alkali said is right—she's just about got the election in the bag!"

When Almeda and I went into the office for a couple of hours, people on the street shouted out greetings. Mr. Ashton was all smiles, and when we saw Marcus Weber a bit later, his white teeth just about filled his dark face in the hugest grin I'd ever seen him wear. The two men did everything but address her as Mrs. Mayor.

Poor Mr. Royce! He had tried being mean, and now he was trying to be nice. But neither tactic made people like him or trust him.

Almeda was silent, unsmiling, even moody. Pa, and I think most other folks, just figured she wasn't feeling well on account of the baby.

But I knew that wasn't it. I knew what she was thinking—she was going to withdraw from the election! After all that had gone on, she had victory in her grasp . . . and now she was going to have to let go of it and hand the election to a man she despised.

It took her the rest of the day to get up the nerve to talk to Pa, because she knew how disappointed he would be. Finally, after supper, she asked him if he'd go outside with her for a walk. He was still smiling when they left. But when they came back an hour or so later, his face was as downcast as hers had been all day, and Almeda's eyes were red from crying. I knew I'd been right. She'd told him, and the election was off.

The instant they walked in the door, a gloomy silence came over the five of us kids. All the rest of them knew something was up, just from Pa's face, although neither Pa nor Almeda said anything about what they were thinking.

Before long we got ourselves ready and off to bed, leaving Pa and Almeda sitting in front of the fire. The last thing I remembered before falling asleep was the soft sounds of their voices in the other room. I couldn't tell if they were talking to each other or praying.

Probably both.

*O*n Saturday, three days before the election, when I got up, Pa was already gone. Almeda was still in bed. Pa finally returned a little before noon. His first words were to Almeda, who was up and about but who hadn't said much to any of the rest of us yet that morning.

"You still want to tell everyone all at once?" he asked her.

"I think it's the best way, don't you?"

"Yeah, I reckon. They gotta know sometime, and it's probably easiest that way."

Then Pa turned to the rest of us. "Listen, kids—we're going to have another meeting of our election committee. So you all be here right after lunch. Don't go running off if you want to hear what your mother and I have been discussing, you hear? Plans have changed some, and we're gonna tell you all about it."

He spoke again to Almeda. "I already told Nick and Katie to come down. What do you think—anyone else we ought to tell personally, so they don't just hear from Widow Robinson and the rest of the town gossips?"

"Maybe it would be good to tell some of our friends," suggested Almeda, "now that you mention it. I'd like Elmer and Marcus to hear it from us."

"And Pat," said Pa. "And maybe the minister—"

"And Harriet," added Almeda.

They both thought another minute.

"Guess that's about it, huh?" said Pa. Almeda nodded.

"Zack, son," said Pa, "You want to ride over to the Shaws' and ask Pat if he could come over around half past one?"

"Sure, Pa."

"Come to think of it," Pa added, "ask him if he's seen Alkali today. Alkali's gotta be here too."

"He was by Uncle Nick's earlier," said Zack. "I heard him say he was going into town."

"Well, we'll round him up somewhere. Between him and his mule, it shouldn't be too hard to find him."

"Corrie, would you ride into town and deliver the same message to Mr. Ashton and Mr. Weber?" said Almeda.

"Can I go see Miss Stansberry?" asked Emily. "I'll tell her."

"Sure," said Pa. "What about Rev. Rutledge? Who wants to ride over—"

"I'll ask him to come too," said Emily. "He'll be at Miss Stansberry's—he's always with her."

"You noticed, eh?" said Pa with a smile.

"Everyone knows about them, Pa," said Becky. "They're *always* together!"

"Okay, all of you get going with your messages. Tell everyone we'll meet here at half past one."

Two hours later, we were all back, and the house was full of the election committee and our closest friends—sixteen in all, probably the most people we'd ever had in the house at one time.

"We're obliged to you all for coming," Pa began. "What we've got to tell you isn't exactly the best news we could have.

But we talked and prayed the whole thing through and this is the way we figure things have to be. You all are family, and the best friends we've got, and we want you to hear how things stand from our own lips instead of just hearing it around town.

"Now in a minute Almeda's got some things she wants you to know about how she's been thinking. When she first unburdened all this to me, I didn't see what the problem was with her being mayor. But I gotta tell you, we done some praying on this dilemma last night, and I went out myself for a couple hours this morning and was asking the Lord some mighty hard questions. And I'm coming to see that maybe what she's doing is the right thing after all.

"You see, we've been thinking mighty hard about this here marriage of ours, and we've been asking God to show us how things are supposed to work between a man and a woman who say they want to live together and try to be one like the Book says they're supposed to be. Almeda figures maybe she hasn't been deferring to me like she ought to have been. At first when she said it, I didn't see how that should prevent her from running for mayor. But I have to respect what she thinks is the right thing to do. And then something began to speak inside me too. I have to hope it was God's voice, just the same as I have to think it's him that's speaking to Almeda's heart.

"I began to see that maybe I had some changing to do too. Maybe I haven't been quite the leader of this marriage that I'm supposed to be. I mean, I don't have any complaint with what Almeda does or wants to do. And I don't want her asking my permission to do things. She's a grown woman, and she's a heap sight more experienced than I am about trying to live the way a Christian should and listening for how to obey what God wants us to do. When it comes to that sort of thing, why she's the one who ought to be leading me! If she comes and says, 'I don't know what to do about such-and-such, and you're my husband and I want to do what you think is best,' I'm more'n likely to answer her, 'You're a grown woman, and I trust you, so do what you think's best.' In other words, I don't figure she needs me telling her what to do all the time.

"Yet I can see that maybe I need to take more responsibility in the way of thinking of myself as head of this family and this marriage. I'm not really sure what that will mean because all this is mighty new to both of us. But I reckon that if you don't start someplace, you're likely never to get the thing done. So we're aiming to start here and now, even though it means having to turn back from something we worked so hard to get. If we got started with this election on the wrong foot, then it's not gonna do nobody any good to keep pushing forward. The only way to make things come out right in the end is to go back and start over, even if it means having to let go of something in the process."

He stopped and let out a big sigh. The whole house was silent as Pa looked around the room. His eyes fell on Almeda last of all. "Well," he said, "I reckon I had *my* say . . . now it's your turn."

"Drummond has really put his finger on what has been bothering me for the last week," Almeda began. "This whole election thing, as he said, got off on the wrong foot. I am coming to see that perhaps I'm a more independent woman than I realized—more independent than I should be. I have been in the habit of doing and thinking for myself, of making up my *own* mind about things, of running my *own* life and never really asking how what I do affects anybody else. And I see that in certain ways I have been headstrong when things stand in my way.

"I suppose it all boils down to the simple question: Is this the way for a woman, a wife, to behave in a marriage? I can't say as I even have the answer. As Drummond told you, neither does he. I don't intend to suddenly start asking him about everything I do. And I know the last thing he would ever do is to start lording it over me like a king. He is the most tender, most thoughtful man I have ever known.

"Yet somehow, we need to make some changes about my being less independent, and maybe him being a little more forceful. Neither of us understands very much about what we're trying to explain, because it's new to both of us."

Almeda then went on to tell how she had made the decision to run for mayor on her own. She shared some of what she and I had talked about, how she realized she had brought her independent streak into the marriage with Pa. And now, she said, she felt that the only way to make right what she had done was to go back and undo it, and then start anew.

"Drummond explained how I feel," she said. "I should have paid more attention to his initial hesitations, but I was determined it was the right thing. You can't make something come out right in the end if you got started with it in the wrong way. You have to go back and start over. The foundation has to be built right, or else everything that comes along and gets put on top of it will be shaky. It's like the old parable of building a house on either rock or sand. And I fear my running for mayor of Miracle Springs was a decision built on sand. Nothing I can do now will change that, or change the sand into rock. I don't know anything to do but go back and rethink the original decision in a new light."

She stopped, drew in a deep breath, and then went on with the hardest part of what she had to say.

"This new light cast on my decision to run for mayor shows me that it was an ill-advised decision—one made independently, maybe even with some pride mixed in, a determination not necessarily to do what was right or what God wanted, but rather to do something that pleased my ego— that is, prevent Franklin Royce from becoming mayor. I never stopped to ask whether running for mayor was right for my husband, for this wonderful family of mine—"

Her hand swept around the room as she spoke, and she glanced around at all of us.

"I just said to myself, 'I can do this. I *will* do it!' And so I did. I made the decision without consulting a soul. Of course I prayed about it. But even my prayers were so full of self that God's voice could only speak to me through a heart that was still thinking independently.

"Well, the long and the short of it, as I'm sure all of you have guessed, is that we feel we must go back and undo that original decision I made.

"Now, no doubt you will all find yourselves full of reasons to try to convince us to reconsider. I know Franklin Royce is a dangerous man to let become mayor. I know every possible thing you could say to try to convince me to remain in the race. I've said them to myself. At first Drummond would not hear of my withdrawing, and he gave me every reason he could think of too. But as we talked and prayed, and as time settled our thoughts, we both became convinced that this is the right and proper course of action. Neither of us can give you every reason why—but we feel it is the right thing to do. So please, don't try to change our minds, unless you truly feel we've missed something God might have wanted to say to us.

"So," she concluded, in a quiet tone full of resolve, "I have decided—that is, *we* have decided . . . together, both of us—that it is best for the name Almeda Hollister to be withdrawn from consideration in the election for mayor of Miracle Springs. Since it is obviously too late for my name to be taken off the ballot, I would like to make a public announcement tomorrow at church, if that would meet with your approval, Avery, and simply tell people that I am no longer a candidate. If despite this, people still check my name on the ballot on Tuesday, I will not accept the position. In any case, Franklin Royce will become the next mayor of Miracle Springs."

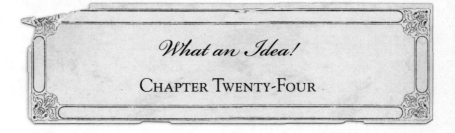

What an Idea!

CHAPTER TWENTY-FOUR

$\mathcal{T}$he room was silent.

Pa and Almeda both felt relieved, I think. I could tell a burden had been lifted from Almeda's shoulders. The peace on her face was visible. And since I had been expecting it, the shock wasn't as great for me.

But for everybody else, the news was awful!

I knew every single person wanted to start shouting out reasons to make them reconsider. But because Almeda had said not to, no one spoke.

The silence went on and on for a minute or two. Finally Rev. Rutledge broke it.

"Does this represent your decision too, Drummond?" he asked. "Is this what you want?"

"I reckon," Pa answered. "At first I didn't like it any better than the rest of you. And she's right—I spent an hour trying to convince her that I *did* want her to be mayor. But then after a while I saw what she'd been driving at. And so I reckon I do agree that maybe a woman—at least a wife, who's carrying my baby!—ought not be mayor. I'm not saying that *no* woman should do something like that. But we got ourselves a family here, and it's gonna be an even bigger family in a few months. We got our hands full without her trying to manage a town's business besides. So yeah, Reverend, I'm in agreement with this decision, even though I can't abide the thought of Royce being mayor any more than the rest of you can."

The silence fell again, and Rev. Rutledge seemed satisfied. A long time passed before anyone said anything.

"Well, I reckon there ain't but one solution t' this here fix," cackled Mr. Jones at length.

Pa looked over at him with a blank expression. I know he was expecting one of his old friend's wisecracks.

"And what's that, Alkali?" he asked.

"Fer you t' take the lady's place. Hee, hee, hee!"

As his high-pitched laughter died down, silence again filled the house. We could all *feel* an unexpected energy of hope rising out of the disappointment of only seconds earlier.

Faces gradually started glancing around the room at each other. Eyes grew wider and wider.

Mr. Jones' words were like a stick of dynamite exploding right in the middle of the room! For the first few seconds everyone wondered if they'd heard him right.

Then light began to dawn on face after face!

Uncle Nick was the first to say what everyone else had felt instantly. "If that ain't the dad-blamedest best idea I've ever heard!" he exclaimed, jumping out of his seat. He walked over to Pa and stuck out his hand.

Dazed, Pa shook it, still hardly believing what he'd heard. The moment he took Uncle Nick's hand, everyone in the room began letting out cheers and shouts of approval. The next instant we were all out of our seats and crowding around Pa, who still sat bewildered.

"Drummond," said Rev. Rutledge somberly, "I think Mr. Jones has hit upon an absolutely wonderful idea."

"The perfect answer!" chimed in Katie and Miss Stansberry almost in unison.

"Will you do it, Drummond?" asked the minister. "We're all behind you 100 percent."

Almost in a stupor in the midst of the sudden excitement, Pa still didn't seem to grasp what all the fuss was about.

"Do what?" he said.

"Take Almeda's place, you old goat!" said Uncle Nick. "Just like Alkali said."

Still Pa's face looked confounded. The idea was just too unbelievable for him to fathom.

Finally Almeda turned from where she was sitting beside him. She took one of his hands in hers and looked him full in the face with a broad smile. "Drummond, what these friends of yours are saying is that they want *you* to run for mayor . . . *yourself*."

"Me . . . run for mayor?" he exclaimed in disbelief. "The notion's crazier than Alkali shaving his beard and taking a bath!"

"No crazier than me being hitched and having a family, Drum," rejoined Uncle Nick.

"This here's Californeee, don't ya know! Things is done a mite looney out here. Hee, hee, hee!"

"Times are changing. You might as well change with them," added Mr. Shaw.

"But I'm no politician," objected Pa. "I don't know anything about that kind of stuff."

"Nobody else does either, Drummond," said Almeda, growing in enthusiasm over the idea herself. "I'm no politician either, and Franklin is only running so that he can gain more power for himself and his bank. Surely you don't want *him* to be elected?"

Her words sobered Pa and quieted everybody down.

For the first time the look on Pa's face indicated that he was giving serious thought to the reality of the possibility—as outlandish as the whole thing still seemed to him.

"My name's not even on the ballot," he said at length.

"If enough people voted for me and I should happen to win," suggested Almeda, "I could then step down and appoint you mayor."

"Is that legal?" asked Miss Stansberry.

"Royce would probably challenge it and call for a new election," said Katie. "Something similar happened in Virginia a few years back."

"And then once that happened, he'd think we'd deceived him and would no doubt start in again with his shenanigans and financial pressure on everyone," said Almeda, thinking aloud.

"There's got to be some way to get Drum elected mayor," said Mr. Shaw, "even if the election's only three days off."

The room got quiet for a minute. When Almeda spoke next, her voice was soft and earnest. It was almost as if the two of them were alone, continuing a conversation they'd been having in private.

"Drummond," she said, "it seems to me that this could be exactly what the Lord has had in mind all along. Perhaps this is the reason things have worked out as they have, and why he unsettled my heart about my being out in public view trying to make something of myself. Maybe all along God wanted me, and perhaps the whole community, to be looking to my husband for leadership. I see God's hand in the way events have unfolded. And I can't think of a better way for me to defer to you, and for you to move up a step in taking hold of the firm hand God might want you to exert, than for me to step aside so that you can take the lead in this election."

She paused, and her eyes were filling with tears of love as she went on. "I can't tell you how pleased it would make me," she said softly. "It would make me feel as though these past two months had not been in vain, that maybe God was even able to use my independence to accomplish his purposes. But of course," she added, "it has to be your decision, and I will understand and stand by you whatever you think is best."

She stopped, and now all eyes rested on Pa as he considered everything that had been said. A long time—probably two or three minutes—passed before he said a word.

"Well, you're all mighty convincing," he said finally. "And I have to say it's flattering that you'd think I could even do the thing—that is, if I had a chance in the first place."

He paused and took a breath.

"But it occurs to me," he went on, "that one of the first things a mayor probably has to do is make decisions of one kind or another. And it occurs to me, too, that if I'm gonna start taking more of a lead in this marriage partnership Almeda and I are trying to figure out, then I have to get more practiced in finding out what the Almighty wants me to do, instead of just taking things as they come, or figuring that Almeda's supposed to handle most of the spiritual side of things, while I just go on without paying much attention.

"All that is my way of saying that I guess I *do* have to make the decision myself. I appreciate all your thoughts and advice. And I'd appreciate all of you praying for me, because I'm gonna need it. But first I have to get alone and ask God what decision he wants me to make, and then hope that he'll put the thoughts into my heart and head plain enough that I can figure out what he's saying."

He let out a deep sigh, then hitched himself to his feet.

"So that's what I'm going to do before I say anything else, and before you all try to do any more convincing."

He went to the door, opened it, and walked outside.

Gradually those of us left in the house started talking a little. Katie had to entertain little Erich, and Becky and Tad had had enough sitting for one stretch and had to get themselves moving again. Almeda went into her and Pa's bedroom and closed the door, to pray for Pa and the decision he was wrestling with.

About twenty minutes later Mr. Shaw was about to leave, and Rev. Rutledge was helping Miss Stansberry with her coat, when the door opened and Pa walked in.

From the look on his face, every one of us knew instantly that he'd made his decision.

Almeda had heard him return and emerged from the bedroom just as he spoke. "It'd be a shame to waste all those good 'Hollister for Mayor' signs and flyers," he said with a big grin. "So if it's not gonna be one Hollister, it might as well be the other! Move over, Royce—I'm in it now too!"

"Now the varmint'll find himself in a *real* scrape!" cackled Alkali Jones. "Hee, hee, hee!"

More hollering and handshaking went around the room, while Mr. Shaw and the others took off their coats again. Over to one side of the room I could see the person more involved in this turn of events than anyone but Pa, and she wasn't yelling or whooping it up.

Almeda closed her eyes briefly and softly whispered the words, "Thank you!" Then she opened them, and walked forward with a smile to join her husband in the midst of the commotion.

Devising a Strategy
Chapter Twenty-Five

*W*ell, I suppose you'll still be wanting to make an announcement at church tomorrow," said Rev. Rutledge at length. "Although it looks like it will be quite different than what you first had in mind, Almeda!" he added with a big smile.

"I don't know, Reverend," replied Pa hesitantly. "I don't know if it strikes me as quite right to use your pulpit to further my own plans. Seems like it might have been okay to make a public announcement like Almeda was fixing to do. But without Royce having the same advantage, it hardly seems like it'd be fair for me to do it."

All this time Pa had been so angry at Mr. Royce for everything he'd done, and now all of a sudden he was worrying about being fair—even to him. It didn't take long for him to start thinking like a politician—and a good one at that, not like the kind who are always trying to twist things for their own advantage. Maybe Pa was gonna be cut out for this kind of thing after all!

"Aw, come on, Drum," said Alkali Jones. "How considerate has that snake been t' you an' yer missus here?"

"All's fair in love and war—and politics—that's what they say, Drum," added Mr. Shaw.

"Now let's have no more of this, the rest of you," said Almeda. "My husband has made his first decision as a candidate for mayor, and I think we should support him to the fullest in it. And besides that, I think he's absolutely right. Ethically speaking, it would give him an unfair advantage to speak in church."

"Not to mention mixing religion and politics," added Miss Stansberry.

"Even if there weren't anything wrong with it," Pa said, "Royce'd squawk and complain of an unfair advantage and might get so angry he'd start causing who knows what kind of mischief all over again. Just because I have to be fair to the man doesn't mean I trust him any more than I ever did— which isn't much. No, there's not gonna be no speaking out about this change of plans in church. If I'm going to win this election, I'll do it fair and square, so that Royce hasn't got a straw of complaint to stand on."

The room got quiet and people sat back down again. Only Pa remained on his feet, slowly pacing about, as if he had to keep moving while he was trying to think. But when he spoke, since he was standing and all the rest of us were sitting, it was almost like a speech, although I knew speechmaking never crossed Pa's mind. I couldn't help being intrigued by the changes I saw coming over him already! He was taking command of the situation, just as Almeda had said she had hoped he would.

"And that brings us straight back to the question I asked a little while ago," Pa went on, "which seems to be the crux of the whole matter. My name isn't even on the ballot. I don't see how I *can* run against Royce for mayor, even if I want to. There just isn't enough time."

Silence fell again. He was right. Time was short. What could be done? The ballot obviously couldn't be changed.

"What about a write-in vote?" suggested Katie after a long pause.

"What's that?" asked Pa.

"A write-in vote. People write in someone's name who isn't officially running. You hear about it all the time in the East—although nobody ever wins that way because they just get a few votes."

"That's it! That's the perfect way!" exclaimed Almeda excitedly. "What do you think, Drummond?" she asked, turning toward Pa. "We'll get word out that everyone who was going to vote for me should write in your name on the ballot instead."

"That's a lot of folks to get word to," replied Pa, "because I still don't want an announcement made in church."

"We could do it, Pa," said Zack, getting into the spirit of it. "Look how many of us there are right here. We'll just go out and tell everybody!"

"He's right—we could!" said Almeda. "With eight or ten of us, each calling on five or six families, telling them to let it be known—why, the whole community would know in no time."

"What are we waitin' for?" cried Uncle Nick. "Let's get the horses saddled and the buggies hitched and be off!"

"Hold your horses!" said Pa loudly. "I figure if all this is going on because of me, I ought to have some say in it too!"

Everybody quieted down and waited. Pa thought for a moment. He was still standing up and slowly walking back and forth.

"All right," he said finally, "like I said a bit ago, I'm in this thing, so maybe Zack's got himself a good idea. If you're all of a mind to help, then you've got my permission to tell anybody you want—"

A fresh round of whooping and cheering went around the room. Even Rev. Rutledge dropped his normal reserve and got into the act with some noise.

"Wait a second . . . hold on!" shouted Pa. "Don't you go chasing off before the wagon's hitched! I was about to say you could tell anybody you want . . . *but* ye gotta keep word of this quiet—just one person to the next. I don't want this being talked about on the streets of Miracle Springs. I don't want Royce getting wind of it. You just tell people to spread the word around quietly and not to make a big ruckus about it, but just to walk into that schoolhouse on Tuesday and do what they feel they oughta do. The less Royce knows the better. I don't want to give him any more fuel to try anything else that's gonna hurt somebody. After the election's done, he can come and see me if he's got a complaint."

"That sounds easy enough," said Uncle Nick. "Now can we git going, Drum?"

"Nobody goes anywhere till after church tomorrow," answered Pa. "I don't want it talked about, you hear? Tomorrow afternoon, once folks are back home, then we'll see what can be done. But we're all going to go to church as usual, and we're not going to say anything. You all promise?"

Everyone nodded, although Uncle Nick and Alkali Jones didn't like the idea much. I think they would have liked to go and shout the news in the middle of the Gold Nugget so the whole town would know everything in five minutes!

Rev. Rutledge rose from his chair and walked over to Pa. "May I be the first to offer you my congratulations, Drummond?" he said, extending his hand. "I think you have chosen a reasonable and a wise course of action, and I want to wish you the best."

"Well, I reckon we'll see what'll come of it in a few days!" replied Pa, shaking his hand. The two men looked at each other for a couple seconds as their eyes met. I can't say it was a look of love so much as a look of mutual respect, and even friendship. They had sure come a long way together.

We went to church the next day, like Pa had said, but we all sat there with half smiles on our faces, as if we all knew a secret we were keeping from the rest of the town.

Which, of course, we did!

But we didn't keep it from them for long. That afternoon, everyone who had been at our place the day before—everyone except Pa, that is. He didn't feel he ought to go to people and ask them to vote for him—rode on horseback or by buggy all throughout the community to pay short visits to everyone we could. Almeda and Miss Stansberry and Rev. Rutledge had planned out where we would all go. Even Tad and Becky had their calls to make.

The visits continued on Monday, although Almeda and I went into the office and tried to conduct a normal day's work in spite of the distraction of knowing the election was the next day. Smiles and nods and whispered words of hope and encouragement as the day progressed told that the word of Pa's write-in candidacy had spread through the town as quickly and successfully as anyone could have imagined.

Late in the day, Franklin Royce paid another call. He came into the office, asked for Almeda, then extended his hand and shook hers in one last election formality.

"Well, Almeda," he said, "by tomorrow evening this will all be over. So may the best man win, as it were."

Almeda smiled, thinking to herself—as was I—that he could not possibly have realized the significance of his own words. He obviously knew nothing about Pa, or Almeda's decision to remove herself from the race.

We all went to bed tingling with anticipation and excitement . . . and a little fear besides!

The next morning, the fateful day of November 4, 1856, we all got up and rode into town in the wagon with Pa, so he could cast his vote.

Election Results

CHAPTER TWENTY-SIX

*T*he voting stopped at six o'clock that night.

The government man from Sacramento, Rev. Rutledge, and a few people they'd gotten to help locked the door right then and started to count the ballots. They figured to be done and announce the results by eight-thirty or nine o'clock.

By eight a pretty big crowd was beginning to gather around the schoolhouse. Lots of people had come back to town, whole families in wagons, carrying lanterns and torches. At eight-fifteen, Mr. Royce drove up in his fancy black buggy. We were all bundled up warm in the back of our wagon. People came over now and then to speak briefly to Pa and Almeda, but mostly we just waited nervously. We tried to figure out how many voters there were. Pa and Almeda thought there would be somewhere between three and five hundred men who lived in and close enough to Miracle to vote for its mayor. There were probably another hundred or two hundred men who lived farther away who would have come to town to vote in the presidential election.

At about eight-forty the door to the schoolhouse opened. Some men came out, and everybody who was waiting came and clustered around the stairs to hear the news. The government man held a paper in one hand and a lantern in the other.

"I have some results to report to you," he said, and silence fell immediately over the crowd. "First of all, in the election you're most interested in, that for mayor of Miracle Springs, we have tallied the unofficial vote as follows. These will have to be reconfirmed, but this is the first count. For Mrs. Almeda Parrish Hollister, the first name on the ballot, there were 67 votes cast."

A small ripple of applause scattered about. Already I could see a smile starting to spread across Mr. Royce's face where he stood not too far away.

"For the final name to appear on the ballot, Mr. Franklin Royce, we have a total of 149 votes."

Again there was some applause, though it was not as loud as Royce had expected. His smile grew wide. The turnout was not very high, but he was willing to take the victory any way it came. He began making his way through the crowd and toward the steps where he was apparently planning to address the people of Miracle Springs with a short victory speech. He had just taken the first two steps when he was stopped by the sound of the man at the top of the landing again.

"And in what is a most unusual and unexpected occurrence, we have a third unregistered candidate. . . ."

Everybody could almost feel the chill sweep through Mr. Royce's body. The smile began to fade from his lips.

"This candidate has received a sizable number of write-in votes. In fact, by our unofficial tabulation, a certain Mr. Drummond Hollister, with 243 write-in votes, would appear to be the winner. . . ."

Before these last words were out of his mouth, a huge cheer went up from the crowd gathered there in the darkness. Instantly scores of people clamored around Pa and Almeda, shouting and shaking hands and clapping and whooping and hollering. In the middle of it, suddenly Mr. Royce appeared. His smile was gone, and even in the darkness I could see the rage in his eyes.

"I don't know what kind of trick this is, Hollister," he said. "But believe me, you won't get away with it!"

Without waiting for a reply, he spun around and walked back to his buggy. No one took any notice as he turned his horse and cracked his whip and flew back toward town. Nothing ever came of this last threat. There was not a thing he could do. Pa had won the election fair and square!

Looking Past the Election
CHAPTER TWENTY-SEVEN

After the headlong rush of events for the four or five months leading up to the election, the months of November and December of that year seemed like a sudden calm. Like a river tumbling over rocks and through white, foamy rapids, our lives suddenly opened out into a calm pool.

Everyone, myself included, felt like just sitting back and breathing out a sigh of relief. It was good to know there were no more stories I had to write immediately, no more dangers facing anyone, no more elections, no more trips, no more handbills to pass out. The next morning I lay in bed for a long time, just enjoying the quiet. I didn't want to get up, I didn't want to write, I didn't want to think about anything!

The whole town seemed to feel that way. People seemed relaxed, but they were talking plenty about the election results! The men spent a lot of time hanging around the street in front of the Mine and Freight, although we hardly had a customer for three days. They weren't interested in seeing any of *us*, or in doing business. They were waiting to catch sight of their new mayor!

When Pa rode into town that Wednesday afternoon, I knew by the look on his face that he had no idea what was waiting for him. He was such a down-to-earth and humble man that he still didn't realize that he was suddenly a local hero. He had hardly gotten past the first buildings of Miracle Springs when word began to spread, faster than the time it took him to ride the rest of the way in. By the time he got off his horse and was tying the reins to the rail in front of the store, fifty men and women had gathered around him—shouting, cheering, throwing out questions—with kids running through the streets like miniature town-criers, telling everybody that the new mayor was in town!

Pa just looked sheepishly at everybody, confused and not sure what all the fuss was about. After a minute or so they all quieted down, as if they were waiting for Pa to make a speech or something. But when he finally spoke, all he said was, "Tarnation, what are you all raising a ruckus about? I just came to fetch my wife, and I can't even get through the door!"

———

Almeda wasn't due until April or May, but Katie, who was due earlier, was starting to show a lot. And once the election was over, the anticipation of two new babies on their way into the Hollister-Belle-Parrish clan started to take more of everybody's attention. I could see both Pa and Uncle Nick treating Katie and Almeda with more tenderness, pampering them more than usual. Katie still could be reserved and distant, and every once in a while she would say or do something that made me wonder whether she liked Almeda at all. Sometimes I saw a look on Uncle Nick's face as if he might be thinking, "What's going on inside this lady I married?" Nick tried to be gentle with her, helping her across the bridge with his hand, or fixing her some soup when she didn't feel well. Sometimes she'd be appreciative and smiling, but at other times she seemed to resent it, and would snap, "Let me alone. I can take care of myself!" Uncle Nick would stomp around muttering, or go off for a ride or a walk alone in the woods if Katie got after him. It was obvious he didn't know what to do. Being a husband was still pretty new to him. But Almeda never seemed to take it personally or be hurt by it. Once she said to me quietly after Katie and Uncle Nick had left and we were alone for a minute, "I know what she's going through, Corrie, and I know how hard it is."

"What is it?" I asked. "You mean with the baby and feeling sick and all?"

She smiled. "Oh, that upsets our system a bit," she answered, "but there's more to it than that. The Lord is at work in your Aunt Katie's heart, Corrie, and she doesn't like it. We must continue to pray. Her time is coming."

That was all she ever said. But ever after that, when I'd look into Almeda's face when Uncle Nick and Katie were around, or when we'd go up to visit them or to help Katie, I saw an even more tender look in Almeda's eyes. Maybe she was praying at those times too. After what she'd said to me, I noticed Almeda paying all the more attention to Katie, looking for every opportunity possible to help her or do something for her. I wondered if she would say something to Katie about God as she had with me several years before. But as far as I know, nothing was ever said.

In the meantime, more visitors began to show up around our place, men coming to ask Pa's advice about things. They came both to the claim and to the office in town. Sometimes it was about a little thing that didn't have anything to do with Pa, but maybe they figured that since he was mayor and was a man they could trust, he was the one to ask. And once he realized this was going on, something in Pa's bearing began to change. There seemed to be a confidence growing inside him. Around town, people would greet him with, "Hey, Drum!" and he'd wave and answer back. Gradually he seemed to get used to the attention folks paid him and quit minding it so much, as if he realized it was his duty now to be something more to them than he had been before.

Dirty Politics

CHAPTER TWENTY-EIGHT

*I*t took some time before we found out the results of the national election. We knew the following week that Mr. Fremont had lost his home state of California, but it was weeks before we found out that he had lost the rest of the country too. James Buchanan had been elected the fifteenth President of the United States.

By that time I was sure my story had never run in the *Alta*. I was disappointed for the Fremonts, and I didn't know what to think about my story. I was sure it would have helped counteract all the rumors and lies being told about Mr. Fremont during the campaign. And Mr. Kemble had seemed to want the information so badly. I couldn't imagine what had happened. I wrote to Mr. Kemble to find out, but it was well toward the end of November before I got a reply from him.

Dear Miss Hollister,

I understand your concern over your Fremont article, especially after the hard work and dangers you undertook on the *Alta*'s behalf. It was a fine bit of legwork you did, and now that I have been able to extract more of the full scope of what happened from your colleague, Mr. O'Flaridy, I realize just what a powerful article it was and how fortunate I am indeed to count you as one of my reporters. I commend you once again for a fine piece of journalism!

Unfortunately, as it turned out, I was unable to run the story in the Alta prior to the election. Apparently your man Gregory got back to the *Globe* and immediately began trying to cover his tracks with accusations against you and our paper. I received a not-so-friendly visit from the editor of the *Globe*, and he told me that if we tried to run a pro-Fremont piece there was sure to be trouble, for the paper as well as for you. I told him I didn't believe a word of it and that I fully intended to stand by my reporter and run the story. The world needed to hear, I said, that what was being said about John Fremont was nothing but a pack of lies. He left in a huff, and I made plans to print your story just as you gave it to me.

However, the next day my publisher ordered me to kill the story. "What?" I said. "They didn't get to you, did they?" He didn't say anything except to repeat his order. "Listen," I told him, "the country's got to know the rumors and charges against Fremont are unfounded. It could turn the election!"

"It doesn't matter now," he said. "You just kill that story. John Fremont will have to take care of himself without any help from us. If we run that story they could ruin us—both you and me and the paper, do you understand, Kemble? And they could hurt your young reporter friend too. We have no choice. They've made that clear, and I don't intend to see how far they're prepared to back it up."

"Goldwin?" I asked.

"Goldwin . . . and others," he answered. Then he left the room.

So I'm sorry, Miss Hollister, but he left me no choice. My publisher's a strong man, and a major influence in this city. I don't know how they got to him, but whatever they were holding over his head, it must have been powerful. I've never seen him so beaten down and defeated. But it was for your good as well as the paper's that we didn't run it, as much as it galled me to see the *Globe* get away with printing Derrick Gregory's phony interviews. I truly believe your story could have influenced the election, if it had run in time to be picked up by the Ohio and Pennsylvania papers. But sadly, we will never know.

Perhaps John Fremont will be able to make another run at the White House in 1860, and we can try to help his cause again. In the meantime, I hope you will be working on some articles for me. You have shown a flair for politics as well as human interest. I would be happy to see you pursue more along that line in the future.

> O' Flaridy sends his regards.
> I remain
> Yours Sincerely,
> Edward Kemble, Editor
> San Francisco *Alta*

I almost expected my reaction to be one of anger. Most of Mr. Kemble's letters aroused all kinds of hidden emotions in me and put me through all kinds of ups and downs and doubts and questions. But this time I just put down the letter with a deep sense of sadness and regret. It almost confirmed everything Derrick Gregory had told me about politics being a dirty business where everything depended on money and what people wanted out of you rather than truth. Was that really what political reporting boiled down to? If so, then I for one didn't want to have any more to do with it. However flattering Mr. Kemble's words might have been, I would stick to human interest from now on. And as for Robin O'Flaridy's regards—those I could do without!

During the next several days I alternated between being upset, then depressed and disillusioned all over again. I had spent so much time and had invested such effort in that story, not to mention risking my life! And for what? The bad guys had won anyway. The powerful senator had used his influence to get his way and to keep the truth from being printed. A slave supporter would be in the White House for another four years. And all I *thought* I had accomplished seemed wasted. It really made me stop and question why I wanted to be a newspaper writer in the first place.

But then I got to thinking about the *other* election I had been part of. Who could deny that good *had* come through in the Miracle Springs mayor's race? It wasn't that I had much to do with the outcome—I probably hadn't at all. But the truth did come out in the end. The most truthful person, Pa, had won the election. And so in this case at least, politics wasn't a dirty business at all. The good guy had defeated the underhanded banker!

I never did come to much of a conclusion about myself and whether I would do any more writing about politics. But I finally realized that politics itself wasn't necessarily a bad thing. If you're going to run a country or a state or a town, you've got to have elections and officials and presidents. And I was glad that Pa was mayor now rather than Franklin Royce. Maybe what was needed was for good men like him to be in politics, not men like Mr. Royce and Senator Goldwin. I just hoped Mr. Buchanan would be a good man too, and a good president, and that someday someone would get elected who would free the slaves like Mr. Fremont had wanted to do.

I wrote to Ankelita Carter about returning Rayo Rojo to Mariposa. I had wanted to do so before the election but there hadn't been time. I told her about the article being scuttled and how sorry I was for the way the election had turned out. When I heard back from her, shortly before Christmas, she was furious. She said she was sure the election would have turned out different, especially in California, if people had known what she told me. She'd written to the Fremonts before the election and told them about what I was trying to do. She hadn't heard back from them since news of the loss, but she knew what Jessie and Mr. Fremont must be going through, and she said she intended to write them that very day with news of what had happened with the *Alta* story. There was nothing Mr. Fremont could do about it now, but he ought to know what Senator Goldwin had been able to do, even in far off California. She wanted to see me again, whenever it might be possible, and if I wanted to do *another* article on the Fremonts, she would be more than happy to oblige. There was no hurry about getting Rayo Rojo back, but when I was able to come, I should plan to spend at least two or three days with her.

She wrote as if I were her friend, and it set the wheels of my mind in motion again. Why couldn't I do an article on Mr. Fremont about the lies that had been told? It might not win him the election now, but at least it would vindicate his reputation and might help him in the future.

Time would tell. In the meantime, I wanted to think of some less controversial subjects to write about.

Preparations for the Holidays
CHAPTER TWENTY-NINE

*O*ur Christmases always seemed to be times of exciting announcements, high-running emotions, family, friends, guests, food, and the unexpected. The Christmas of 1856 was no exception.

We had been looking forward to Christmas all the month of December. Almeda had such a way of making the holiday a happy time, and of course my sisters and I couldn't have enjoyed anything better than being part of all the preparations. We made decorations out of ribbons and popped corn, colored paper, and greenery cut from the woods, bells, and dried berries.

And what Christmas celebration would be complete without a feast, and people to share that feast with? So along with everything else, we were thinking of who to invite to our place for the day. Pa and Almeda always included all five of us kids in most of the talking and discussion that had to do with our family. Sometimes they'd talk alone, walking together, or whispering in low tones in their room late at night, but they included us in everything they could. It really made us all feel that we were a *whole* family. And both of them would include *me* in even a more personal way in their decisions too. To say I had a *friendship* with my own Pa sounds a little funny, but in a way, that's what it was. He *was* my friend! And so was Almeda—friend and mother and an older sister all rolled up into one.

And so we talked and planned the Christmas as a family. Of course we intended to invite our friends like Alkali Jones and Rev. Rutledge and the Stansberrys, and of course Uncle Nick and Katie and little Erich. Zack said he'd like to invite Little Wolf and his father, and after a brief glance at Almeda, Pa looked back at Zack and replied, "I think that's a mighty good idea, son. You go right ahead and ask them if they'd join us for the day!"

Pa fell silent for a few moments. I hadn't noticed the look that had come over his face, but when he next spoke I could see in his eyes that he'd gone through an intense struggle just in those brief moments. The tone in his voice spoke much more than the words that came out of his mouth.

"You know, Almeda," he said quietly, "there is someone else we might pray about asking to join us."

"Who's that, Drummond?"

Pa paused again, and when he answered her, though his voice was soft, the words went like an explosion through the room.

"Franklin Royce," he said.

Becky and Zack immediately let out groans, but Almeda's eyes were fixed on Pa with a look of disbelief and happiness at the same time.

"You're right," she said after a moment. "He is a lonely man, with probably no place to go on Christmas."

"It just seems like the right thing to do," Pa added. "I'm not all that anxious to strike up a friendship with him after what he's done. But we have to put the past behind us, and I believe it's got to start with us. One thing's for sure—he's not going to be inviting us to his place anytime soon!"

Almeda laughed. "I think it's a wonderful idea, Drummond!"

The rest of that week before Christmas we did lots of baking—wild huckleberry pies, an *olia podrida* (a stew with a lot of meats and vegetables mixed together), and honeyed ham. Then Christmas morning we baked biscuits, potatoes, carrots, yams, and two pumpkin pies.

There was also a lot of sewing and stitching and trying-on to be done too, everyone pretending they didn't know what it was all for. Almeda made Pa close his eyes to try on the new vest she was making him, telling him to pay no attention to anything that was going on. I did the same for a shirt I was making for Zack. We kept poor Mr. Bosely so busy that week—buying extra bits of linen or cotton fabric, lace, buttons, and thread.

It was so funny to watch Pa going about Christmas business of his own, and with Zack and Tad. Men have such a hard time knowing how to do and make things, especially for wives and sisters and daughters. Most of the preparations at holiday time came from the women. But Pa entered into the spirit of it, and kept his little secrets too, and would sometimes shoot a wink at one of the boys about the things that *they* were planning that none of us knew about. I could tell it made Almeda love him all the more to watch him try to do his part to make it special.

A Christmas Day to Remember!

CHAPTER THIRTY

*C*hristmas morning everyone was up at the crack of dawn.

It was one of those crisp, sunny winter days that made me love California so much. And as the day wore on, though it would never get hot, I knew it would warm up enough to draw the fragrances up out of the earth and from the trees and out of the grasses and pinecones and dew. Days like that always made me want to go find a quiet place in the sun where I could just sit down and lean my back up against a tree trunk and read a book or draw or just think.

While Pa stoked up the fire with a new supply of wood and Almeda put the ham in the oven to bake, Tad scurried around making sure the rest of us were up and ready. Then he was off across the creek to fetch Uncle Nick and Aunt Katie to make sure they got down to our place the minute they were dressed. He didn't want to have to wait one second longer than he had to before Pa turned him loose in the pile of packages and presents next to our Christmas tree.

If the giving of gifts at Christmas is an expression of a family's love, then there couldn't have been a greater outpouring than there was that year. Pa gave Zack a beautiful new hand-tooled saddle with a matching whip. If Zack could have carried the saddle around with him all day, he would have. He *did* carry the whip, feeling its tightly wound leather handle, smelling it, examining every inch with his fingers and fine eye. He was truly a horseman, and nothing could have pleased him more.

Almeda gave me a beautifully bound copy of *The Pilgrim's Progress*, and a new journal. Like Zack, I carried around my two new books most of the day, just looking at them and feeling them.

She and I had made dresses for Emily and Becky. We three girls, with Katie's help, had nearly completed a new quilt for Pa and Almeda's bed, with a big "H" in the middle of it. But we had to give it to them not quite finished, saying we'd get the stitching done later.

There was a new doll for Becky, scarves for all three of us girls, a harmonica for Tad, Pa's new leather vest, and other smaller things—candies, fruits, nuts—as well as what we gave Uncle Nick and Aunt Katie.

Two of the most memorable gifts of the day were given to the two mothers. Almeda had bought a small New Testament. She had been praying a lot for Katie, and trying to find ways to talk to her about her life with the Lord. And so I knew how deeply from the heart the gift of the small book was. But when Katie opened it and saw what was inside the package, she was very quiet for a moment. "Thank you," she finally said, her words stiff and forced. When I glanced over at Almeda, I saw clearly the disappointment on her face from Katie's lack of enthusiasm.

Pa had made Almeda a nice wood shelf for the wall in her kitchen. It had three levels, with a decorative top-piece he'd carved out with a design. Almeda raved excitedly about what fine workmanship it was and all the things she would put in it. But then Pa pulled out one last wrapped package, one he'd kept hidden somewhere.

"Well, you've gotta keep a place on one of the shelves for this," he said as he handed it to her. "This is what gave me the idea of making the shelf in the first place, so you'd have somewhere to put it so you could see it."

She took it from him and opened it. Out came a beautifully painted little china replica of a two-story house, like I'd seen drawn in books and magazines of city buildings in the East.

"I ordered it from one of Bosely's catalogs," Pa said, and I could tell he was excited. "It's called 'Boston Home.' The minute I saw it, I wanted you to have it."

Almeda fought back tears. "Thank you, Drummond," she said finally in a soft voice. "It is beautiful."

"And look there behind," said Pa, taking it from her hand and turning it around, "here's a place for a candle, so it lights up and looks like there's lights in the windows. I hope you like it," he added. "I thought it would remind you of your home back East."

She looked up at Pa, then reached forward and kissed him.

"Whenever I look at it," she said, "it will remind me of how grateful I am to be here with *you* in California!"

Then she stood up and left the house for a few minutes. There *were* tears in her eyes by now. The room was silent for a short spell, then Pa tried to liven things up again.

"Play us a tune on your new mouth organ, Tad, my boy!" he said.

That was all the invitation Tad needed! He started blowing furiously with puckered lips, which was enough to send the rest of us scattering. Pretty soon we were all occupied with looking over our new things, and I didn't even notice when Almeda came back in. I happened to glance up from my book about ten minutes later and there she and Pa were over against one wall trying to find the best place for Pa to nail up her new shelves.

The rest of the morning we spent cooking—Almeda checking on the ham from time to time, the rest of us cutting up vegetables and peeling potatoes. Becky and I mixed up the biscuit dough. Katie and Uncle Nick went back to their place for the morning, until all the others came for dinner in the afternoon.

Alkali Jones was the first to arrive, and as always he kept things pretty lively the rest of the day. Then Rev. Rutledge and Harriet and Hermon Stansberry came, all together, Hermon riding his horse behind the carriage. When the minister helped Miss Stansberry down, I'd never seen him so gentle with anyone. Of course with her crippled leg, she needed assistance getting in and out of carriages and climbing steps. But he took hold of her arm so firmly, yet with such a kind look in his eye, I could tell she felt really safe. It was easy to see that he cared a great deal for her.

About half an hour later, Little Wolf rode up with Mr. Lame Pony, each of them on beautiful horses. Little Wolf always seemed to be riding a different animal, always spirited but well behaved, always groomed and shining. It was obvious the Indian father and son took great pride in their animals, and loved them as if they were part of their family.

Pa and Lame Pony shook hands, and Pa made every effort to make him feel welcome and at home with us. After tying up his horse, Little Wolf walked over to see me and Zack. We chatted a while, then he said, "This is a hard thing for my father. But the more he knows your father, the more he will trust him."

"Look," I said, "it won't take long." I pointed to Pa, already leading Lame Pony toward the stables to show him our horses. Pa had his arm slung around the Indian's shoulder and was talking good-naturedly. I knew he would win Lame Pony over and make him a friend in no time. Pa was like that with people nowadays.

When Katie and Uncle Nick came back down from their place not too long after that, however, I wondered if the spirit of Christmas was going to be spoiled. Little Wolf had been around enough that Katie had gotten used to him, although she never spoke to him or was very friendly. But now when Pa introduced her to Little Wolf's father, she was noticeably hostile.

"Nick, you know our neighbor from over the ridge," said Pa as he and Lame Pony walked toward them as they approached from the bridge over the creek.

"Best horses in California," replied Uncle Nick, giving him a shake of his hand. "Nice to see you here, Jack."

"Katie," Pa went on, turning to her, "this is Jack Lame Pony, Little Wolf's father. Jack, this is—"

Lame Pony nodded his head in acknowledgment toward Katie as Pa spoke, but before Pa could complete the introduction, Katie turned toward Uncle Nick and abruptly said, loud enough for everyone to hear, "What's *he* doing here?"

"He's our friend and neighbor, that's what," answered Uncle Nick hastily, obviously embarrassed by her rude comment, and a little riled at her at the same time.

"Well, neither of them are *my* friends," shot back Katie, and then marched off toward the house, leaving the three men standing there, Pa and Uncle Nick mortified at her behavior. And poor Lame Pony! What was *he* supposed to think after such an outburst?

But Pa didn't wait for the dust to settle around Katie's words. He said something about wanting to show Lame Pony something at the mine, and then I heard Uncle Nick trying to apologize for Katie, and adding something about women doing funny things when they're carrying young'uns. By dinnertime everything seemed to be smoothed over, although Katie was pretty sullen all day.

None of the rest of us could understand why she was so prejudiced against Indians, especially with what a good friend Little Wolf had been to our whole family. But we had learned to accept that Katie didn't think like the rest of us. She'd never been very friendly toward Rev. Rutledge either, as much as she knew he meant to the rest of us all. And although she was usually pretty tolerant, every once in a while she'd make some comment that let everyone know how ridiculous she thought trying to live like a Christian was.

"Going to church is one thing," she said once. "And though I don't have much use for it myself, I don't mind folks going themselves. But all this talking about God in between times, and praying, and trying to act religious about everything else you do—that's just taking it too far. Church is one thing, but you've got to live life without trying to bring God into every little thing. I've got no use for that kind of thinking. It's just not natural."

Almeda had been praying for her and hoping to find opportunities to share with her how she felt. I didn't know what Uncle Nick thought of it all. He never said much.

Mr. Royce was the last one to arrive, all alone in his expensive black buggy. Pa and Almeda greeted him as if he were an old family friend, and the look on his face made it clear he didn't know *what* to make of it. What he thought of getting the invitation in the first place I don't know, but being greeted and welcomed as a friend was altogether too much! Maybe he was so used to folks being suspicious of him that courtesy and friendliness made him uncomfortable. He was pretty reserved the whole day, yet entered into the spirit of the occasion as much as he was able to.

Once everybody had arrived, we went inside the house. The whole place was filled with delicious smells! The table was set as fancy as we had been able to make it, but Pa asked everyone to sit around in the big room where the chairs were rather than at the table.

"Almeda says the ham still has about half an hour," he said, "so that's why I arranged the chairs out here. There's some things I want us to talk about before we get down to the business of the dinner."

Everyone took a seat and it got quiet. Pa stood up in front and everybody waited for him to continue.

"Ever since me and the kids got together four years back," Pa began when everyone was situated, "we've kept up the tradition of reading the Christmas story together, kind of in memory of our Aggie, the kids' ma, and in memory of what this day's supposed to be all about."

Pa turned behind him and took down Ma's white Bible and flipped through the pages.

"This is our fifth Christmas together in California," he went on. "And, Avery, with all respect to you being our preacher, I think I'm going to keep this privilege all to myself today."

"Wonderful, Drummond!" said Rev. Rutledge with a smile. "It is a great blessing for me to be able to listen to you."

"So I'd like to invite all the rest of you to listen, though I guess I'm mostly reading this to the five of you kids. And you be sure to remember your Ma when I read, 'cause she got us going with this tradition, and I don't doubt for a minute that it's on account of her prayers that we're all together like this, doing our best to walk with the Lord like she did."

He drew in a sigh. I looked at Almeda out of the corner of my eye as he spoke. The radiant smile on her face was full of such love! I knew there was no confusion in her mind—or in anyone else's—over the love Pa had for both her *and* Ma, and the special place both the women God had given him held in different corners of his heart.

"And it came to pass in those days," began Pa with the familiar words out of Luke, "that there went out a de-cree from Caesar Augustus, that all the world should be taxed. And this taxing was first made when Cyrenius was governor of Syria. And all went to be taxed, every one into his own city. And Joseph also went up from Galilee, out of the city of Nazareth, into Judaea, unto the city of David, which is called Bethlehem; (because he was of the house and lineage of David:) To be taxed with Mary his espoused wife, being great with child. And so it was, that, while they were there, the days were accomplished that she should be delivered. And she brought forth her first-born son, and wrapped him in swaddling clothes, and laid him in a manger; because there was no room for them in the inn. And there were in the same country shepherds abiding in the field, keeping watch over their flock by night. And, lo, an angel of the Lord came upon them. . . ."

As he read the story, Pa's voice filled the room. Everyone sat quiet, not just listening, but *absorbing* his words. It was a different voice than the one who had read the Christmas story four years earlier, just after we had arrived in California. This was the voice of a man of confidence, afraid of nothing—not even afraid to stand up and talk to other people about his God and the birth of his Son. Just listening to him read—well, it was no wonder that the people around here had come to respect and admire him. Now it was *Pa* reading from the Scriptures, and Rev. Rutledge sitting and listening with a smile on his face, as if he was proud of Pa and what he was becoming. Pa's voice seemed to have a *power* in it, even though he was reading softly.

As we sat there listening, I looked at the faces around me. What did Mr. Lame Pony and Little Wolf think of our Christmas religious practices? Franklin Royce's eyes were fixed on Pa as if he was trying to make sense of this man who was extending forgiveness toward someone who had done his best to destroy him. I saw something in that lonely banker's face, and a little spark of love for the man stirred in my heart.

Alkali Jones sat there more still than I'd ever seen him. He was staring down at the floor, so deep in thought he looked like he was a thousand miles and forty years away. I wondered what memories he was reliving as Pa read. Had *his* mother read him this passage as a child? What *was* going through that old mind? And Katie—she sat there, still looking solemn. I couldn't read a thing in her eyes. But I knew she was thinking.

Pa's voice pervaded the room, and the very sound was weaving a mood upon us. I don't think I've ever been so aware of what it might be like for God to be speaking through a man as I was that day. I felt as if God himself was telling us the story of Jesus' birth, and using Pa's voice to do it. It was hard to imagine that Katie had a hard time believing, or that Mr. Royce had ever been Pa and Almeda's enemy, or that there could possibly be enmity between Indians and white people. There was such a good feeling in the room, a sense of oneness. The story of Jesus' birth was so alive that we were all sitting on the edge of our seats to hear how it would all turn out.

". . . And when eight days were accomplished for the circumcising of the child, his name was called JESUS, which was so named of the angel before he was conceived in the womb."

Pa stopped, and the room remained silent. Pa closed the Bible, and then after a short pause started talking again.

"I don't aim to start infringing on our good Reverend's territory. That'd be just a different kind of claim jumping, wouldn't you say, Avery? But it strikes me that a few more words might be in order on a day like this. Since this is my house and you all are our guests, then I reckon nobody'll mind if I take the liberty of delivering them myself."

A few people chuckled, and everybody relaxed in their seats. "You go right ahead, Drummond," said Rev. Rutledge. "I'm sure these good folks are sick of my preaching and will welcome the change!"

"Well, I thank you," replied Pa, "but I ain't gonna preach, and I don't aim to keep them as long as *you* do on Sundays!"

More laughter followed.

"I guess I just figured this was a good time for me to say a thing or two about what Christmas means to me," said Pa. "And what my family means. Somehow you need to say these kinds of things to other people once in a while for it to get all the way down to where it's supposed to go. So I'm going to tell you who're here with us today."

He paused, took a breath, then continued.

"Christmas is a time for giving and good food and friends," Pa said. "And for the youngsters there's always some toys and gifts and candy. So now and then we can get our eyes off what's the *true* meaning of this day. On this day God's Son, the little baby Jesus, was born. We need to remember that, because without his coming to the earth when he did, and living his life and then giving it up for us, there wouldn't be any life for the rest of us.

"But then I've been thinking, there really *is* something special about families at Christmas. So I just want to say how thankful I am that God gave me this family of mine—every one of these kids that Aggie gave me, God bless her. And for Almeda and the one that she's bearing right now, and for Nick and Katie and their family. I just feel about as full and blessed as any man ought to have a right to feel. And I'm thankful for the rest of you too, because you're what you might call a part of our bigger family.

"So, God bless you all—thank you for sharing Christmas with us. Let's not forget that Jesus was born on this day a long time ago. And let's never forget that good friends and family are what makes this world a pretty special place."

Pa stopped and sat down. In earlier years he might have shown a little embarrassment at making a speech like that. But not this time.

"Amen to every word, Drummond!" said Rev. Rutledge. "We are blessed to be part of your family, and that you are part of all of us too."

Pa nodded while a few other comments filtered around.

"And now, might I be permitted a word or two also?" the minister added, glancing first at Pa and then at Almeda.

"Of course, Avery," said Almeda.

"This won't take long," said Rev. Rutledge, standing up and then clearing his throat. He sent a glance and smile in Miss Stansberry's direction.

"I have a little announcement to make," he went on, "and I—that is, we—thought it would be nice to wait and tell you all about it all at once. And what more fitting time and place than here on Christmas day?"

He took in a big gulp of air, then plunged ahead. "And what I've got to tell you is this: Harriet and I are engaged to be married. . . ."

I think he was going to say something more, but before he could get another word out of his mouth, Almeda was on her feet nearly shrieking with delight.

"Oh, that's wonderful!" she exclaimed, hurrying over to Miss Stansberry and taking both her hands in a tight clasp.

In the meantime Pa and Uncle Nick had joined the minister and were shaking his hand and slapping him on the shoulder. In another minute everyone else was on their feet joining the hubbub and well-wishing.

"Couldn't keep from stealing the show, eh, Reverend?" laughed Uncle Nick.

Rev. Rutledge knew he was being kidded only because of how happy everyone was for him, and joined in another loud round of laughter with the men. His boisterous laugh could even be heard above Alkali Jones' *hee, hee, hee*! The fact that Pa and Uncle Nick and Avery Rutledge were laughing and joking and talking together like they were showed how much things had changed in those four years since our first Christmas together. Who could have foreseen it all?

I glanced over at Almeda. She'd been talking with Miss Stansberry, but then looked over across the room at the men.

For once she wasn't looking at Pa, but at Rev. Rutledge. She had tears in her eyes. She had cared for him, in a different way from Pa. And I knew his happiness meant a lot to her.

But she only watched the celebrating men a moment, then clapped her hands a few times and raised her voice above the din.

"Enough everyone!" she cried. "You can do the rest of your visiting and carrying on at the table. It's time to eat, and the food's hot! Come now, find your places!"

*W*hat a group that was!

Pa stood up by his chair at the head of the table and raised his hands to quiet everyone down for the prayer.

"Before you take your seats," said Pa, "let's all bow our heads and give thanks to God."

Everyone calmed down. A quiet settled over the room.

"God, we thank you for this day," said Pa solemnly. "Help us all never to forget what it means. And help us every day of the year to remember how much you loved us, and the whole world, to give us your Son. And thank you for family and friends, and the good food and fellowship you give us together. Amen."

"Okay, everyone," said Almeda, walking toward the stove while everyone got into their seats, "we've got ham and sweet potatoes, biscuits, stew, vegetables, and a special treat that Lame Pony and Little Wolf fixed for us—what did you call them, Jack?"

"*Pozoles*" answered Little Wolf's father. "That is Mexican word. Little Wolf and me, we just say pig's feet."

"So all of you try one of Jack's *pozoles*," added Almeda—handing two large pewter platters, one to Pa, one to Mr. Royce—"while we start this food around the table. But save room for the pies!"

It didn't take long for everyone's plate to be piled high, and within five minutes the sounds of eating and conversation and laughter echoed around the table. There was a harmony in it, almost like music. I sat with Becky on one side and Little Wolf on the other, trying to listen to Mr. Jones on the other side of Becky and Rev. Rutledge a little further away. I was especially curious about what Pa and the banker were talking about. So the whole meal for me was a mixed-together jumble of half conversations, laugher that I didn't know the cause of, words, smiles, and always passing food and exhortations from Almeda to eat up on the one hand but to save place for dessert on the other.

Alkali Jones was in good form, as always, and must have told two or three of his famous "totally" unbelievable stories. But as interesting as they always were, on this day I found myself most eager to hear what was going on across the table, and I strained to listen whenever I could.

"Glad you could be with us today, Franklin," Almeda had said.

"I must say your invitation came as a surprise."

"Why's that?" said Pa. But when the banker turned toward him to answer, I couldn't hear what he said.

". . . put it in the past," I heard Pa say next. "Learn to live like neighbors and brothers. . . ."

"What my husband is talking about, Franklin, is forgiveness," put in Almeda. "Don't you think it's time to let bygones be bygones?"

Mr. Royce said something, but I couldn't hear it. He didn't seem altogether comfortable with the direction of the conversation. It was as if he didn't know how to react to it being so personal.

"That's exactly what I was trying to say," added Pa. "I figure if I'm gonna be mayor, even though you wanted to be when this whole thing started, then I've got to be your mayor too. And that means doing the best I can for you just like everyone else. And so we figured the best place to start was to invite you to our home and shake your hand like a friend and neighbor, and say, 'Merry Christmas, let's put the past behind us.'"

". . . kind of you—kind of you both," Mr. Royce said, "certainly more hospitality than anyone else in this town has ever shown me."

"We want to be your friend, Franklin," said Almeda, and although I was too far away to see into her eyes, I knew from her tone what kind of look was on her face.

"Even though I tried to put you out of business and have opened a store to compete against you? A Christmas meal may be one thing, but do you seriously think I can believe you want to be my friend?"

"Believe what you want, Royce," answered Pa, and now it was quieting down a bit around the table as more of us were listening to this most interesting conversation. "Whether you can understand it or not, we're supposed to be your neighbor and to try to do good to you and to love you. That's what the Lord God tells his folks to do, and it don't matter what they do back to you in return. So Almeda and I've been praying for you, and we want to do good for you however we can. I don't reckon I've been too neighborly to you in the past, and I hope you will find it in your heart to forgive me for that. In the meantime, I aim to change. I aim to forgive you for what you've done, to keep praying for you, and to do my best for you however I can."

He stopped, and the table was silent for just a moment. Mr. Royce just shook his head and muttered something at the same time as Alkali Jones let out with a cackle, "Hee, hee, hee! If that don't beat all! Mayor and preacher all rolled up into one!"

Then Tad asked for another biscuit and Almeda started passing food again, and pretty soon the conversation was once more at a loud pitch, although I never heard any more serious goings-on between Pa and Mr. Royce.

The only person who didn't enter much into the lively talk was Katie. She hardly said a word, and didn't seem to be enjoying the Christmas celebration at all. She was either feeling mighty poorly, or else had something brewing in her mind.

When the meal was done, the men went outside to light pipes and talk about horses and weather and whatever else men talk about. We girls and Miss Stansberry and Almeda got busy cleaning everything up, talking and chatting away, mostly about Rev. Rutledge's and Miss Stansberry's surprise news, and when they were planning the wedding and what kind of dress she would wear. Katie still didn't participate much. Claiming to be tired, she left and went back up to their place.

An hour or so later, when we had the place looking tidy again, the men came back in and we cut into the huckleberry and pumpkin pies. Uncle Nick had a piece of pie, then took little Erich and went to check on Katie.

By this time even Jack Lame Pony seemed to be feeling real comfortable and he and Pa and Rev. Rutledge were talking freely. Hermon was asking lots of questions about the horse-breaking work they did and was even planning to go up to their place in a day or two to look for a new horse. Zack and Little Wolf and Tad were off shooting their guns. Franklin Royce was even entering in a little to the conversation, though I still don't think I'd seen him smile the whole day. But at least the scowl that I'd always associated with him was gone from his face, and every once in a while I'd hear him say something to one of the other men. He seemed a little out of his element, however, with the others talking about such man-things as working and mining and shooting and horse taming, and him there with his suit and white hands that hardly looked like they'd seen a day of work. But you almost had to admire him for entering in as much as he did.

Mr. Royce was the first to leave, late in the afternoon, but the others stayed a while longer, drinking coffee and nibbling now and then at the ham or one of the pies.

Around dusk, Uncle Nick and Katie and little Erich came back down the path, holding a lantern. The most memorable part of that Christmas was about to begin.

Katie's Outburst

CHAPTER THIRTY-TWO

*K*atie was still quiet and sober. Everyone greeted her kindly, but she didn't say much. Uncle Nick looked a little nervous, and would glance at her now and then, although he entered into the spirit of the evening with everyone. I wondered if they had an argument, because they didn't say much to each other.

Everyone but Mr. Royce was still there. The day cooled off quickly. Pa stoked up the fire, and we sat around the hearth talking and chatting. I don't think I'd ever seen Rev. Rutledge so jovial and in such high spirits. Even he and Alkali Jones laughed together more than once about something one or the other said. Mr. Lame Pony was a little more reserved when Katie got back, and every once in a while I'd catch a glimpse of him glancing over at her, probably wondering what she thought. But he stuck around, visiting with the men, and I was glad of that. I hoped he and Pa might become friends!

As the evening progressed, the talk got more subdued and quiet, even serious at times. How different Pa was! He talked with Rev. Rutledge about spiritual things on equal footing, not as a miner talking to a preacher.

"What do you think, Avery," Pa was saying, "about how God lets folks know what he wants them to do?"

"Do you mean how he speaks, how he guides in our lives?"

"Yeah. How can you tell if God's telling you something or if it's just your own thoughts? Like me being mayor. I figure something ought to be different about my mayoring if I say I'm trying to follow God in what I do. It ought to be different than me just following my own nose like most folks do, and like I spent most of my life doing."

"That's exactly what being a Christian is, Drummond, bringing God into all you do."

"It's easier for you, because religion's your business, ain't it, Reverend?" piped in Uncle Nick.

"Just the opposite, Nick," replied Rev. Rutledge, turning toward him. "Maybe you're right in one way," he added slowly. "It is easier for me to *talk* about things of God because people expect it of me. But it's no easier for me to have God's attitudes inside than anyone else. And, you know, I sometimes think being a preacher is a handicap."

"How's that?"

"Because my very presence gets it into people's minds that there is a difference between religious and nonreligious people. Like I said, they expect me to be religious. After all, I'm a preacher, I get paid to talk about God. I can never go into any situation, any discussion, any group of people and just be myself—Avery Rutledge, a man with feelings and thoughts like everyone else."

The others were silent for a minute. Even the quiet showed that what Rev. Rutledge said was true, and that they *hadn't* thought of him as anything but a preacher. I knew that was true about me. The only ones among us who had really seen him as a *person* beneath the minister were probably Almeda and Miss Stansberry.

"I reckon you're right, Avery," said Pa after a minute. "That is how folks see you, and that's me too. I reckon maybe I owe you an apology."

"Think nothing of it, Drum," laughed Rev. Rutledge. "I wasn't looking for sympathy, only telling you how it is with me."

"Still, I aim to take your words to heart. So if I ever forget and start talking to you like you're only a preacher, and you need me to be a friend just as one man to another, then you stop me and say something. I want you to do that, you hear, Avery?"

"Agreed," smiled Rev. Rutledge, and I could tell Pa's words meant more to him than he was letting on.

"That goes for me too, Reverend," added Uncle Nick. "You can count on the two of us as your friends, whether it's preacher-business or not."

"I thank you too, Nick."

Alkali Jones and Mr. Lame Pony and all the rest of us were watching and listening to this exchange with a sense of wonder. Men rarely talk honestly and about their feelings with one another, and we'd never heard these three men talk like that. I knew what Almeda was feeling. I didn't even have to look at her. And I suppose something of the same mood was upon all of us. Christmas had brought a gift nobody had been looking for, the realization that these men weren't just "acquaintances" who got together for dinner, but *friends*.

"Okay then, well *I* got a question fer ye," piped in Mr. Jones, to everyone's surprise. I'd never heard a single word even hinting at religion from his mouth. Heads turned toward him. "How *do* you figure to bring God into yer mayoring, Drum? Sounds like a kinda crazy notion if ye ask me."

"I don't know, Alkali," Pa answered. "That's why I was asking the Reverend here. But there *oughta* be a way to do things different if you're trying to walk with God."

"So whatcha got in mind, Drum?" Mr. Jones asked again. Still he hadn't let out one of his cackling laughs. He seemed genuinely interested in the answer.

"I don't know. I figured maybe if there was something I had to do, or some decision to make that affected the town, I ought to pray about it, or maybe get together with some of the rest of you and Avery here, and try to find out what the Lord wants to happen. It seems like that'd be a better way to go about things than just barging ahead and doing whatever I think of to do. Nick and I did that for a lot of years, and I can't say as it always turned out so good. Maybe it's time I tried to learn a new way of going about things. The idea's just a little new to me. It'll take some getting used to. I don't know my way around too well yet with thinking like this."

"None of us do," said Almeda, speaking now for the first time. "Look at how long I've been trying to live as a Christian, and yet only a few months ago there I was out chasing my dream of being mayor without ever stopping to ask what God or my husband might have to say in the matter."

"It is easy to hitch our own horse to the wagon instead of letting God be the horse and us being the wagon."

"That's a good one, Reverend," laughed Mr. Jones. "Hee, hee, hee!"

"You could put that in your next sermon, Avery," added Pa.

Now it was Zack's turn to get into the discussion. "I'm not sure I see what you mean about the horses and wagon, Rev. Rutledge," he said. The serious expression on his face showed he was really trying to grasp the deeper meaning.

"I was only saying that sometimes we've got to stop and take a look at who's doing the leading and who's doing the following," replied the minister.

The puzzled look on Zack's face didn't disappear.

"Come on, Avery," said Pa good-naturedly. "If the boy takes after his Pa, he's likely a little thick-headed." As Pa said it he shot a wink in Zack's direction to show he meant only fun. "He's gonna need more explanation than that."

"You don't want me to preach a sermon, do you, Drum? You've got to be careful what kind of openings you give a preacher, you know."

Pa and the rest of us laughed.

"Don't try to fool us, Reverend," laughed Uncle Nick. "You'll take any chance you can get to convert us sinners! Remember that first Christmas in town at Almeda's?"

A huge roar of laughter followed. Now that they *were* friends, they all remembered that awkward discussion around the dinner table with affection for each other.

"I *did* do some preaching at you that day, didn't I!"

"I never wanted to see your face again," said Pa, still laughing.

"I figured it'd be up to me to save the new minister's life, hee, hee, hee!" said Mr. Jones. "I'd never seen ol' Drum so riled up!"

"Well, those times are all over now," said Pa, "and I for one am thankful for that. I was a plumb fool about a lot of things back then, and I don't want to remember it any more than I have to. So on with your sermon, Avery. Tell us about horses and wagons. We're all waiting."

"Are you sure? You know what I'm like on Sundays. Once you get me going, I can't stop!"

"Course we're sure. You still wondering about your question, son?"

"Yeah," answered Zack. "I'd like to know what you have to say, Rev. Rutledge."

"You listen to these men, Avery," said Almeda almost sternly. "They are all your friends, and they *want* the benefit of your experience and insights."

Rev. Rutledge took in a long breath. "All right," he said. "I suppose you asked for it. But I'll try to make it a *short* sermon."

"Agreed," said Pa. He looked at me with a quick smile and wink, as if to say, *Bet me, eh, Corrie! He'll never keep it short!*

"I've always thought the horse and wagon picture perfectly illustrated our relationship with God," Rev. Rutledge began. "It's easy to talk about what we call 'following the Lord,' but how we actually go about living through the day is much different. In practice, we try to be the horse, and we drag God along behind us as if he were the wagon. When it comes to deciding where to go and how fast to go and which forks in the road to take, *we* lead the way, just like a horse pulling a wagon.

"What God wants, of course, is that we allow him to take the lead and let *him* be the horse. He can do a better job of leading than we can. He knows how fast to go, which roads to take. Our responsibility as Christians is to follow."

"How do you follow horse you not see?" said Mr. Lame Pony, speaking up for the first time in a long while. He had been listening to everything intently.

"That is both the difficulty and challenge of life as a Christian," replied Rev. Rutledge. "It is no easy task. We have to unlearn a lot of habits because our natural inclination is to just gallop off, like Drummond said a while ago, following our *own* nose. That's the way we're made—independent. When

Drummond says to himself, 'I want to find out what *God* wants me to do about this instead of what *I* might have thought to do,' he changes the whole order of his life around. He says, 'I'm going to become a wagon now, and stop being the horse.' And it takes a great deal of practice because we're not used to thinking that way. At least most adults aren't. I suppose children follow their parents when they are young. But then once they get out on their own, they take charge of their own lives. The way God really intended it, however, is for adulthood just to mean that we change horses—from letting our parents do the leading in our lives to letting God lead. It's a hard thing to do—especially because, as Jack says, we often cannot see the horse. We don't know what God might be saying to us about which path to take here or there. It takes a lot of practice, many new habits. It's a challenge that lasts a lifetime."

He fell silent and nobody spoke for a few seconds.

"Do you see what I mean, Zack?" Rev. Rutledge added. "I don't suppose I was real specific about *how* it all works. That's something God has to show every person individually, because he leads all of us on different paths and in different ways. But do you see what I mean about the principle of the horse leading the wagon?"

"Yes, sir," replied Zack.

"So in answer to my original question," said Pa, "about how God lets us know what we're to do, you're telling me that you don't exactly know what he's gonna be saying to me, but that I have to keep listening anyway so I don't accidentally get out in front of the horse, is that it?"

"Like I did before the election," added Almeda.

"I suppose that's about it," answered Rev. Rutledge with a smile. "An answer that maybe isn't an answer you can do much with until the time comes when you have to ask God for yourself what he's saying to you."

I found myself thinking back to the words of his sermon about how God speaks to us through our thoughts, and about pointing our thoughts and prayers toward God so that he could point his toward us. But before I had a chance to think too much about it, Tad's voice broke the silence.

"Who's driving the wagon?" he said.

Everyone laughed.

"That's the trouble with any illustration," said Rev. Rutledge. "There's always someplace where the parallel doesn't work. Maybe God is driving the wagon, and the horses are Jesus or the Holy Spirit. They're who we're supposed to be following, while our heavenly Father directs everything. It's difficult for it to make exact sense. But I think we all see the principle involved in trying to apply Proverbs 3:6: 'In all thy ways acknowledge him'—that's the part of letting him be the horse, the driver, the guide of our lives—'and he shall direct thy paths.' But thank you for your question, Tad. We need young fellows like you to keep us on our toes."

The whole conversation had been lively and warm. Just from the looks on their faces, I could tell everyone felt involved and felt the same thing I did, that it was all the more special this time since the men were open and talking freely with each other. Everyone except Katie, that is. She had been sitting the whole time a little ways off from the rest. I didn't want to look at her, but out of the corner of my eye I could see that she wasn't enjoying it. I couldn't tell if she was sick or angry. She'd had a sour look on her face all day. I felt bad for her not feeling well on Christmas.

Pretty soon Almeda got up and made some fresh coffee, and the conversation picked up again in other directions.

Little Erich was waddling around talking to himself. I listened more closely and heard the words, "God drive wagon . . . God make horse go." Just then Uncle Nick walked by and scooped his son up and tossed him up into the air.

"What's that you're saying, boy?" he said, catching him and burying his face in the plump little belly.

Erich just giggled.

"He was talking about God driving the wagon," I said. "He must have heard what Rev. Rutledge said."

"A little preacher in the making, that's what you've got, Nick," said Almeda with a smile as she held out a cup of coffee for him.

"That'd be a mighty hard one for my father to imagine!" laughed Nick. "Why the very thought of it—"

He never finished his sentence. Katie had had enough, and was suddenly on her feet.

"The thought of it's enough to make me completely sick!" she yelled. "You stay away from my son with any more of your talk of making him a preacher, do you hear, Almeda? And as for you," she added, spinning around and glaring at me, "you mind your own business, Corrie!"

In an instant there was silence in the whole house.

"Now wait a minute, Katie," said Uncle Nick, trying to calm her down. "They didn't mean no harm. There's no call to go yelling at—"

"You stay out of it, you big lout!" she snapped back at him. "You're the worst of the lot, talking about horses and wagons and God and the Bible like there was anything to any of it. It's all such ridiculous trash, you talking away with that minister and that Indian like you're some saint! You big hypocrite! I know you better than anyone here, and I daresay *you're* not holy!"

"Just you quiet down a minute! Just because you're not feeling so good doesn't give you the right—"

"I'm feeling fine!" Katie retorted, shouting louder now. All the rest of us were shocked silent. It was terrible to be in the middle of such an argument, especially with her having just yelled at me and Almeda, and now pouring out all her anger on Uncle Nick. "I'm not going to quiet down. I've been quiet too long! All this talk about God and religion—I hate it! I can't stand it one second more! Hypocrites, that's what you all are, and you're the biggest fool of them all, Nick, if you believe one word of all that! I'm getting out of here!"

She grabbed little Erich out of Uncle Nick's arms, and turned around for the door before anyone could say a word.

"Katie, you just wait," said Uncle Nick, going after her. "You may be able to say what you want to me. But you ain't got no right to go shouting at Corrie and Almeda, or calling the minister or anyone else names. If you're bound and determined to go, then you owe them an apology."

"An apology! The only thing I'll apologize for is coming back down here at all. I should have stayed home! You and this family of yours are nothing but a pack of religious do-gooders, and I hate every bit of it!"

She was out the door with the final words trailing behind her. The door slammed in Uncle Nick's face with a loud crash. He opened it and went after her, leaving the rest of us in stunned silence. The only sounds in the whole room were the faint noise of the fire and the boiling water on the stove.

A Talk about God's Timing

CHAPTER THIRTY-THREE

*A*lmeda was still standing there holding the cup of coffee she had meant for Uncle Nick. Her face was deathly white. I suppose mine was too, after what Katie had said to both of us. But neither of us felt anger, only hurt and sadness to find out what Katie had been keeping inside all this time.

Slowly Pa got up, walked over, took the cup from Almeda's hand, and led her to a chair. "Don't think anything of it," he said. "It wasn't you she was upset at."

Almeda nodded and sat down. "I know," she said. She took in a breath and let out a long sigh. "Poor Katie," she said softly. "She's got so much turmoil inside, and so many mixed-up ideas. She thinks God is her enemy, when really he's the only source of life she's ever going to find."

"Why don't you tell her that?" I suggested.

"Now?" replied Almeda, looking over at me. "Oh no, Corrie. She's in no frame of mind to hear it now—especially from me. Right now she needs some time to cool off and settle her mind down. And I'm sure she and Nick will have to work some things through after this, and he needs to be the one standing beside her."

"But she needs to know God's not at all like what she thinks."

"All in good time, Corrie," said Pa. "God can't be rushed in what he's about with people. Look at me. Sometimes it takes a good long while for him to break through the outer layers people have got up all around them. And from what I know about Katie, I reckon she's got a few for him to break."

"That doesn't sound too pleasant," I said.

Rev. Rutledge went to stand next to Pa. A look of deep concern filled his face.

"Pleasantness isn't always what the Lord is after, Corrie," he said. "His purposes are beyond what someone feels— whether they're happy or sad on a given day. He's after hearts and lives he can get inside of and possess more than he's after making a person happy."

Almeda let out a sigh. "I think we need to pray for our dear Katie," she said softly, then looked up at Pa.

He nodded, then sat down and immediately started to pray. I'd never heard Pa pray for another person like that. He seemed totally unconcerned about everybody else in the room listening. And everybody joined in silently, I could tell, even though only Pa and Almeda and Rev. Rutledge actually prayed out loud.

"Lord, we ask you to take care of Nick and Katie, and to calm Katie down so she can see how it really is with all of us."

"Oh, yes, God," Almeda went on. "And let her see how it is with our Father. Let her see that you love her, and that our lives are deeper and richer because we live them with you."

A short silence followed, then the minister prayed.

"Heavenly Father, we join together in asking for your touch to be upon Nick and Katie and their small family— right now, even as we pray. Give Nick the words to say to soothe and comfort his dear wife. And we pray that in your own way and time, you would draw Katie and open her heart to the influences of your life and love."

"Give us opportunities to show her that love, Lord," added Almeda. "Let your Spirit flow out from us to her. Help Katie to know that we do love her."

"Amen," said Rev. Rutledge.

As the room fell silent, gradually some of the others began getting ready to go. The mood of the wonderful Christmas we'd spent together was broken, and no one seemed inclined to try to be jovial any longer.

Hermon Stansberry got up and slowly put on his coat. Little Wolf and Lame Pony got up also and gathered their hats and coats.

"I suppose we ought to be heading back to town as well," said Rev. Rutledge, smiling toward Miss Stansberry. "But we will be in prayer for the situation here."

"Thank you, Avery," said Pa, shaking his hand. "And thanks for being part of our Christmas."

"*Thank you*, Drummond," rejoined Miss Stansberry.

"Oh, and we are so happy for the two of you!" added Almeda.

The minister and schoolteacher smiled. Almeda gave them each a big hug, and Pa led them to the door. In another few moments only our family was left inside, and everything was quiet. It had been a wonderful Christmas, but suddenly none of us felt very much of the Christmas spirit. Nobody said anything as we slowly gathered around the fire. Katie was weighing heavily on our hearts.

A few minutes later, Uncle Nick came back through the door.

"Well, I apologize to you all for what happened," he said with a sigh, taking off his hat and plopping down in a chair.

"Think nothing of it, Nick," said Pa. "It wasn't your fault. Just one of those things."

"I didn't make it any better by trying to shush her up. I shoulda just kept my mouth shut. But it's done now. I just wish I coulda said something to the others, though I did see the minister and Harriet outside."

"I'll go talk to Little Wolf and his father tomorrow if you'd like," said Zack.

"Would you, boy?" said Uncle Nick. "I'd be obliged to you if you did. You give them my apologies. That'd mean a lot to me."

"Sure, Uncle Nick."

Uncle Nick sighed again. He was really looking sad and downcast, more than I'd ever seen him.

"It's going to work itself right in the end, Nick," said Almeda after a bit, reaching out and laying a hand on his arm. "This is often the way God works. The storm has to come to clear the sky, and the rain falls to bring life. God is at work in your wife, Nick."

"I don't know how you can figure that, Almeda. She hates any mention of God. Didn't you hear what she said—she was sitting here stewing and fretting and getting more and more annoyed at all our talk."

"Those are only surface reactions, Nick. Down inside, God's Spirit is moving, making her think, and—I believe with all my heart—drawing her. The more people resist and argue against God, and the more they dislike hearing Christians talk about the way their lives are *with* God, the more they are actually being drawn by God. The resistance is a natural human tendency when we feel change in the wind blowing toward us."

"Hmm, I reckon I see what you mean," replied Uncle Nick slowly. "Though I can't say as I could picture Katie *ever* having anything good to say about religion. She can't stand any mention of it. I sure ain't no religious kind of guy, but I got my beliefs like anyone else, though my father'd probably be surprised to hear me say so! But alongside Katie you'd think I was a preacher. Why, just last week she got mad 'cause I tried to teach little Erich to pray before we ate. It was just a harmless little prayer, but she wouldn't have a bit of it."

"Her time will come, Nick. Everyone's time comes eventually. We all have to face God personally and decide what we're going to do with him. I don't think that time's come yet for your wife. She sounds so much like I was before I gave my life to the Lord."

"You?" said Uncle Nick, glancing over at Almeda with a surprised look on his face.

Almeda laughed. "You should have heard me back then! You wouldn't have even known me. I was pretty bitter about God myself."

"Bitter?" I said. I couldn't imagine Almeda being bitter about anything.

"I had plenty to be bitter about—in my thinking, at least. My life hadn't been easy, and I took it out on God. So I know what Katie's going through."

"That's what I asked before," I said. "Don't you think it would help Katie if she knew that?"

"And your father's answer shows what a wise man he is, Corrie," replied Almeda with an affectionate smile. "It's all about time, Corrie—God's time. God wants *every* single person to know about him. But he's got to get a person ready so that he can hear the good news properly when that time does come. Some people's ears are so plugged up with wrong and distorted notions about God that even if Jesus himself were to appear to them and tell them about his Father, they *still* wouldn't hear, wouldn't be able to receive it. They would hear the words, but their minds and hearts would be so mixed up they might turn and walk away from the very Giver of Life himself."

"I know that's right," said Uncle Nick, " 'cause I was like that when I was young. Such a fool hothead I was! And now things are making more sense to me than they ever did, things I recollect my father telling me, and my Ma, things I learned in church. But I don't understand why it's gotta be that way. Is it just growing older?"

Almeda glanced in Pa's direction, seeing if he wanted to reply.

"Don't look at me, woman," he said laughing. "I'm still too new at this myself to know what to tell him. You're the philosopher here. You've been at this Christian life longer than any of the rest of us. So since Avery's on his way back to town with his wife-to-be, I reckon you're the most qualified. You just speak on!"

Almeda laughed.

"You married a long-winded woman, is that what you're trying to say, Drummond Hollister? Who, if she can't be a politician, will keep on being a woman-preacher!"

"You said it, not me!"

We all laughed, and it felt good after the tension and uneasiness following Katie's outburst.

After the laughter settled down, Almeda became serious again.

"Growing older's part of it, Nick," she said after a moment. "But not the most important part. Circumstances have a great deal to do with it. Through circumstances God gets us to a place where we're ready to listen and really *hear* his voice.

You see, we hear with our hearts, not our ears. And our hearts have to be ready. It's exactly what Drummond said when you were gone with Katie. It takes a long time for God to break through the outer layers so he can get inside us. He uses the events of our lives to break down the layers of our resistance. Then, when the time is right, he comes and shows himself. If we have been listening and paying attention, and if our heart is open at that time, then we are able to receive his love, and say yes to him."

"Like you and me chasing around the country, getting into trouble, making fools of ourselves," said Pa. "Who knows but that God was using all that to get us ready for this time now when we're listening to him a mite better than back then."

"Sometimes it takes a crisis, a real moment of heartbreak, before our inner ears—our hearts I should say—are unplugged enough to hear God's voice. For you, Drummond, I suppose it was that moment when you learned your wife was dead and you were standing staring at your five children. Suddenly all you'd run away from came back upon you in an instant."

"You're right there," said Pa. He had a faraway, thoughtful gaze in his eyes. "All the layers of toughness I had tried to surround myself with all those years just started to break and crumble away in that moment."

"So that God's life could begin to come in," added Almeda. "Do you see what I mean, Nick? Circumstances. For Corrie," she went on, glancing at me with a smile, "there was her mother dying in the desert and her feeling of aloneness. Out of that pain, God was able to enter into her life in a greater way."

"What about me? There ain't been no great big thing like that for me. You saying I've still gotta face some awful thing before God's gonna be able to do anything with me?"

"Not at all. It doesn't work that way for everyone. God can also come into lives slowly, a little at a time. The more a person listens to him, the more he or she becomes open to God's influences. It's different with everyone. But *sometimes* it takes a crisis, some major change in outward circumstances, to open a person's heart to be able to listen. And judging from Katie's agitation and hostility right now toward spiritual things, I have the feeling God is speaking more and more loudly to her. I hope she will listen. I hope and pray she doesn't have to be broken by circumstances any more than she already has been. But I do have the sense that God is speaking to her and that she is trying to resist."

"Well I hope it don't take too long for him to get through," sighed Uncle Nick. "I don't know how much more I can take of her being so irritable."

"Have patience. Besides, she's carrying your child."

"I know, and I do all I can for her. But sometimes she can be the most ornery woman!"

Almeda laughed softly, then became very thoughtful. "I will talk to her, Nick. I've been praying for an opportunity. Perhaps this is it."

"I'd be mighty obliged, Almeda," said Nick.

"All in God's time. You just join me in prayer for the right opportunity."

$\mathcal{W}$e didn't see Katie or Uncle Nick much the whole week after Christmas. Katie kept to herself in their house up across the creek. No more was said by anyone about what had happened, but it was obvious she was avoiding us. From Uncle Nick's behavior it was clear he still felt mighty bad about what had happened. And from the look on his face it didn't seem that things were so well between him and Katie either. He'd walk down to our place most evenings, and although he didn't say much, his face said plenty. He loved Katie, I could tell that, but when she got in one of her moods, he didn't know how to help. Eventually it started to bother him that she wouldn't pay any attention to what he tried to say or do. And of course none of the rest of us were too anxious to get involved. Katie had made it plenty clear what she thought.

After a week and a half, one afternoon Almeda finally said, "Well, it's been long enough. I'm going up to see Katie. If she's not ready to see me yet, she ought to be. This isn't doing anybody any good."

She packed up some food, asked Becky to carry it up for her, and took a small pot of soup she'd made. The two of them headed for the bridge. We'd been sending things up with Nick, but this was the first visit any of us had paid in person.

They were back in about fifteen minutes. Almeda's face wore a smile.

"How is she?" I asked.

"The same," she answered. "Sullen, quiet. I didn't get a single smile and hardly two words out of her. But it's an open door, Corrie. Before long, when the time is right, I'm going to sit her down and have a long talk with her. And by then I think she'll be ready to listen."

"With the heart?" I said with a smile, recalling our conversation of the other evening.

"Yes," she smiled back in return. "Katie's heart is nearer the surface than she lets on. I saw something in her today, Corrie, for the first time since I've known her—hunger. Something in her eyes tells me she knows she isn't as self-sufficient as she wants everybody to think. She *is* being broken and made ready. I can see it! It's exciting. The Lord is tilling her soil, making her ready for the moment when he comes to her and says, 'Katie, it's time to let me in.' "

"But what about everything she said about God?" asked Becky, who was still standing beside Almeda. "She said she hates it when anybody even mentions him."

"Oh, but Becky, that's the best part of all!" replied Almeda. "The closer the Lord gets to a person's heart, sometimes the more that person resists and shouts and complains. That can take many forms, like Katie's outburst the other night. It's just a sign that God is getting ready to take hold of her heart. It's a sign that circumstances are pressing in closer and closer around her, that thoughts and ideas about God are on her mind, that she is watching and observing all the rest of us, seeing the part God plays in our lives. You see, Katie is aware of all that, aware that we are trying to live in a certain way. She says she hates it because way down deep inside she actually *wants* God living with her too. She wants him but she doesn't want him at the same time."

"How can that be?" said Emily, joining the discussion. The two boys were off with Pa at the mine, and it was special, just the three of us girls talking with Almeda.

"The human heart is a complicated thing, Emily," said Almeda with a smile. "It finds no difficulty at all in wanting and not wanting the same thing at once. That is especially true of a woman!

She chuckled, obviously thinking something to herself, then laughed outright. "If you doubt that, girls, just ask your Pa!" she said, still laughing. Gradually she got serious again, and then went on.

"It's also especially true in spiritual things, because just like love, our spiritual beings live in our hearts, not our heads. We both want God and don't want him. He created us to need him, to hunger for him. Life can never be complete unless we are living in a relationship with God. That's the only way we can be fulfilled as human beings. The *only* way. But at the same time, we've all got a stubborn streak. And that part of us wants to keep hold of our independence. We want to *think* we don't need anyone—God included. We want to think we're self-sufficient and strong.

"That's the great conflict down inside all of us—every man or woman, every boy or girl—until the time comes in our lives when we realize we need to walk *with* God, not independently from him. It's just like the minister was saying about horses and wagons. And I think Katie's time is coming, and so the independent part of her is fighting and resisting and complaining and yelling inside."

"Inside *and* outside," added Becky.

We all laughed.

"Yes, Becky," said Almeda. "But it's not any of us she's angry at. She's not really even angry at God. It's just her independence fighting to keep control, while all the time her Father in heaven is drawing her heart closer and closer to his, so that he can pour out his love to her and give her his life."

"But what if she doesn't want his life, doesn't want to be a Christian?" asked Emily.

"Then God may keep bringing circumstances to her that are harder and more painful, until one day she finally comes to the point of realizing happiness and freedom and contentment are not qualities she can have without him."

"So it's just a matter of time?" I asked.

Almeda shook her head. "Maybe. But God never forces people to accept him. Katie still has a choice—we must pray that she chooses to accept God instead of rejecting him."

We were all silent again, thinking about Almeda's words.

"Can we pray for her now?" said Becky.

"I think that's a wonderful idea."

We all bowed our heads and closed our eyes, and softly we prayed for Uncle Nick's wife. Almeda prayed for an opportunity to speak with her, the rest of us prayed that she would be open to God's voice and that we'd have chances to do things for her and show her how much we cared about her.

Praying with other people you love always makes you feel closer to them—especially when you are joining together to pray for someone else you love just as much. The rest of the day I found myself thinking about people praying together. I wondered if that was one of the reasons Jesus told us to pray in groups of two or three. In addition to the answers to the prayers, maybe praying itself brings those two or three people closer together.

Our prayers did get answered, although we sure couldn't have seen ahead of time how it was going to happen. It's a good thing Almeda told us about God sometimes using painful circumstances. That way, when the time came, at least we were a little more prepared for it.

Deep Pain Surfaces

CHAPTER THIRTY-FIVE

$\mathcal{S}$everal days later, out of the blue, Almeda said to me, "Come on, Corrie, we're going to see Katie."

She began gathering up some things in the kitchen, then to my questioning look added, "It's time, Corrie. From the moment I woke up this morning, I had the strong sense that today was the day."

"The day for what?" I asked.

"For doors to open."

The puzzled look on my face didn't go away with her answer.

"I can't even say that I'm sure myself what that means. But sometimes God puts within you a sense of purpose, a sense of urgency, a sense that it's time to *do* something, say something, take some action that will move things in his kingdom."

"Are you saying you think Katie will be open to God today?"

"I don't know. That's something I have no way of knowing. God holds the keys to our hearts, and nothing we do can open or close *those* doors without there first being nudgings and promptings and openings from his Spirit. I don't know what's going on in the deepest regions of Katie's heart. That's God's domain, not mine. Our responsibility is to obey his promptings *in us*, not concern ourselves with what he is saying to others."

"So what is it you think will happen today?"

"I have no way of knowing that. I wouldn't even want to. God is in control of Katie's destiny, and her heart, not me. Yet sometimes God will place inside us an urge to do or say something that fits in with the groundwork he is doing inside someone else. The result is that a door opens. It's impossible to say what exactly that means, how it will come about, or what will be the eventual outcome."

"What will you say?"

"I won't try to plan that. To speak of holy things at the wrong time, before someone is truly ready to receive them, can do more harm than good. We must rely on God's guidance to provide the fit opportunity, and we must move slowly. I don't know what Katie needs to hear. God knows that. So I just want to be available."

We packed up some food, and two knitting projects we had been working on, and then set out for Uncle Nick and Aunt Katie's—just the two of us. All the way there Almeda said nothing. From the intense look on her face, I knew she was praying.

When we arrived, Katie was alone with Erich. Uncle Nick was at the mine with Pa and Zack. All the other kids were in town at school. It was the middle of the morning, and the men would be working for another two or three hours before lunchtime.

Katie did not seem particularly overjoyed to see us, but she went through the motions of being hospitable.

"How are you feeling?" Almeda asked.

"Well enough, I suppose," Katie answered.

"We brought you some fresh bread. I know sometimes it's difficult to keep up with baking when you're not feeling so well."

"I tell you, I'm feeling fine," replied Katie, a little crossly. "I don't need your help, Almeda. I'll get through this fine on my own. Just quit worrying about me so much."

Almeda looked away for a moment. "I'm sorry," she said after a bit. "I'm only trying to be a good sister-in-law to you, and a good neighbor, and I know how it feels to be alone and far away from—"

"Look Almeda," Katie interrupted. She turned and faced Almeda. Her face did not seem to be angry, but there was no trace of a smile to be found anywhere on it. She was cool, distant, reserved, and obviously not interested in returning Almeda's friendliness. "I know what you're trying to do. I know you feel sorry for me. But just don't bother. I can get along fine without you or anybody else's sympathy. Keep your bread and all your religious notions about neighborliness to yourself, and just leave me alone!"

The words stung Almeda; and the slight wince that flitted across her face showed that they had stabbed her right in the heart. I would have done anything to disappear right then and not be in the room with them.

How thankful I was for Erich. Little children are so innocent, and sometimes they can stumble right into the middle of a hornet's nest without realizing it. On this particular morning he toddled in and rescued us from any further embarrassment.

"Look, Aunt Corrie," he said, holding something up to me, "Papa make me wood bear."

I stooped down to look at the piece of wood he was holding, so relieved for *something* to do. After I'd seen it, he marched over to show it to Almeda. She had looked away after Katie's rebuke, but now she stooped down, put an arm around his shoulder. Though her face was still a little pale she flashed him a bright smile and asked two or three questions about his toy "bear," which looked like a stick that had been whittled on. Katie went about something on her stove without another word, and Almeda and I talked for a few more minutes with Erich.

When he finally waddled off to another part of the house, Almeda threw me a glance which was followed by a deep sigh. This did not seem to be turning out to be much of a visit.

Slowly we rose, still holding the things we brought. Almeda walked over toward Katie, whose back was still turned toward us.

"I brought the stockings I've been making for Erich," Almeda said quietly, "and the sweater for your husband. I thought you might like to see them."

Katie did not reply for a moment. Then, still not facing us, she said, "You can leave them on the table if you wish."

"They're not finished. I thought you might like to see how I'm planning to—"

"Then take them with you and finish them any way you like. Leave them if you like, or take them. I don't care."

Almeda winced again, as if she had been struck across the cheek.

Almeda stood still, facing Katie's back, looking helpless. She wanted so badly to be Katie's friend.

Finally she drew in a breath and said, "I suppose we'll be going now. I'm so sorry, Katie. I didn't mean to cause you any pain, or to intrude where I don't belong. Please, if you can find it in your heart to forgive me, I would appreciate—"

"Forgive you!" repeated Katie, spinning around. Her face was red and her eyes flashing. "Forgive you for what?"

"I don't know," stammered Almeda. "For upsetting you, for intruding when you wanted to be alone." I'd never seen Almeda so flustered and unsettled. "I'm just sorry to have caused you any more grief."

"The only grief you cause me is by trying to be so good and self-righteous all the time!"

"Oh, Katie, I'm so sorry," said Almeda in a quavering voice.

"Sorry . . . forgive . . . don't you ever get sick of being so *good*? Do you ever stop, Almeda? Don't you ever want just to be normal and let people live their own lives, without always being nice, always smiling, always doing things for them, always preaching to them with all your holier-than-thou notions of God? Sometimes you make me sick with all your talk of God and forgiveness, and that happy smile on your face— always with a kind word, always doing somebody a good turn, never getting upset, never getting angry!"

I sat shocked at what I was hearing, my eyes glued to Katie as she poured out her fury. Poor Almeda just stood standing in front of her, defenseless, tears pouring down her cheeks.

"Do you know what it feels like to be around someone like you who's always so good?" Katie went on. "It makes me resent every word I ever hear about God! What about the rest of us, Almeda, who can't be as good as you? What does God have for people like us? I'm sick of it, do you hear? I hate God, I hate you, I hate California, I hate this stinking house, I hate the whole rotten business, and I never want to hear another word about God as long as I live!"

I don't know if she was going to say anything else. Before her outburst was finished, Almeda ran out the door, one hand held over her face. The bread and knitting lay on the floor where she had dropped them.

The sound of her footsteps and sobs woke me from my trance. I looked hard at Katie and saw tears in her eyes too. The next instant I ran out the door after Almeda.

She was hurrying away from the house, but not down the path to our place. She stopped on the edge of the woods, and I caught up with her leaning against a tree.

She was sobbing harder than I'd ever seen before, from the depths of her heart. I walked up to her slowly and laid my hand on the back of her shoulder. It was hot and wet. She kept crying but reached up and grasped my hand with one of hers, clutching it tightly.

We stood there, alone and quiet next to that tree, for several minutes. Gradually her weeping calmed down, then finally stopped.

Slowly she turned around, looked deeply into my eyes, and attempted a smile.

"I am so thankful for you, Corrie," she said softly. "I don't know what I'd do right now if I didn't have you here to share this with me."

I had no words to say. I just put my arms around her and held her.

"Do you know what's the hardest thing of all, Corrie?" she said at last.

"What?"

"Being so misunderstood . . . having your motives—which you thought were good—questioned as if you had some selfish end you were trying to gain."

"She didn't mean to hurt you," I said.

"Oh, I know. She has no idea what she's done. But to have love turned back on you as if you were trying to injure rather than help and minister . . . that's such a painful thing."

We were silent another minute.

"But of course she didn't mean it," Almeda went on. "I have no doubt she's hurting more right now than I am. And it must be especially bitter for her in that she has no place to turn, no source of help. I do. But she is alone with her anger and her frustrations. So of course I don't blame her for lashing out at me." Her voice was soft and clean, as if the tears had washed it.

"It's not you anyway, is it?"

"No. Katie's not angry with me. She just doesn't know where to turn for help."

By this time we had stepped back, and Almeda was leaning against the tree again. I could tell she was thinking about the last words she had said.

It was quiet a long time. Then Almeda took a deep breath, looked at me, and smiled.

"We do know where to turn for help, don't we?" she said. "Maybe this is the door I had the feeling the Lord was going to open. It just might be time I told Katie some things. As painful as it will be, I think the time has finally come. Let's go back to the house, Corrie."

She turned and led the way back toward the cabin.

I followed Almeda through the door. She didn't knock or wait to be invited in. Katie was sitting in a chair staring straight ahead, her face white.

"Katie, I know you and I haven't always seen eye to eye on some things," Almeda said. "And I know our views on religion are very different. I'm sorry if I've hurt you or done things to bother you. I've honestly tried to be a good neighbor and friend to you. I'm sorry if it's seemed otherwise to you."

Katie just sat there saying nothing. She looked spent, like the storm of her anger had left her weak and with no more words to say.

"But there's one thing you've got wrong, Katie," Almeda continued. "And that's about me being good. When you said 'someone like me who's always so good,' your words felt like a knife piercing right through my heart. And so whether you like it or not, Katie, unless you actually demand that I leave your house, I want to tell you what I used to be. You've got to know some things about God that you have all mixed up in your mind. After you've heard what I have to say, then if you still think faith is ridiculous and want to hate it, that will be your choice. But I intend to tell you what I have to say."

She paused for a breath. She was still standing, looking straight down at Katie. Katie sat with her eyes focused on the floor. But she said nothing.

Almeda sat down in front of her, took another deep breath, and began to speak.

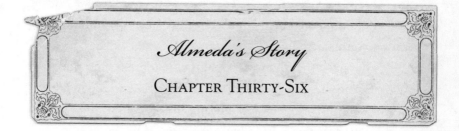

$\mathcal{T}$he person I was many years ago in Boston," she began, "was a different person than you have ever known me to be. Completely different, Katie. Do you understand what I mean—black and white, night and day different?"

Almeda paused momentarily, but apparently she wasn't waiting for any answer, because she went right on.

"My father was a wealthy Boston merchant. I was one of three daughters—I hesitate to say it, but three *beautiful* daughters. I was the eldest. My father was a conniving man who would do anything—including sacrifice his own daughters—to turn a profit or to make a deal that would pad his bank account."

A painful look passed across Almeda's face as she said the words. Then she took in a deep breath, as if she was trying to gather courage to continue.

"I have to tell you that even after all the years I have been a Christian and have been trying to forgive him deep in my heart, the very thought of what he did to us still causes resentments to rise up within me. He was not a good man. For many years I despised him. At least now I can say that is no longer true. I have learned to accept what happened, and his part in it, and to know that through it I discovered what I might not have discovered otherwise. To say that I am thankful for my past would not really be truthful. But I do accept it, and have come to terms with it.

"What my father did was to flaunt us before his important clients. From the time I was fourteen or fifteen he would make me put on scanty dresses and alluring silk stockings, then he would pour perfume on me and take me out in the evening with him. There he would meet men I always assumed he was doing business with. I was too young at first to have any idea what was happening to me. I just went along obediently. There I would sit or stand beside my father while he would talk or drink. Sometimes it would be for dinner. Other times we would go to saloons or taverns. Soon enough I realized that he was talking to the men about *me*. They would look me over, and there would be laughing and winking and whispered comments, then more laughing, all with a lewd, suggestive tone to it. My own father was hinting to his various associates that he would let me be available to them in exchange for their business.

"At first it wasn't so awful. The men would try to joke with me or take me alone over to the bar to buy me a sparkling water to drink while they had their whiskey. But it got worse the older I grew. They wanted to touch me and put their arms around me and feel my hair, always leering at me through toothy grins and evil eyes.

"I hated it. I hated the men, and I hated my father. But there was nothing I could do except go along with it. If my father thought that I wasn't being 'friendly' enough, or wasn't doing enough to please his associates, he would yell at me and hit me when we got home, and say horrible and abusive things to me. Sometimes he beat me even when I had done my best to be agreeable, just because a certain client decided to take his business elsewhere. One time—"

Even as Almeda spoke, the memory made her shut her eyes and a momentary shudder passed through her. She took a deep breath and continued.

"One time, he stopped the wagon on the way home, shoved me down from my seat, jumped down after me, and struck me over and over, knocking me to the ground until my nose was bleeding and my dress was torn and I was covered with dirt and mud, then threw me in a heap in the back of the wagon. I had learned years before not to cry aloud in his presence. He hated it when I cried, and he would beat me all the more. So I had to learn to stifle my whimpered sobs, and bury the agony of pain from his beatings.

"That night riding home in the back of the wagon, blood and dirt on my face, my ear and shoulder splitting with pain from his blows, I realized, perhaps for the first time, that my father was not a good man, and that I hated him. And from that moment, something began to rise up from inside me, a determination to escape from his clutches whenever and however I could.

"But it wasn't as if I could just leave home. I was only sixteen, and I was still completely dependent upon my parents. They never gave any of us any money. What could I do, where could I go? We had no relatives, no friends I could turn to. My mother knew what he was doing to us, but she was just as afraid of him as we were. I could never understand why she didn't stand up for us and protect us from him. But as I grew older I saw that she felt just as helpless as we. I tried to confide in her about what he did when he took us out in the evenings, but she would only suffer with us in silence. I don't doubt that she had more than her share of beatings from his hand as well. Probably if she had tried to say or do anything, he would have punished us all ruthlessly—all of us. So she just must have figured it best to keep silent and hope we could endure it.

"Once I even tried to talk to my father. It was late in the afternoon, around dusk. He was out in the barn working on a new saddle he'd bought. How naive I must have been to think he would listen, that he would care. But something had come over me that day with more clarity than ever before that what he was doing was just *wrong*. It was so plain to me all of a sudden, with my little girl's trusting heart, that if I could just say it to him he would see it too. I was wrong.

"I walked up to him slowly. He had his back turned. I don't even know if he heard me approaching. I stopped a few feet from him, terrified. I mustered all my courage and blurted out, 'Daddy, I want you to stop doing what you're doing to me. It's wrong. I don't want to go out with you again to see any more men.'

"That was all I said. I stood there trembling, just looking at his back in the quiet of the barn. He said nothing, and what seemed like a long time passed, though it was probably only a minute. Then he slowly turned around and bore his eyes into me. His face was blank. It was not even a look of anger, just a total lack of feeling, an emptiness, a void. Then slowly a cruel smile spread over his lips. He just looked at me with that horrid half smile. It was the same kind of expression I'd seen in the men he made me be friendly to. Then slowly he turned back to his saddle, never uttering a word.

"I don't even remember when or how I left the barn, or how I spent the rest of the afternoon. But I remember the night distinctly enough. He took me into town again, and it was an absolutely horrible evening. My father joined with the men in saying things about me—half of them I didn't even understand, but I felt ugly and small and dirty just from the looks and laughs and winks that went along with their words. And that night he made me go to a man's room alone. Nothing much happened; I suppose once he got me alone the man felt sorry for me because of how young I was, and he was almost nice to me when he saw how terrified I was.

"So he took me back downstairs to my father a little later. And then on our way home, out somewhere desolate where even if I did scream no one would hear me, my father gave me the worst beating of my life. He never said a word. He didn't have to. The message was clear enough: I must never speak boldly to him again like I had that afternoon in the barn. I had to stay in bed for two days. My mother hardly even came into my room except to give me something to eat. I knew she felt guilty, but powerless at the same time. So she did the worst thing of all—she did nothing. She didn't even offer me so much as a look or a smile of consolation, not even a glance to say, 'I understand . . . I'm sorry.'"

Almeda stopped. Her voice had grown quiet, and now she looked down, took a handkerchief from her pocket and dabbed her eyes.

"You know," she went on in a moment, her voice soft and husky, "during all the years I was growing up, I never once remember hearing the words I love you. Not even from my mother. Love was nonexistent in our family. I don't know what my two sisters felt. But all my life I felt unwanted, that my parents would have gotten rid of me the moment I was born if they could have."

She paused again, crying now.

"Do you have any idea what it's like," she said through her tears, "never once all your life to be told that you are loved— by *anybody?* Not once. Never to be touched except in anger. Never to be held . . . never to feel arms wrapping themselves around your shoulders in tenderness . . . never to—"

She couldn't continue, but finally broke down and sobbed, her face in her hands.

I don't know what Katie was thinking. Part of me didn't want to look at her. Besides, I was far too occupied with my *own* thoughts and feelings. I was shocked, of course, but that was only part of my response. I could feel the hurt, the ache, in her voice. And because I *did* love her—oh, so much!—it made what she'd gone through so much harder to hear. I just wanted to go back and take that girl she had once been in my arms and wrap her up and protect her from any more hurt and any more unkindness.

On another level, as I listened I could hardly believe what I was hearing. From the very day I had first seen her, Almeda had been to me the absolute picture of strength and Christian virtue and maturity. I had never seen her "weak." There was never a time when I didn't know she could be depended on, no matter if everyone around her fell or faltered or even ran away. To hear her describe her past was like looking into a window inside of someone else. And I couldn't manage to make the two images come together into the single person I had always known. Suddenly there were two pictures of Almeda—the stately, solid lady, full of grace, capable and mature, and the young girl, frightened, alone, and unloved.

How could the two be the same person? Yet there sat Almeda, the same loving woman I had always known, my stepmother now, opening up this window into her soul.

Slowly I got up from where I was sitting and walked over to Almeda. I knelt down in front of her, took one of her hands in mine, and looked into her face, red with tears and the anguish of reliving the ugly memories of the past.

"Almeda," I said softly, "I love you . . . I love you more than I can ever tell you!"

At the words a fresh torrent of weeping burst out from Almeda. I put my hand around her waist and tried to comfort her, but she had to go on crying for another minute or two.

"Oh, Corrie," she whispered at length, "you'll never know how precious those words are to me! Your love is such a priceless treasure to me . . . words cannot express the joy you give me."

She blew her nose, then looked down at me with a radiant smile. I guess it's true that pain makes a person more capable of love. Almeda's face at that moment was more filled with love than any face I'd ever seen. Our eyes met and held. I felt I was looking right through her, not into her heart or into her past life, but into the deepest parts of *her*—the whole person she was, the person she had always been, the person she was still becoming. Maybe in those few seconds I had a tiny glimpse of what God sees when *he* looks deep into us—a glimpse into the *real* person, the *whole* person—apart from age or appearance or past or upbringing.

All these feelings passed through me in just a second or two. Then Almeda gave me a squeeze and took a deep breath.

"I want to finish," she went on, "or I might never get this far with it again. And I want both of you to hear what I have to say. I care about the two of you, and I want you to know me—to know *all* about me."

I stood up and went back to where I had been sitting.

"It's difficult for me to describe what I was feeling back then," she continued, "because I suppose I didn't even know myself. I was terrified, and yet at the same time I was growing more and more determined to escape from that awful life. I suppose there was a part of me that was a fighter. I've been called headstrong more than once, as you know, Corrie, from the very first day when we saw each other."

She looked over at me with a smile.

"You weren't afraid of anybody when you went into the saloon looking for Uncle Nick, that's for sure," I said.

"No, I don't suppose I was," she replied. "And as afraid as I was of my father, by the time I was sixteen a part of me inside was biding my time until I saw an opportunity. And after he'd done it once, my father started trying to make me go upstairs alone with men again. The next time it happened, knowing what I was in for, I refused to go. 'I just won't do it,' I said, which silenced the joviality around the table where we were sitting. And the look of daggers my father threw at me told me there was a beating waiting for me, the likes of which I'd never felt.

"And of course after that, nothing my father could say would make the man he'd been talking to take me away anyway, even if I'd given in. So I just sat there in silence, trembling about the ride home.

"Luckily my father had an appointment the next night with another man, a whiskey distributor I'd met before. I had never liked him one bit. The smiles he would give me, and the pinches and little jabs, were so horrible. It never took long in that man's company to know what kind of man he was. My next younger sister still had a black eye from the hand of my father, and he wanted to make sure I was presentable because whiskey was one of my father's main sources of income. So he didn't beat me that night, although he made sure I knew full well that as soon as the *next* night was over, I was going to be so black and blue I would be in bed for a week and would never refuse to do anything he asked of me again.

"All the next day I plotted my escape. I stole what money I could find in the house, packed a few clothes in a bag, and hid it in a field nearby. Then I waited for evening to come, filled with fear and anticipation all at once.

"This time I was as nice as I could be, and I just smiled when the men called me 'Honey,' as if I enjoyed it, and I went right upstairs with that awful man. But on the landing I managed to get ahead of him, and since I knew what room we were going to, I ran in and locked the door behind me, then climbed out the window onto the landing and scrambled down to the alley.

"I ran away from there as fast as I could, hardly even knowing what direction I was going. I ran and ran, through alleys and streets, but always with the vague intent of moving in the direction of our home, which was on the edge of the city.

"After that it all becomes a blur. I can't even say how I spent the rest of that night or the next few days and nights. I managed to retrieve my bag of things, but where I went and what I did after that I honestly can't even recall. There are just images that sometimes flash into my mind—a face, a place, or a set of surroundings.

"Actually that's all I remember for the whole next year. How I survived I don't know. Now I can say that the hand of God was upon me, but then I knew nothing of God, and certainly cared even less. If I thought it had been bad at home with my father, now my life turned black indeed. I don't even want to remember all the things I did, or what I got myself mixed up in. I lived on the streets, sometimes in the countryside, in saloons and cheap hotels, getting what jobs I could find. I stole, I drank, I used people if I thought it might get me a free meal.

"I knew my father probably hated me all the more for making him look foolish, and that he was no doubt looking for me. But I didn't care. I told people who I was and exactly what I thought of him. Over the next several years, as I got older and more capable, I was able to hold jobs for longer, and even to do a man's work when I had to. Living like I did made me tough and independent. I could take care of myself, and I wasn't afraid of my father finding me. I knew he'd never be able to get a hold on me again. I suppose I even had something of a reputation as a pretty hard, tough young lady—which no doubt is how Franklin found out about my past last year.

"To make a long story short, when I was about nineteen or twenty I fell in with a man who more or less took me under his wing. He was a confidence man, a card shark, a high-stakes swindler, but he lived a fast life, and I found that appealing. I didn't love him, and I know he didn't love me either. I was just a pretty girl for him to have around. I had no idea what love was and at that point in my life never stopped to even ask if such a thing as love existed. Life was survival. To survive you had to be tough, you had to take advantage of what opportunities came along, and you had to put yourself first. If other people got hurt in the process, that wasn't my concern. Life had dealt me a pretty bad hand, and I wasn't about to start getting pangs of conscience over anyone else.

"So I lived with him for a while, stole for him, set people up for him, and in the process lived better than I had for several years. At least I knew I was going to have a roof over my head, a warm bed, and a good meal. It was the closest thing to stability I had known in a long time. How much longer it might have gone on like this, or what might have become of us in the end, I don't know. Because then something happened which changed everything."

Again Almeda stopped, and again I knew from her face and the tone of her voice that she was struggling within herself for the courage to say something that was painful.

The room was silent for a minute or two. I chanced a quick glance in Katie's direction. She was looking intently at Almeda, listening to every word. Every trace of anger was gone from her face.

"There was a child," Almeda said at last. She stopped again and hid her face in her hands.

I saw Katie gasp slightly, and I felt myself take in a quick breath. I couldn't believe what I'd just heard!

"I'm so ashamed to tell you what I have to say next," she went on, crying a little again. "The minute he learned I was pregnant, I was nothing to him but baggage. I woke up one morning in the hotel we'd been staying in to find myself alone with nothing but my carpetbag and a few clothes left in the room. I never saw him again. He left me ten dollars, and I was back on the street.

"I was too angry even to cry. It just drove my bitterness toward men—toward the whole world, and I suppose toward God too—deeper. The old hard determination rose up in me again, and I struck out after that day all the more mistrusting, all the more independent. I was a different person, I tell you—selfish, hateful, caring for no one but myself.

"When the baby was born—God forgive me!—I took it to an orphanage. I didn't want to—"

Almeda broke down and wept. I wanted to comfort her, but I was so stunned by what she'd said that I couldn't move.

"Oh, how many times I've relived it in my memory, wondering where I might have changed this course I was on, wondering if I did right or wrong. I was so unprepared to be a mother. Yet something in me has often wished—"

Again she stopped to collect herself, then continued.

"The birth of my baby sent me lower still. By now I was in my early twenties and something in that hard independent spirit slowly began to break. Guilt over what I had done began to set in. Gradually it ate away at me, burrowing deeper and deeper into my heart. I didn't realize it at the time, but now I see that all the hard, determined independence was only my young way of covering up my desperate hunger to be loved. The more I tried to assert my strength, the more my soul was being torn apart. I didn't have any idea who I was. My whole identity had come from my father. To him I was just an object to be used. No one had ever loved me. How could I do anything but despise myself? And even the most precious thing a woman has—that purity which is the only thing she has to offer her husband—I let slip away. And I gave away the child that should have been the wonderful outcome of love between a man and a woman. I was no better than my father! I didn't even want my own baby! Oh God . . . how could I have been so shameful . . . how could—?"

Again she broke down and sobbed quietly.

"There is no way I can tell you what that time was like for me," she finally said after a while. "I felt so guilty, yet I tried to hide it. Inside I was slowly dying to all that life should be, sinking into a pit of despair, yet making it worse by the obstinate hard-bitten image I tried to keep up.

"I started drifting, caught trains to New York and Philadelphia. I worked here and there, stealing what I needed, living among some really rough men and women. I even got to be pretty handy with my fists when I had to be. It was a dreadful life! It wasn't life at all, it was a living death."

She paused once more. By now her tears had stopped. She breathed in deeply, and looked out the window off into the distance. As if she had suddenly become unaware that Katie and I were in the room with her, she seemed miles and years away. I'd seen that look before, a look of mingled pain and remembrance. Now at last I knew why those clouds had passed across her face.

She continued staring out the window for a long time, then suddenly came back to the present and turned and focused her gaze onto Katie.

"So you see, Katie," she said, "when you spoke of me as someone who's always so good, as if God was somebody I could understand but you couldn't, do you see why your words bit so deep? I *wasn't* good, Katie! I was about as despicable a person as they come. For the first twenty-five years of my life, I did everything wrong! I did not know love. I was miserable. I was mean and bitter and vengeful. I hurt people, I did more horrible things than I could count.

"If you're going to think of Christianity as something that's only for a certain kind of person, then you'd better leave me out altogether. If you think God reserves his life for churchy 'good' people, where does that leave me? All those things you said about me—nice, always smiling, holier-than-thou, forgiving, doing good turns, never getting upset, never getting angry . . . don't you understand, Katie—none of that was me at all! The person you think you see, the person you have known these last couple of years, wasn't me at all not so very long ago. I don't say that to be critical, Katie. But if you're going to criticize me for how I am now, then I think you should know the whole story. And that's why I wanted to tell you."

Still Katie just sat numbly, not saying anything.

"So what happened?" I asked finally. "How did you . . . I mean, how could everything have changed so much?"

Almeda turned toward me and smiled. Her eyes were a little red still, but the radiance that was normally on her countenance had returned. Having told us everything, reliving it as she did, she was ready for the sun to come back out.

"That," she sighed, "is almost an equally long story."

Encounter with a Shopkeeper
Chapter Thirty-Seven

One day," Almeda began again, "when I was back in Boston, I was walking in one of the better sections of town. I don't even remember why I happened to be on that particular street because it really wasn't a part of town I went to very often. Fate, I suppose I would have called it back then. I would call it something else now.

"In any case, I walked into a shop that sold a mixture of many things—dry goods, some fine linens, with one glass case of some very expensive jewelry. I wandered in, probably looking every bit the street-tramp that I was. I must have stood out like a sore thumb, but I didn't really think of that myself.

"As you might imagine, my eyes immediately focused on the case of jewelry. I sauntered toward it, saw that it was filled with expensive gold and silver rings and necklaces and pendants. The proprietor of the shop was occupied along one of the far walls with a lady who was picking out some fabric, and the jewelry cabinet was out of the man's direct line of vision. All I would need would be a second or two. If I could get my hand inside the case and snatch three or four pieces, I'd be able to dash out the door and all he'd see was the back of my heels. I'd done the same sort of thing a hundred times and had the utmost confidence in my cunning and my speed once I lit out. The only question was whether the case was locked.

"I moved up to the case and searched quickly for a lock but didn't see one. The back seemed to be open. I eyed the pieces I thought I could nab. Then with one motion I stretched over the top of the case and reached into the back. My fingers grabbed two or three rings. I hurriedly put them in my other hand, then stretched out again and reached for two pearl necklaces that were close by. Just as I'd laid hold of them and pulled my arm back, ready to make a dash for the door, I felt the grip of a strong hand seize my shoulder.

"The store owner had sneaked up behind me and now he had me red-handed. I winced from the pain because he'd grabbed me tight. His only words were, 'Drop them on the counter, Miss.' There was no anger in his voice, only a calm tone of command. I instantly did what he said. I had no choice.

"He relaxed his grip slightly, but still held on. The other lady had left the store and now we were alone. Still holding on to me, he walked me over toward the door and locked it. I was too feisty and stubborn to be scared. I squirmed a little, but he was strong and it did no good. I couldn't have escaped if I'd tried, and now with the door locked I settled down and decided just to wait and see what would happen next.

"The man was younger than I'd first realized, only a few years older than I was—in his midthirties. He led me, still with a strong hand, back behind the counter of the shop and into another room, which was his home, attached to the store. He sat me down in a chair, then finally let go of my arm and shoulder. He took a chair himself and sat down opposite me. He must have seen my eyes darting about already plotting my escape.

" 'There's no way out, young lady,' he said. 'All the doors are locked, and even if you did manage to find a key to one of them and get out, I'm quite a fast runner and I'd catch you before you were halfway down the street. And the sheriff's office is only two blocks away. So if I were you I'd just sit still for a moment or two.'

"His voice still had that calm, deep tone of authority. I couldn't help but find myself arrested by it. And though I slouched back in my chair with a look of angry resignation on my face, already I found myself wondering why he hadn't yelled at me or wasn't already on his way to the sheriff's with me.

"The longer I sat there, the more confused I became, although I wouldn't have shown the man a bit of what I was thinking. He just sat there for the longest time and stared into my eyes. I found his gaze annoying and looked away. I kept looking all over the room, but still he kept focusing in on my eyes and my face. It was very disconcerting. Yet at the same time I couldn't help thinking that there was something in his expression that I had never seen before, though I had no idea what it was.

"Finally he spoke again.

" 'Why did you try to steal from me?' he asked.

"I shrugged.

" 'If you were hungry, why didn't you just ask me for some food? I would have given it to you.'

"I still had nothing to say.

" 'If you needed money, why didn't you come in and tell me about it? Perhaps I could have helped.'

"*What is this?* I wondered to myself. *If you're going to have me thrown in jail, then get it over with.*

"Yet inside curiosity was already starting to well up in me about this strange man who didn't seem bent on condemning me but instead sounded as if he was interested in me.

"Well, I sat there for the next hour while he continued to question me and talk to me, always in the same calm voice, with his eyes probing into me in a way no one ever had before, and gradually he began to coax some words and then some whole sentences out of me. By the end of the hour, we were actually carrying on a conversation. Over and over he kept saying, 'I don't think you really want to be a thief. I think you want to be a lady, but you just don't know how.'

"I hardly knew what he meant. But the compassion and caring in his voice was real enough, and the commanding tone and the purposefulness of his eyes slowly began to speak to me. I found myself listening with more than just my ears. I found myself *wanting* to listen, wanting to hear more of this strange man's words . . . wanting to *believe* that he was right, wanting to believe that perhaps he really did see something of worth and value as he looked into my face, saw something that maybe I didn't see, and had never seen myself."

Almeda paused and took a breath, but quickly kept right on going.

"After a while he offered me something to eat. I took it eagerly. I hadn't had much to eat all day and was famished. He heated me some soup on his stove, and poured me a cup of coffee.

"'How about a slice of bread to go with it?' he asked. 'I made it just yesterday.'

"I nodded between spoonfuls of soup, half glancing up now and then with one of my eyebrows raised in puzzlement over this strange man who was treating me so nicely.

"I must have looked like a ravaged animal sitting there!"

She chuckled and the faraway gaze came into her eyes again.

"When I said earlier that my father had three beautiful daughters, I meant no boast in any way. Our faces were a curse, if anything, because they made men look upon us differently than they would have otherwise. A plain face is a young girl's greatest gift and greatest protection against many of the cruelties of this world, though most never discover that fact for forty or fifty years. But as I sat there in that man's kitchen, I can tell you I was anything but beautiful. My face had grown bitter, hard, calculating. There was a perpetual scowl on my brow. My cheeks were sunken, my hair ratted and messy, my clothes dirty, even torn in places. It was not an attractive sight. That man had absolutely nothing to gain by befriending me. I hadn't bathed in two weeks, and the plain fact of the matter is that I was foul. I looked and smelled ugly, inside and out.

"But he—"

Almeda paused and looked away, suddenly overcome again with emotion. I saw her handkerchief go to her eyes once more.

"But he saw something in me. Why . . . how . . . I hadn't any idea. I know now it was because God's love resided in him, but I didn't know it then. He *saw* something in me! Something that he considered of *value*. And you just can't understand what that did to my starved, confused, lonely, encrusted heart. It was as though he took hold of my eyes, looked deeply into them, and then said, 'Look, young lady. Look here—into my eyes. Gaze deeply into them, and you will find someone who has compassion on you, someone who cares about you as a person.'

"As I ate his food, he just kept watching me, quietly talking, and I'm sure praying too, though I was oblivious to that. And that same message kept coming through, even in his silence: *Here is someone who cares about you.*

"And then another strange and unexpected thing happened. As I was finishing up my second bowl of soup and starting to think about being on my way—that is, if he was going to let me go instead of having me thrown in jail— the man got up, pulled a book from a shelf nearby, sat back down, and said, 'Did you know there's a description of you in the Bible?'

" 'No,' I answered.

" 'Well there is,' he replied, 'and I want to read it to you.'

"No harm in that, I thought as I kept eating.

"He flipped through the pages, stopped, and then began to read: 'Who can find a virtuous woman? for her price is far above rubies. The heart of her husband doth safely trust in her, so that he shall have no need of spoil. She will do him good and not evil all the days of her life.'

"I found myself listening more than I let on. Was this the man's idea of a cruel joke, calling me virtuous? Me! Couldn't he see that I was anything but good? I didn't even have a husband, but if I did I'd be the last person on earth anyone would say such things about! I had just tried to rob this storekeeper, and now he was reading words like, 'She will do him good and not evil,' and saying it was a description of me!

"But when he got to the end, he paused a moment, then looked intently into my eyes with a piercing gaze and said: 'Many daughters have done virtuously, but thou excellest them all. Favor is deceitful, and beauty is vain: but a woman that feareth the Lord, she shall be praised.' That's when I suddenly knew beyond any doubt that I'd landed in the house of a man whose wits had left him. There was that word *virtue* again! I knew how black I was inside! That hidden part of me that I tried so hard to keep anyone from seeing—I knew that part was selfish and horrid through and through!

"But even if he was a madman, he had been nice to me, after all. So I simply finished up my soup, then stood and asked if I was free to go.

" 'If you want to,' he replied. " 'But the day's almost over. It's going to be cold tonight. Do you need a place to stay?'

"*So that's it,* I thought to myself. *All this just to lure me into his lair! He's no different from everyone else!*

"Then he added, 'I have a guest room. I'd be happy to put you up for the night. You could take a hot bath, have breakfast with me in the morning, and then be on your way.'

"I eyed him carefully, squinting to see if I could detect some motive. But try as I might, I could see nothing. I don't think the man would have been capable of taking advantage of another. And even if he did try something, I thought, I could take care of myself.

"So I shrugged, and said, 'Sure, I suppose a bath and clean bed would feel good for a change.'

"That night changed everything, and altered the whole course of my life. The man could not have been a more perfect gentleman. He treated me like a queen, heated water for my bath, gave me clean clothes to sleep in, fixed me tea and brought it with some crackers to my room before I went to bed. I didn't know it at the time, but when I was bathing he took my clothes out to be cleaned by a lady around the corner.

"You can imagine the changes I was going through in my mind as I lay there that night. One part of me was laughing inside that anyone could be such a sap. I would sneak down in the middle of the night, find my way into the store again, and make off not with just three or four pieces of jewelry, but with everything in the case. My head was resting on a nice clean pillow cover that would hold everything.

"But somehow another part of me was feeling things I had never felt in my life. This storekeeper—madman or sap or religious nut, whatever he was!—had treated me with courtesy and respect and kindness and graciousness like no other human being in the world ever had. So the deeper part of me was hardly anxious to leave! It felt good to have someone care and treat me kindly. I was not consciously aware of these feelings at the time. Inside I was still pretending it was all ridiculous.

"But he had shown me my first real glimpse of love. He had reached out, looked into my face, and said, 'I see a person of value and worth inside there.' He'd even used that silly word *virtue* and said the passage he read was a description of me. No matter how I might rave and bluster on the outside about it all being syrupy and stupid, I couldn't help feeling cared about and loved.

"So even though I lay there plotting and scheming my escape and all the loot I would make off with, the deeper part of me gradually went contentedly to sleep. And I slept like a baby and didn't wake until I heard the man's familiar voice. I opened my eyes. Sunlight was streaming in through the window, and there he stood with a tray in his hands and a cup of steaming coffee on it, and saying with a bright expression, 'Good morning, young lady. I hope you slept well!'

"In just a few short hours, this place—a place I had walked into to rob, run by this man standing there whose name I didn't even know yet—had become more like a true home to me than any I had ever known. And as I lay there, suddenly the most unexpected thing happened. I felt tears in my eyes. I looked up at him, blinking them back as best I could, and then another unexpected thing happened. A smile came across my lips, and I said, 'Yes, I did. Thank you.'

"He left the coffee, and I lay back in the bed and cried. But they were like no tears that had ever come from my eyes before."

Almeda glanced over at me and smiled. Her eyes were glistening.

"Needless to say," she went on, "I didn't leave immediately, or rob him, or anything like that. I stayed for breakfast and for all that day, then for another night, and before I knew it I had been there a week. He gave me new clothes from his shop. He fed me. I had a bath every day and a room completely to myself. Within a couple of weeks he moved me into a boardinghouse just down the street and offered me a job in his store.

"The long and the short of it is—I became a new person. Life such as I had never known began to come up out of me. I began to notice things that had been dead to me before. People took on a whole new meaning, and I found within myself a desire to reach into them and find out about them.

"Well . . . if you haven't guessed it by now, the man who took me under his wing and helped me to believe in my own worth was none other than Mr. Parrish. The year after I first wandered into his shop I became his wife.

"What a transformation took place within me during that year! That wonderful man simply reclaimed me from Boston's gutters, pulled me up, gave me a place to stand, loved me, believed in me, spoke encouragement and worth into me, and showed me how to *live*. He was God's provision for me. I was dead to all that life was, and he rescued me. I became a new person, thanks to him—completely new, the person the two of you know today.

"Do you know what he did?" Almeda smiled tenderly at the memory.

"After that first day, he read that passage from Proverbs 31 to me every day until we were married. He kept reading it to me, over and over, and kept saying to me, 'You *are* that woman of virtue, Almeda. You are virtuous and pure and capable.' He kept telling me that, and kept reading those words to me, until they began to sink into my soul. God began to wash me clean with those words, and with many other passages from the Bible. Washed me clean from my past, at the same time as he was implanting within me a new picture of the person I could become. It was really quite a wonderful process, nothing short of a full transformation. The old fell away under the influences of this man's love and God's love, leaving the new free to emerge and then eventually to spill out onto others. All my life I had lived under a dark cloud— first from feeling unwanted, then from the awful things my father did, and then finally the cloud of my own blackness of heart that I had been carrying for many years. The clouds were swept away. Someone *did* want me and *did* love me. The horrible memories of my father were replaced by the present reality of a man who was caring and compassionate, a man who loved me and would never hurt me. And the blackness in my heart was cleansed and healed by his belief in me, and by his gentle and tender and encouraging words. The sun came out for the first time in my life. He gave me a place to stand in life, a place of warmth and smiles, and a contented feeling when I went to sleep at night.

"Of course, on a deeper level what was really happening was that he was giving me my first glimpse of God's nature and character. For what he did was exactly what Jesus did when he encountered people—he looked into their eyes and reached down inside them to touch the *real* person down at the core. That is what God is always trying to do in people's lives, in a million ways, sometimes using other people, sometimes on his own. He has a million ways to love us, a million ways to try to get through to us, if we're only able to hear that voice that is sometimes so hard to hear. We are locked away in the cocoons that life surrounds us with. Yet all the while the freedom of the butterfly lies hidden deep inside, and God is constantly trying to find ways to loose our wings and let us soar and be happy in the flight of his life.

"That's what Mr. Parrish did. He looked inside me and said, 'You are someone special. You are a gem that can shine—all we have to do is polish it a bit.' And he went to work polishing.

"At first it was just his words, his kindness, his caring, his love. He made me believe in myself, and believe that he loved me. I listened to him read the Scriptures, and I listened to everything he said about God, but the Lord was still distant. God was not someone who had yet touched my life in a real way. I listened and I probably absorbed more than I realized. But it was still some time later when I awoke to the immediacy of God's relation to *me*—me personally! It took some time for God to steal closer and closer, until that moment when I was ready to surrender my heart to him, as well as to Mr. Parrish."

ow influences from our Father in heaven begin to penetrate our consciousness," Almeda continued, "is one of life's great mysteries. I know ever since the moment I met Mr. Parrish, God began speaking more directly to me. But for a long while, as I said, I was not aware of it.

"We worked together in the store, then expanded the business a little, and by and by built a pretty good life there in Boston. I was obviously not what you would call a 'society lady,' yet in a way my husband did succeed in making a lady of me. He would take me to the theater and sometimes to social gatherings, without the least shame in the kind of person I had once been. He knew everything about my past—about my father, about the men who had been in my life, about the baby. Yet nothing could stop him from continually saying to me, 'You, Almeda, are a woman of virtue and uprightness and righteousness. God made you in *his* image. He loves you, and I love you. Yesterday's gone. Your past has been washed clean.'

"All that couldn't help but make all of life new to me. The sun was brighter. The raindrops sparkled with a new radiance. Flowers took on such a wonderful new meaning. One day a little bee flew against our window and stunned himself and fell to the ground. I scooped him carefully into my palm, and just gazed upon him with a tenderness I didn't even know was in my heart. When he began to come to, I lifted him into the wind and blew him off my palm. And as I watched him fly away, tears came to my eyes, although I didn't even know why.

"Life was happening all around me, but it wasn't an *impersonal* life. Somehow everything was very personal. It all seemed to touch my heart so. To breathe in deeply of the fragrance of an orange or yellow rose touched chords in my being I can't even describe. The smell itself was holy, as if it went back to the very foundation of the world itself, and then had come into being just for me, that I might smell that rose on that particular day. There are no words to convey what I felt. The smell was almost sad in a way, calling forth a yearning for something more than just the aroma of the rose's perfume, but a longing for something that could never be had, never be found. I think that's what it was with the bee too, a longing after something, a hunger—oh, I don't know!—to somehow be a sister, a friend, to that bee in the shared life of the creation we were both in. Yet the bee was just a bee, without the capacity to let me share his life, without even the capacity to know that such a thing as people existed. And somehow as a result I found tears in my eyes.

"Birds in flight held my gaze, something about their seeming freedom called out to me to join them. Sunrises, sunsets . . . even tiny green blades of grass—*everything* began to speak to me. Not speak in words, but speak in feelings. Just to see the intricacies of creation was to find feelings of love rising up in me for those things—for the rose, the bee, the bird, the blade of grass—each unique and so beautiful in its own way.

"Yet there always were tears to go along with the love. For a long time I didn't know why. But then a day came when at last I did.

"The moment came when we were on our way here to California. My husband got a business scheme in his head, and we sold everything and booked passage to join the rush to California.

"One night I was standing along the rail, gazing out across the expanse of the Pacific. It was late, and I was alone. There was a bright moon out, and its light spread glistening out across the water as far as I could see. A few clouds now and then slowly went across it, dulling the reflection for a few moments, and then it would return.

"All these things I have been telling you were filtering through my mind, images out of my past, the changes that had come, how alive and full I felt, such a great thankfulness that the downward path of my former existence had been stopped and that I'd been turned around. And I was thinking of the bee too, and wondering why it had caused me to weep. All the time I was gazing out upon the glow of the moon on the water. The ocean . . . the moon . . . the water . . . the clouds . . . the mystery of the silence . . . it all began to have a saddening, yearning effect on me, and as I stood there, I found tears welling up in my eyes.

"But it only lasted a moment. The next instant a voice spoke to me. I don't mean out loud, but it was so clear in my heart it might as well have been an audible voice. It said: 'It's *me* your tears are meant for. *I'm* the one who put my life into the things I have made, and it's that life which calls out to you. All along I have been calling out to you through the fragrance of the pine tree and the buzz of the honey bee and the winged freedom of the butterfly . . . and this very moment I am calling out to you through the moon's light on the sea.'

"And I knew it was the voice of God speaking to me. And suddenly I knew that he had been there all along, all my life, speaking, calling out to me, trying to love me and touch me and heal me—and care for me. I knew that he knew all about my father and everything that had happened to me. And I knew that he had sent my husband to help pull me up and make a woman of me.

"Yet somehow, even in knowing these things, I continued to weep. I was filled with a sense of remorse because I hadn't seen God before this moment, even though he had been beside me, so close beside me since the day I was born. I had smelled the roses and picked the blades of grass, but I had never seen the *life* that was in them, the life that was God, so close as to be in my very hand, yet unseen.

"In that moment, in a sense, my whole life swept through my memory, and I saw for the first time my own responsibility in what I had allowed myself to become. Even as awful as my father had been, I saw that if I had seen that God *was* with me even then, and had listened to his voice, I could have shared that time with him, and that he could have protected me and kept me from what followed in my life. But my independence kept my eyes on myself, and until Mr. Parrish came along I just looked at nothing else but *me*.

"Right there on the ship, I dropped down onto my knees. And still clinging with one hand to the railing, I began to pray to God from the depths of my heart.

" 'O God,' I prayed, 'I want to live! And I want to live with you. I want you to be my Father. I said I'd never let anybody near me . . . I didn't think I could trust anyone, not even you! All those painful years growing up, people were so cruel . . . they only wanted me for what they could get out of me. I learned to be tough, and when anyone tried to come close, I'd just push them away . . . but inside I was truly afraid . . . I only wanted someone to love me. But there's been no one . . . until this dear man you sent me to . . . and *you*, Lord! Please forgive me . . . it just hurt *so* bad. But now I see how much I've always needed you. Be the Father to me I never had. O Lord, forgive me for my stubbornness and independence when I was younger. I'm so sorry I didn't know you were there, didn't pay attention. Help me now to live, and to live for you! Help me to get my eyes off myself and onto others. Let me be a help to those who may not know love, just as I didn't. O God, please help me. I want to be your daughter. I want to be your woman. Do whatever you want with me, Lord, whatever it takes to transform me into the person you want me to be.'

"When I was through praying I got up and went back to our cabin. I knew there had been a change. And from the moment we got to California, I was a new woman. Mr. Parrish had begun the process by picking me up off the ground. Now the Lord continued the transformation deep in my being, all the way through every part of me.

"And it goes on every day. I still have to struggle with my independence, as you both know from the events of the election campaign. But as I said when I began, even though the work God has to do in me goes on every moment, the difference between fifteen years ago and now is like night and day. You, Corrie, are very fortunate to have begun so early in your life to make the Lord part of your life. I hope and pray that you will one day give your heart to him too, Katie. Because there is no abiding contentment in life apart from him. I can tell you that, not because I am a good Christian lady, but because I've known life without him too, and I know how empty it is."

Almeda stopped. We had been sitting for nearly an hour and a half. It was the most moving story I had ever heard anyone tell, and I still could hardly believe Almeda was telling about her *own* life! She was visibly drained.

"What about all those rumors Mr. Royce was spreading around town last fall?" I asked finally.

Almeda smiled—a sad smile, yet without bitterness.

"There were elements of truth in everything that was said, Corrie, as you can now see for yourself. But like all rumors, it was half fact, half fiction, with usually the fiction parts being those aspects of it people are most eager to believe. All that ridiculous talk about meeting Mr. Parrish on the ship and marrying him practically the next day—I don't know where some of that was dredged up from."

"Does Pa know all this?"

"Everything," she answered. "I wouldn't have let him marry me without making sure he knew what he was getting. I told him every detail. And do you know what he said? He said, 'Everything you tell me just makes me love you more, not less.' He's quite a man, Corrie, that father of yours!"

I nodded and smiled.

"I suppose there's no disrespect in saying this," she went on. "But I'm just now seeing just how much I really do love your father. Mr. Parrish taught me that I could *be* loved. He showed me love. He gave me love. He opened up so much of himself to me. But once I came to know your father, Corrie, I found hundreds of new things opening in *me* that weren't there before. Or at least if they were there, I hadn't noticed. In knowing him, suddenly love began to pour out of me in a new way. Of course I loved Mr. Parrish, but—well, I suppose I just wanted you to know that your Pa is special to me in a completely unique way. There is a part of my heart that is only for him and no one else."

Again she was quiet. Still Katie sat without moving.

Almeda rose. "I suppose it's time we were going home," she said.

Then Katie rose and finally spoke. "Almeda," she said, "I am sorry for the things I said. I had no right."

Almeda smiled. "Think nothing of it, Katie. I just wanted you to understand." She gave Katie a hug, which Katie only halfheartedly returned, and then we left.

"What do you think she thought?" I asked as we walked home.

"That's something only God can know," Almeda answered. "He does everything in his own time, especially in the matter of the human heart. Katie's time will come just as surely as mine did on the ship. But what did you think, Corrie?" she added.

"I guess I'd agree with Pa," I said.

"How so?"

"That your story makes me love you more, not less."

She slipped her hand through my arm and we walked the rest of the way in silence.

The Town Council

Chapter Thirty-Nine

*A*lmost the moment we got back to our place, exhaustion came over Almeda from all the energy it had taken to pour herself out like she had. She slept for two or three hours that afternoon, and I went into the office in town. When I came back that evening and our eyes first met, she smiled at me, and there was something new in her look. I suppose I saw for the first time how much depth there had always been in that smile. And I could tell she was glad that I knew everything. It was like a smile exchanged between sisters who know each other completely.

Nothing much changed otherwise. Things returned to normal with Katie. No more sullenness, no more outbursts, but neither was there any exuberance or special friendliness. I was sure Katie had been touched by Almeda's story, but you could see nothing of it on her face or in her actions. I hoped something was going on inside her.

Meanwhile, business at the Mine and Freight hardly seemed to suffer at all on account of Mr. Royce's competition up the street. Now and then we'd hear of some sale he made to someone, or of something he was doing. But most of our customers remained loyal to Almeda. And of course the way the election turned out and what Pa and Almeda had done for Shaw and Douglas and had promised to do for the others—all that just deepened people's allegiance to them.

I thought that after Christmas dinner Mr. Royce might eventually close down his store. But he kept it open, although he was pretty subdued about promoting it. He probably knew it wouldn't do much good anyway, and I think he was starting to realize that maybe Pa and Almeda weren't the adversaries he had always imagined them to be. He also stopped making so much noise about making trouble for Pa and his claim. Maybe getting beat in the election sobered him into recognizing that he wasn't quite as all-powerful in the community as he had thought. He made good on his promise to call no more notes due. In fact, just shortly after the first of the year he lowered the interest rate on a few of the larger ones, not wanting folks to be mad at him for what they'd heard about Pa and Almeda's arrangements with Mr. Shaw.

Mr. Shaw kept paying them, and they kept paying the fellow in Sacramento, and so in the long run it actually worked out better for the Shaws than it had been before.

As it turned out, I didn't get the chance to visit again soon with Ankelita Carter. She wrote saying that she was sending some men to Sacramento for supplies, so Zack and Little Wolf and I arranged to go to the capital and meet them and return Rayo Rojo without having to ride all the way down to Mariposa. But I still hoped to meet the Fremonts someday!

Even with Christmas and the beginning of the new year behind us, I still couldn't get myself in a frame of mind to do much writing. Somehow the motivation was missing after the events leading up to the election and disappointments about my article and Mr. Fremont's loss. I tried to write a few articles throughout the first months of the year, but they were nothing I wanted to send in to Mr. Kemble. I found myself wondering if I'd ever write much again. I drew lots of pictures and kept writing in my journal, and otherwise spent most of the day-time in town at the Mine and Freight. Almeda kept working too, although by the beginning of March her pregnancy was far enough along that she had to slow down and take most afternoons off.

Several interesting things happened in town during those early months of 1857. Some meetings were held in Sacramento about town planning. Now that the gold rush was gradually giving way to the growth of California and the concerns of statehood and settlement, the state's lead-ers in the capital seemed to think communities like Miracle Springs needed some help figuring out what to do with them-selves. Because of my articles, someone there had actually heard about the election and knew of the outcome. And so Pa received a personal invitation to come to the meetings. They asked if he'd be willing to make a short talk about the problems and difficulties he felt *he* had in being a leader in a former gold-boom town that was now growing into a more diverse community.

When the letter first came, everyone was excited about it, and Alkali Jones was laughing and cackling about Pa running for president himself next. Everyone was excited, except Pa. His response was just what you might have expected—casual and disinterested.

"I can't see what you're all making such a fuss about," he said. "They most likely sent this same letter to a hundred other men just hoping that *one* of them would show up with something to say."

But inside I could tell Pa was mighty proud, and a time or two I caught sight of him alone rereading the letter, so I know he was thinking about it more than he was willing to let on.

He did go to Sacramento, and he did speak a little to the meeting of town leaders who were there, although he downplayed that when he got back, too. But it was obvious that he was different after that—more serious about being mayor, talking more about problems that needed solving in the community, thinking about the impact of things on the people he served as well as his own life and family.

One of the results of Pa's going to Sacramento was a town council.

"It's the way a town ought to be run," Pa told us, "so no one man can tell everybody else what to do. They can vote on things, and that way it doesn't all just rest on the mayor's shoulders. And besides that, the council gives the mayor someplace to go for advice, other men to talk to—"

"Other *men?*" repeated Almeda with a sly smile. "Are only men allowed on the council?" The rest of us laughed.

"You're dang right, woman!" said Pa with a grin. "You don't think after what you put this community through last year that anyone's going to stand for a woman on the town council!"

"They just might! And I suppose you're going to tell me that only men can vote for the council too?"

Pa smiled, drawing it out a long time, waiting until everyone quieted down and was watching for what he would say next.

"Well, actually what they recommended," he answered finally, "is that the mayor himself pick the people to be on the first council, instead of trying to call an election."

"And so no women will get selected?" persisted Almeda.

"I think you've just about got the gist of how California politics works at last," said Pa.

We all laughed again, Almeda louder than anyone.

"Seriously, Drummond," she went on, "are you really going to pick the council yourself? How will you choose?"

"I don't know yet. But I gotta have some folks I can talk to besides just you and Nick and Corrie and Alkali and the rest of you. That was all right for trying to decide about the election last year, when we all just got together and discussed everything. But what would folks think if that's how I did my mayoring, just getting my advice from my family? One thing's for sure, I'd never get re-elected! No, folks want to know their voice is being heard somehow. That's what they called 'representative government' in Sacramento. We all know that everybody votes for president, but they said the same thing's important in a town too, that the mayor and council represent all the people, not just their own interests."

Pa was starting to sound like a politician!

"They said those towns without a council yet ought to get one appointed so they can get it working and get the bugs worked out of how town government's supposed to function. Then in two years—that'd be in fifty-eight, when the next state elections are held—they can have people run for town council and mayor, and make it all more official."

"How many are on a council?" asked Zack.

"Oh, depends, son. In big cities, maybe ten or twelve. But for a little place like Miracle Springs, four or five, maybe six, is plenty."

"What does a town council do, Pa?" asked Becky.

"I reckon they just help the mayor decide things."

"But who says what the mayor decides and what the council decides?" I asked.

"Well, another thing they talked about in Sacramento is a town drawing up a set of what they call bylaws. That's like a set of instructions of who does what and how rules and laws are made. So that's something we got to do too, after we get a council. They've got some from other places we'll be able to look at and work from."

"What if the council votes and it's a tie?" said Zack.

"That's why you have to have a wise mayor who knows what he's about," replied Pa with a smile. "In cases where they can't make a decision, the mayor casts the deciding vote and they do what he says."

As it turned out, Pa wasted no time in getting together the first Miracle Springs town council. He went around and talked to folks, got lots of opinions and suggestions of who people'd trust to sort of be their community spokesmen and leaders. The first man he selected was Mr. Bosely, the owner of the General Store, and then Simon Rafferty, the sheriff. Those two surprised no one because they were men most folks knew and respected. Next there was Matthew Hooper, a rancher who lived about five miles from town. Pa said he wasn't sure if him being on the council was exactly legal, since he didn't actually live in town. But that could all be straightened out later, he said, and if it wasn't, then a change could be made at the next election. For now he and most folks around thought Mr. Hooper would be a real good help for speaking up for ranching interests. And to represent the miners, there was Hollings Shannahan, who had been in Miracle since 1850. But the last two—Pa had decided on six for the council—

shocked everybody. The first was Almeda, and she was the most surprised of all!

"What will people say, Drummond?" she said. "Picking a woman's bad enough . . . but your own wife!"

"I don't care what they say, woman. You're one of the most qualified people around here, and everyone knows it. You ran for mayor. And what anyone thinks is their own business. I want you on my town council."

But his final selection made everyone for miles throw their hands up in the air wondering if Drummond Hollister had finally gone loco once and for all. He wouldn't say anything to any of us ahead of time, and on the day when he made the announcement of the council members to a gathering of people in town, he saved the surprise name for last.

"As the sixth and final person to help look over this town," Pa said, "I name a fellow I've had a difference or two with, but who I reckon has just about as much a say in the things that go on around here as anyone—Franklin Royce."

So that was Miracle Springs' first town council—Bosely, Rafferty, Hooper, Shannahan, Parrish-Hollister, and Royce—with Drummond Hollister mayor over them. As time went on, everyone saw Pa's wisdom in picking the people he did. Everyone came to have a real confidence in the council to make decisions that were for the whole community's good. Even Mr. Royce began to be seen in a new light. I think it meant a lot to him that Pa had picked him, although he wouldn't do much to show it.

The first meeting of the town council was a celebrated affair that was held, of all places, in a back room of the Gold Nugget, which they cleaned up for the occasion. Lots of people were there, curious to see what was going to happen. But for the meeting itself, Pa wouldn't let any spectators in.

"There may be time enough one day for all you gawkers to see us do some of our town counciling. But for this first time together, we aim to just talk among ourselves, and get a few matters of business settled."

Then he shut the door and disappeared inside, leaving all the onlookers in the saloon to drink and talk and wonder out loud what there could possibly be for a Miracle Springs town council to talk about, anyway.

When Uncle Nick was telling us about it afterwards, he said, "There was more than one of the men that said, 'What in tarnation's got into Drum, anyhow? He's done got hisself so blamed official about everything since the election! He ain't no fun no more!'"

But mostly Uncle Nick said the men had a lot of respect for how Pa was handling the whole thing.

When Pa and Almeda got back later that evening it was already pretty late, but we were dying of curiosity. Pa didn't say much, but Almeda went on and on about it.

"You should have seen him!" she exclaimed. "Your father ran that meeting like he was the governor himself! Why, he even had to shut me up once or twice."

"You told me to treat you like all the others and not to give you preferential treatment on account of us being married," said Pa in defense.

"I didn't mean you had to silence me in midsentence."

"You were carrying on, Almeda," said Pa, "and I didn't see anything else to do but shut you down before you made a fool of yourself by what you were saying."

"A fool of myself!"

"You were talking like a woman, not like a town councilman. And maybe you are a council*woman*, not a council*man*, but you still gotta act like a councilman. I'm just trying to protect you from getting criticized by any of the others."

Almeda didn't say anything for a minute, then added, "Well, even if I am still vexed with you for what you did, I still think you ran that meeting like the best mayor in the world, and I'm proud of you."

"What did you talk about, Pa?" asked Emily.

"Oh, not too much, I reckon. A town this size hasn't got all that much that anyone needs to decide. We just looked at a copy of some bylaws I brought from Sacramento and talked about some of the stuff, trying to decide how *we* ought to do things here in Miracle."

One of the things they decided over the course of the next few meetings had to do with growth and new businesses that might come to Miracle Springs in the future. With the way the state was growing so fast—and this was something Pa said they talked a lot about at the meetings in Sacramento—communities like ours had to make some decisions early about how much they wanted to grow and in what ways. Pa and the council members decided that the council would vote on any new businesses that wanted to come and start up in Miracle, so that they'd have the chance to determine if they thought it was a good idea or not.

As it turned out, this decision was one of the first ones to be tested, and the results were different than anyone had expected.

Pa's First Big Decision

Chapter Forty

*A*s a result of all the ruckus the previous autumn about money and foreclosures and all the threats Mr. Royce had made about calling notes due, an unexpected turn of events landed Pa and the rest of the council in the middle of a controversy. Pa and Almeda were even more in the middle of it than anyone else.

When Almeda's friend from Sacramento, Mr. Denver, had helped to arrange with his boss, Mr. Finch, for them to borrow the money to help Patrick Shaw, the incident had apparently stirred up Mr. Finch's old antagonism toward Franklin Royce. Mr. Denver told Almeda that there was a time when his boss had thought about expanding their financial holdings into the northlands, and now it seemed that uncovering his old grievances had brought that desire to life again.

One day out of nowhere Carl Denver rode into town to see Almeda. Almeda's first thought was that something had gone sour on their arrangement with Mr. Finch and that he was about to call Pa and Almeda's money with *him* due. But that wasn't it at all, Mr. Denver assured her.

"Finch couldn't be more pleased to be involved with you people up here," he went on with a smile. "In fact, he's hoping this is but the beginning. Which brings me to the reason for my trip."

He reached into his coat pocket and pulled out several papers. From where I was standing in another part of the office, they looked like legal documents of some kind.

"Mr. Finch wants to open a branch of Finchwood Ltd. right here in Miracle Springs!" he announced. "He's already had all the documents drawn up, and he sent me up to find a site and begin making specific preparations."

"That's wonderful," replied Almeda. "But I can't imagine . . . why Miracle Springs? Finchwood is a sizable investment firm. What can there possibly be here to interest you?"

"All of California is growing at an explosive rate. Mr. Finch is a shrewd businessman, and loses no opportunity to get in on the ground floor, as he calls it. He's convinced that Miracle Springs will one day become a sort of hub for this region north of Sacramento. And I have to tell you, Almeda," he went on, "no small part of that has to do with your impact upon him. He was quite taken with you—with your resolve, your determination. He's watched what went on here, followed the election, and then saw your husband at the recent town-leader meetings down in Sacramento."

"Mr. Finch met Drummond?"

"No, they didn't actually meet. But Mr. Finch has been considering a move of this kind for some time, so he went to the meetings to explore possibilities. He heard your husband address the meeting, and was duly impressed with him as well. Out of all the growing communities represented at those meetings, he came away thinking more strongly than ever that Miracle Springs was the town he wanted to invest in—with a new bank, with investment opportunities for the miners who happen to be doing well and need a place for their funds, and perhaps with other businesses as well."

"I must say, Carl, I'm . . . I'm rather speechless. It's so unexpected—to think that Miracle Springs could one day grow into an actual city."

"There's no *could* to it, Almeda. If Mr. Finch has his way—and he usually does—there will be no way to stop Miracle Springs from growing by leaps and bounds. A population of ten thousand or more within three to five years would not be out of the question. And you know what that means?"

"I imagine it would mean a great number of things," replied Almeda slowly, her expression turning very serious. "But what do you think it means, Carl?"

"It means money, Almeda, opportunity, jobs. Your business, even if no changes were made, would positively explode. But as I said, Mr. Finch is very taken with you and your husband. He would lose no chance to make some very attractive and lucrative opportunities available to you. He would like to help you expand your business. He told me to convey that to you personally. He would invest money in your husband's reelection campaign when the time comes. He even hopes to persuade one of you to join him in Finchwood in some capacity or other—perhaps with a stock option—in order that you and your husband might be influential in securing Finchwood access into the community, so that we would be able to gain people's trust, as it were."

"I see," responded Almeda, thinking heavily.

"It's a once-in-a-lifetime opportunity, Almeda. If the growth happens as Mr. Finch is convinced it can with his money pouring into the area, in five years you and your husband could wind up in a very secure position—even wealthy, by the standards of most people. Your husband would be mayor of one of California's leading small and growing cities. And who knows what opportunities can open up politically, with your being so close to Sacramento. Not to mention the vast influence you would both have right here in your own community. You would become its first man and first woman, with the prestige and wealth to accompany it!"

Almeda was silent a moment. It was clear Mr. Denver didn't understand her hesitancy.

"There is one thing you have perhaps not considered in all this," said Almeda at length.

"What is that?"

"The town council."

"Oh, not to worry. A mere formality," said Mr. Denver buoyantly. "It's money that runs politics, not politics that runs money, Almeda. Once the people of this community realize all the good to come of the kinds of investments and growth Finchwood will bring, they'll be begging us to come."

"A recent town ordinance was passed which says the town council must authorize any new business within Miracle Springs."

"Yes—and aren't both you and your husband on the council?"

"I am. Not Drummond."

"But he's the mayor. Why, with the two of you behind this thing, it can't lose!"

"There is one person who *will* lose from it, that much is certain," said Almeda.

"Who's that?" asked Denver.

"Franklin Royce," she answered. "His bank won't survive six months once a new one opens its doors."

"Mr. Finch *did* think of that," Mr. Denver observed with a sly smile. "He's been waiting for a chance to put him out of business for years. And ever since you came to us for help last year, he's been slowly hatching this scheme in that clever brain of his."

"Seems a little too bad."

"Too bad! Royce is a no-good crook! You as much as said so yourself. I thought the two of you hated him as much as Mr. Finch does. Hasn't he tried to put *you* out of business?"

"Yes, there's no denying he has . . . several times."

"Then here's your chance to get even and rid Miracle Springs of him forever."

Again, Almeda was silent.

"And from what I understand, he's opened a supplies outlet in direct competition with you," Mr. Denver added.

She nodded.

"Well, now do you see how well this will work out for everybody? Kill two birds with one stone, as the saying goes— drive Royce out of business, and his bank and store with him! And all the while Miracle Springs will be growing and you and your husband will be making money and gaining power. What more could anyone hope for?"

"What more, indeed," repeated Almeda, her voice filled with reservation in spite of Mr. Denver's enthusiasm. "But you do know that Franklin is on the council too?"

"Of course. I've done my background work before coming here. One vote won't hurt us. Five to one is just as good as six to zero. Besides, everyone in the whole community hates Royce too. We'll be performing a service to the whole area by getting rid of him! And just to make sure, I'll be contacting the other council members to outline the advantages to them personally for voting with Finchwood."

Almeda did not reply, and then the conversation moved off in other directions. Finally Mr. Denver left to go to the boardinghouse where he would be staying.

Miracle always seemed to be in the middle of *something* or another that had people stirred up and talking and taking sides. And no sooner had all the election hullabaloo settled down than we were smack in the midst of another upheaval. Carl Denver saw to that! He started right off talking to the members of the town council—all except one. Within a few days it was all over town about Finchwood's plans and all the growth and prosperity that would come to Miracle Springs and how good it would be for all its people.

Folks talked about it a lot, and almost everyone seemed to think it was a good thing. You can't stop progress, Mr. Denver had been telling them, and no one seemed inclined to try. Besides, they said, new businesses and new money and new investments in the community couldn't help but be good for everybody. And if California was going to grow, why shouldn't Miracle Springs get right in and grow as fast as anyplace else?

Undoubtedly the change would do damage to the Royce Miners' Bank, especially because Mr. Denver let it be known that Finchwood would probably lend money for land and homes at lower interest than Mr. Royce. I don't think most people wanted to hurt Mr. Royce, but at the same time they weren't all that worried about him, either. "If he can't keep up with the times, that's his own fault," Mr. Shaw commented to Almeda when he was over visiting. "Wouldn't bother me none at all to see him run out of here for good!"

Of course, Mr. Shaw had good reason to dislike Franklin Royce, but a lot of other people would probably have agreed with Alkali Jones' assessment of the situation: "Serves the dang varmint right, hee, hee, hee!" he cackled. "He ain't been out fer nobody but his blame self for years, an' now it'll just be givin' him a dose o' his own medicine!"

Pa and Almeda were surprisingly quiet through the whole thing. I knew they were talking and praying together, but they didn't tell anyone what they were thinking. Almeda had remained somber ever since the day when Mr. Denver had come into the Freight office. I didn't understand her hesitation, if that's what was making her quiet about it. It seemed to me that it couldn't help but be good for her and Pa and the business. And in a way they'd already thrown in with Finchwood months before with their dealings over the Shaw and Douglas notes. I'd heard them talk once or twice about the possibility of getting even more money to lend to people if Mr. Royce got troublesome again. Pa had even jokingly said something about the new Hollister-Parrish "bank," and then laughed. So it seemed that what Mr. Finch was proposing fit right in with what they'd been thinking of themselves.

A special town council meeting was planned to vote on it, so that Mr. Denver could get the papers signed and finalize everything before he went back to report to Mr. Finch. During the week he was here, he had a sign painted, and the day before the meeting it went up in the window of an empty building two doors down from Mr. Bosely's. It read, *Future Home of Finchwood Ltd.*, with the words, *Investments, Banking, Securities* underneath in smaller letters. No one saw much of Mr. Royce all week.

On the morning of the meeting, I said to Pa at breakfast, "How are you going to vote, Pa?"

"Don't you know, girl, it's the council's decision to make, not mine."

"Then how's Almeda going to vote?"

"You're asking me? She doesn't tell me ahead of time. When it comes to the council, she's not my wife. She's representing the town, not me. And I don't want to know what she's thinking, because then one of us might try to do some convincing for our own side, and that wouldn't be right for the town, now would it?"

"I guess not," I answered.

Just then Almeda walked in from the other room.

"Corrie asked me how you're going to vote," Pa told her.

"And what did you tell her?"

"That I didn't know, which I don't."

"When we're representing Miracle Springs, Corrie," Almeda went on, "we've got to do our best to lay our personal feelings aside. If we're going to be faithful to the town and its people, we've got to vote our conscience, even if it sometimes means being on the opposite side of a certain issue. Both of us have spoken to a lot of people, and we've prayed together for wisdom, but that's as far as our communication on the subject goes."

The meeting of the council was scheduled for six o'clock that evening. Because so many people were interested, Pa had arranged for the tables and chairs in the Gold Nugget to be moved aside and organized so that the meeting could take place in the main part of the saloon—the biggest single room in all of Miracle Springs.

When the time came, the place was full, with another twenty or thirty people milling around in the street outside. The council members sat up in front at a long rectangular table with Pa in the middle. Mr. Denver was full of smiles and greetings for everyone, and sat down in the front row of chairs. It was the first time our whole family had been in the Gold Nugget together since that first church service when Rev. Rutledge was new in town. There were chairs for us and for all the women who came, but most of the men had to stand.

Pa called the meeting to order by banging his fist down on the table two or three times.

"Quiet down!" he called out. "Hey, quiet . . . we have to get this meeting called to order!"

Everybody gradually stopped talking and buzzing. "This is a meeting of the Miracle Springs town council for the purpose of deciding whether to grant this petition—" Pa held up Mr. Denver's papers which had been sitting on the table in front of him. "This petition is from Finchwood Limited in Sacramento to set up a bank here in Miracle Springs."

You could still hear quite a bit of noise coming from the men standing around outside, but Pa ignored it and kept right on going.

"So before we decide, I need to ask if anybody's got anything to say. You've all got a right to speak to the council before we vote if you think there's anything we need to hear before making the decision."

Pa waited. The room was silent for a moment. Then Mr. Denver rose to his feet. He talked for about ten minutes, half toward Pa and the others up in front, but turning around into the saloon a lot too, saying mostly the same kinds of things he'd been saying all week about all the good Mr. Finch wanted to do for the people of Miracle Springs.

When he sat down, Pa said. "Any of the rest of you got anything to say?"

Mr. Shaw came forward.

"All right, Pat. What do you have to tell us?"

"Only this—that I think it's an opportunity we might not get again. And as for the folks of Finchwood, it seems to me we can trust them just as far, if not even further, than some of the people we've been having our financial dealings with up till now."

A small buzz went around at his pointed words. Mr. Royce sat in front not moving a muscle, but everyone knew what Mr. Shaw was talking about. Since Patrick Shaw had almost been thrown off his land by Mr. Royce, if anyone had a right to be saying what he was, it seemed that Mr. Shaw did.

"So I say we give them all the approval they want," he added, then went back to where he'd been standing.

From the nods and expressions of agreement, it was clear that most of the men present felt the same way.

"Anyone else?" said Pa over the hubbub.

"Get on with the votin', Drum!" called out someone. "We all know well enough what's gonna happen without no one talkin' 'bout it no more."

"Do yer mayorin', Drum!" cackled Alkali Jones. "Hee, hee, hee!"

"Okay, that's enough from you ol' coots," said Pa. "But I reckon you're right. It's time to get this thing decided and over with. So if there's nothing more to be said, I'm going to call the vote."

Immediately there was silence, and Pa called on the council members one at a time.

"Hooper," said Pa. "How do you vote—yea or nay about Finchwood's petition?"

"Yea," said Mr. Hooper. Another round of chatter spread through the room.

"Bosely?" said Pa.

"Yea."

"Rafferty?"

"I vote against it," said the sheriff. At his words the noise got immediately louder.

"What you got against 'em, Simon?" called out someone.

"Quiet down," said Pa. "You can't interrupt the voting like that. You all will just have to keep your opinions to yourself till we're done."

"I just got a feeling about it, that's all," said the sheriff, not paying any attention to Pa but answering the man anyway. "I just can't see all the good it'll do for Miracle to grow so big as they're saying. It'll make my job all the harder, that's for sure. And that's why I'm voting no."

"Royce?" said Pa.

"Nay," replied the banker. Everyone had expected that.

"Shannahan?"

"Yea."

Now it *did* get quiet. Everybody had figured the vote to be five-to-one, with Mr. Royce being the only person to be against it. Now suddenly it was three-to-two, with one vote left. No one had expected it to be close. And they sure hadn't expected what came next.

"Almeda," said Pa. "Looks like you're the one who's going to decide this thing."

"I wish you'd have remembered to let ladies go first, Drummond," said Almeda with a smile. "Then all this pressure would have fallen on one of the other men."

"Couldn't be helped," replied Pa. "It's just the way you were all sitting around the table. Besides, on a town council everyone's equal."

"Well, I'd still feel more comfortable not being last, because I'm afraid I'm not going to clarify matters much. I vote no."

The silence instantly erupted into gasps and oohs and ahs and comments all filling up the room. The certain outcome was suddenly three-to-three—a tie vote on the first major decision the town council of Miracle Springs had to make!

"What you gonna do now, Drum?" someone called out.

"He's gonna vote himself," said Uncle Nick loudly. "That's what we got a mayor for!"

"Well, I reckon now we're about t' see what kind o' stuff our mayor's made of, ain't we?" said someone else.

"What's it gonna be, Drum—yea or nay?"

"Yeah, Drum, don't keep us in suspense! How you gonna vote?"

"Well, maybe I'd tell you if you baboons'd shut up long enough to let a mayor get a word in edgeways!" shouted Pa into the middle of all their hollering and talking.

Gradually the noise subsided, and within another minute the place was dead silent, with every eye in the room fixed on Pa, who was standing up behind the table where the other council members were sitting. He waited a moment longer. I don't know what he was thinking about, but everyone was listening for him to say just a single word—yea or nay. When he finally spoke, he said neither.

"I aim to say a few words before I cast my vote," he said. "You all know I'm no speechmaker. But I reckon a mayor's gotta get used to making a speech now and then, and so maybe now's as good a time as any for me to have a start at it. I didn't plan this out, because I didn't figure I'd have to do any voting today. But since it looks like I have to cast the deciding vote, I suppose I ought to tell you what I've been thinking about this week."

He stopped and took a breath, as if he was getting ready to jump into an icy river and wasn't too pleased at the prospect. Then he plunged ahead. And if I didn't know it was my own Pa, I would have taken him for a downright politician! It was just about one of the finest speeches I'd ever heard!

"We've got a lot of things to consider," Pa finally went on, "if it's gonna fall on our shoulders to say what should be the future of this town of ours. Now I've been talking to a bunch of you this past week, and doing a lot of thinking. Most of you say you figure change and new business and more money would be good for everybody, and so we ought to just let it go ahead and happen. And I guess we all figured that's how the vote would go, too. Probably most of you are a mite surprised that we've got a tie on our hands. And I'm as surprised as anyone. But even as little as I know about it, because I take my mayoring seriously, I did a bit of thinking these last days about what I thought too, and what I'd do just in case I did have to vote. And a couple of things stuck in my mind."

He stopped for a couple of seconds, just sort of looking around the room at all the eyes on him, then went ahead.

"The first thing I found myself wondering is this—if all this change and growth that Mr. Denver's predicting *does* happen, what kind of place is Miracle Springs going to be five or ten years from now? I'm sure he's right, because he knows more than a man like me about bringing in lots of money and new people. And maybe we'd all get rich. But that's what they said about the gold too, and not too many of us in *this* room are getting fat from having so much money stashed in Mr. Royce's bank."

A ripple of laughter spread through the room.

"Maybe we would get rich," Pa went on. "But it still strikes me that we'd have to ask what kind of place Miracle would be with five or ten thousand people here. Speaking just for myself, I'm not at all sure I'd want to be mayor of a place like that, or would even want to live here. Can you imagine Miracle with ten thousand people? Why, tarnation, the place'd spread so far in every direction, the Hollister place would be in the middle of town! We'd have no woods, no creek, no mine! Even half of Hooper's spread would have streets running through it!"

He paused for a minute while everyone laughed.

"Why Miracle would be a dad-blamed city! There'd be no room for mines anymore. Every inch for miles would be taken up with buildings and people! And I guess I'm just not at all sure I like the idea of that. I don't know about you, but I kind of like Miracle Springs the way it is."

Suddenly everyone quieted down as Pa's words sank in. It was obvious nobody had thought about the question quite like that, and Pa's questions got everyone sobered up in a hurry.

"The second thing that bothered me is gonna surprise a few of you. It surprises me to find myself thinking like this too! But you all know that besides my mayoring, I've been trying to take living as a Christian seriously too, so I'm not afraid to tell you that I pray about things a lot more than I used to. And

I've been praying about this vote too. When you pray, every once in a while you find an answer from God coming your way that you didn't expect. And this is one of those times.

"What I got to thinking about was loyalty, and what it means. Loyalty to other folks—not just to friends and family, but to all sorts of others we owe something to. Seems to me loyalty's in short supply these days. Everyone's out to get all he can, and we don't stop too much to consider what we should be doing about those people Jesus calls our neighbors. But he tells us in the Good Book that we're supposed to do as we'd like to be done by. And that means standing by our neighbor whether he stands by us or not. It means being loyal whether someone's been loyal to us or not. It means trying to do good wherever you can, no matter what anyone else has done to you.

"So I found myself thinking a lot about a certain individual in this town of ours by the name of Franklin Royce—"

Another buzz of whispers and movement went around, then quickly settled down. Everyone was anxious to hear what Pa was gonna say.

"Now, you all know that Royce hasn't been a particular friend of mine, or anyone else's around here. He's pulled some pretty low-down stuff, and he's hurt more than one upstanding man with his greed."

I glanced over at Mr. Royce. His face had a scowl on it, but he didn't dare move a muscle. I could almost feel the anger rising up from his reddening neck into his cheeks!

"He's tried to take my place a time or two, and would've taken Shaw's and Douglas' if Almeda and I hadn't stopped him. So I'd have to say that Mr. Royce has been a mean man, and maybe some of you'd just as soon be rid of him and his bank altogether.

"But you know, if it hadn't been for his bank, half of you in this room wouldn't have your houses and farms and ranches. Almeda's store used money from Royce's bank a time or two, and so did I. Much as we don't want to admit it, Franklin Royce has done a lot for this community. Even if we don't always see eye to eye, he's just as much a part of Miracle Springs as I am or as you are. Why, he was almost your mayor! And it was money from Royce's bank that saved the life of my Becky.

"Maybe Mr. Royce, for all his faults of the past, deserves a little of our loyalty too. He's put five or six years of his life into this place, and I'm not so sure I can be party to watching his business get ruined because he hasn't treated me so kindly. Seems like when times get rough, folks have to stick together and show their loyalty to one another. Maybe this is the time when we need to show Mr. Royce that the folks of Miracle Springs can be loyal too."

There was another pause, this time a long one, while people shifted around in their chairs or shuffled their feet.

"So here's what I figure to do," Pa continued finally. "I think we ought to think a little more about what kind of future we want for this place we call our home. Do we want it to stay the nice little town it is, or do we want it to become a city that's growing faster than we can keep up with? Then I want to go have a talk with Mr. Royce. And I want to tell him I'm willing to give him my hand and be a friend to him, and show my loyalty to him, even if he does try to put my wife's store out of business!"

More laughter erupted, and people shifted about nervously.

"What I aim to say to him is this: 'Now look, Franklin, it's no secret that you're charging more interest than some of the big banks in Sacramento. Why don't you be neighborly, and show *your* loyalty to the folks of Miracle Springs, by lowering the rates on everybody's loans to match what Finchwood would give them? They'll like you all the more for it, and then there won't be any reason for a new bank to open up. What do you say, Franklin?'

"That's what I'm going to say to our friend and banker, Mr. Royce, first chance I get," said Pa, glancing around the table where the council sat. Everyone chuckled when he looked straight at Mr. Royce.

"And in the meantime, since we've got town business to conduct right now, I'm going to cast my vote. I vote no."

He was immediately interrupted by sounds throughout the room. I had been looking at Mr. Royce, and my eyes drifted to Almeda, who was sitting right next to him. She was crying. She was so proud of Pa—we all were!

"So, Mr. Denver," Pa was trying to say, "I'm afraid you're going to have to tell your Mr. Finch that the petition's denied for right now. But you tell him how much we appreciate his interest in Miracle Springs. And you can tell him for me, that if he is still interested in Finchwood coming up this way, try us again a year from now. That'll give us a chance to think about all this a little more slowly. And it'll also give us a year to decide whether we think Miracle Springs is in need of some more competition in the banking business, or if the bank we've got seems to be operating to everyone's satisfaction."

Again Pa glanced in Mr. Royce's direction. The banker's face had a look of stunned joy on it, realizing that the man he styled his arch enemy had just saved his bank from another enemy.

I think Pa's final words were lost on Mr. Royce for the moment. But there would be plenty of people to remind the banker of their significance in the coming months!

People began moving around the room, and lots of men were already walking up to the bar to start ordering drinks. The women and children who had been there made haste to leave. The members of the council stood up, and some talking and handshaking followed.

Then almost as an afterthought, Pa shouted out: "This meeting of the town council is adjourned!"

Pa's speech and vote sure did show what the new mayor was made of! Pa had shown his mettle in front of the whole town, and there couldn't have been a prouder, happier bunch of kids and a wife than we were riding home in the wagon that night after the meeting! It didn't even matter about the vote— it was what Pa'd done. He'd been a leader, a mayor. And it felt good to see him strong like that, and courageous to speak out.

Things seemed to change after that. The mayor and town council were more than just formalities now. They had made a real decision that changed something that would have happened without them. And if Mr. Royce did lower interest rates like Pa hoped he would, then as mayor Pa would have done everybody a lot of good. Miracle Springs might not grow as fast as some of California's new towns and cities. But at least from now on, folks around here knew they had people they could trust looking out for them.

One of the other events that happened early that spring before the babies were born was a big town picnic. But first I want to tell you about a conversation Pa and Uncle Nick had. I didn't actually hear it. Pa came in late one evening, got me and Almeda and Zack together by ourselves after the others were in bed, and told us about it.

"Nick's worried about Katie," he said quietly. We all waited for him to explain further.

"She's still quiet and moody. Of course, that's no surprise to any of us," he went on, "because we can see it well enough. But he thinks it's his fault in some way, that he must have done something, or that he isn't being all to her he ought to be."

"Bless his dear heart," said Almeda tenderly.

"I told him it's not his doing—"

"Of course not," added Almeda. "He's a fine husband and father."

"That's exactly what I said," Pa went on. "Why, nobody from the old days would even recognize Nick! He's that different."

"So what did he say?"

"Aw, he just kept going on about how Katie wouldn't talk to him and was sullen and quiet and how he didn't know what to do. He was frustrated, I could tell that much. Seemed like he was ready to get angry with her one minute, but then the next remembered her condition and felt bad for not having more patience. He just doesn't know what to do, that's all."

"What did he say?"

"He said, 'She's been downright impossible lately. When I married her I didn't bargain for no wife that's moody all the time. What kind of marriage is it when you can't even talk together? But she ain't saying nothing no more, and I wind up talking just about the weather and the mine.' He'd go on like that, but then suddenly stop himself and feel bad just for saying it."

"It could be the pregnancy, you know, Drummond. It's harder on some women than others, and she's a good seven months along."

"So are you," said Pa.

"Are you saying I'm fat?"

"Just good and plump," replied Pa with a smile. "And you aren't moping around like you're mad at the world."

"But then I have you for a husband," said Almeda with a loving smile.

"Yeah, I guess you do at that!"

"But it's not really the pregnancy," Almeda mused. "That probably is wearing her out some, especially with little Erich to keep up with. But there's more than that—it's down deep. She's a troubled woman, Drummond. It's her spirit that's in turmoil, not her body."

Pa sighed. "Yeah, I know you're right. That much is plain from one look in her face. She's just not at peace with life."

"Does Nick know that?" she asked.

"I think so. I asked him when it all started. He said that it had been growing gradually for a long time, but it seemed to start getting worse a while back after he'd gotten her to go to church with us one Sunday. Avery preached a sermon about how we've all got to make God a regular part of our life every day, not just here and there."

"I remember the day very well. And now that you mention it, she was particularly quiet that afternoon."

"Nick said he had a feeling she was thinking about it. 'You remember when she first came, I asked him, 'when she said her aunt used to go to church every Sunday and prayed and did all kinds of religious stuff, but then didn't really live by it much the rest of the week?' Then I told him that she was more than likely watching all the rest of us mighty close, and especially him, to see if our religion was something we lived by. 'I don't mean no offense to you, Nick,' I said, 'but you gotta make sure you live by what you believe.'

" 'What do you mean?' he asked. 'I'm doing the best I can. But it ain't easy, Drum, tryin' to be helpful with her grumpy all the time and ignorin' me.'

" 'Calm down,' I said, 'I know what kind of man you are. I'm just saying you can't go on with your business like maybe you done in the past. You gotta go out of your way to help her.'

"I kept reminding him that she most likely had lots of things brewing down deep inside that had nothing to do with him, but with what she thought about God, and other memories out of her past like her aunt. I told him that all those things and attitudes were probably coming back at her now.

" 'Why won't she tell me about it then?' he asked me.

" 'Can't tell you that, Nick,' I said. 'It's not easy to talk about the past sometimes, especially for a woman like Katie who's used to being independent and in control of things. She probably doesn't want to admit to having any kind of trouble inside herself. That's just the way some folks are.' "

"Sounds to me like you gave him pretty good advice," said Almeda.

Pa shrugged, then continued his story. " 'Well what am I supposed to do?' Nick asked me.

" 'You just be as nice and as gentle to her as you can be,' I said. 'And keep remembering that she's carrying your little son or daughter inside her.'

" 'I'll do it, Drum,' he said.

" 'Then you pray for her, Nick,' I told him. 'You pray for her real hard, and you pray for her all the time.'

" 'What am I supposed to pray? I ain't no praying sort like you and Almeda.'

" 'Well then it's high time you became a praying man,' I told him. 'You look here, Nick—that wife of yours needs you now more than she's ever needed anyone in her life. And she needs more than just you being nice—even though she needs that too. She's got something going on down inside her, and she needs God to be her friend. And that probably isn't going to happen without lots of prayer, because Katie's mighty headstrong when it comes to God. And you being her husband, your prayers mean more than anybody else's because you know what her needs are. We'll all be praying too, but you being the man of that house, and Katie being your wife, you're the one who can take charge of the situation with your prayers. So you gotta do it, you hear me? You gotta pray for her.'

"Well, he shrugged and didn't say much for a long time. He wasn't used to thinking of himself like that. He's like most folks with that fool notion that praying's something you hire the preacher to do, and that living like a Christian's something you do on Sunday and forget the rest of the time. But I told him he's got to get to the business of being God's man in that family of his if he wants to pull his wife through this.

" 'But I don't know how to pray, Drum,' he said again.

" 'You can't have forgotten all your ma and pa taught you,' I said. 'Even I knew them well enough to know they taught you and Aggie better than that. You know how to pray well enough. You just got out of practice because you haven't done it all these years. And now it's time you got at it again!'

" 'But what do I *say?*'

" 'There's nothing special you have to say. Just talk to God, that's all.'

" 'Out loud?'

" 'God doesn't care if it's out loud or not, Nick. Just talk to him, like he was right there in the room with you. You don't have to say a lot of words to get his attention. He's there. He's waiting for you to make him part of what you're about. He's not like us, Nick, who can only talk to a few folks at a time. He can be with all his children at once. So just tell him what you're thinking and feeling. And pray for Katie. Pray that he would open up Katie's heart.'

"He was quiet again. He was thinking pretty hard on what I was saying. I think it was like lots of things coming back to him from when he was just a kid, things he hadn't stopped to think about for a long time.

" 'But I don't know what's supposed to happen, Drum.' he said.

" 'Well, if you're praying for God to open up Katie's heart, then that's what's gonna happen,' I told him. 'That's the way it works. That's the kind of prayer God wants real bad to answer.' "

Pa looked around at the rest of us with a smile. " 'Look at me,' I said. 'That wife of mine—before she was even my wife, I don't doubt—and my daughter, and maybe even my son, for all I know—they were all praying for *me*. And lo and behold if some places down inside me didn't eventually open up and I begin to remember things and think about how I ought to be living and how I ought to be listening to God more. And pretty soon, Drum Hollister's praying out loud and trying to live his life as a Christian, and even some of his old friends are calling him *Reverend*.'

" 'So you see, Nick,' I said, 'that's just the way it works. If you pray for somebody, one way or another there's gonna be a change in their life. You remember what kind of man I used to be! It ain't gonna be all that tough for God to get through to a woman like Katie, just so long as you keep praying.'

" 'She can be a mighty headstrong woman,' said Nick. When he said it he sighed, and I could tell he wasn't being critical. It was just that frustration coming out again.

" 'Well, maybe that's so. But we'll all be praying with you, Nick,' I told him. 'And sometime or another, something down inside her is going to tell her she's not as in control of life as she's always figured. That time comes sooner or later to everyone. For me it was Aggie's dying and the kids showing up. All of a sudden, my whole world changed and a little door somewhere inside me opened a crack. And that's when God started poking his head through, and for the first time in my life, I was ready to listen.

" 'Well, that time will come for Katie too. So when I say you have to wait, that's what you're waiting for—that time when the little door inside of her heart opens up a crack and she looks out and says, "Maybe I do need to know God more than I've always thought." Then you can pray with her.'

" 'I'm not sure how,' Nick said.

" 'You're the man,' I told him. 'You gotta take the lead and show her that you can pray. Just ask for God to be in both of you and to show himself to you, and pray that you'll be open to let him do what he wants to do in your hearts. And then if she's willing,' I said, 'then you encourage her to pray that same thing, that God would show himself to her and that he'd live in her heart and help her to understand things better and be a friend to him like she hadn't been up until then. If she'd pray that, I think you'd have yourself a new woman, Nick— one with a smile on her face.'

"He was real quiet again. This was all pretty new to him. I'm not sure he even liked it much. But I could tell he knew it was true, and knew what he had to do."

The cabin got real quiet. From the look in Almeda's eyes I could tell she was far away. But this time it wasn't the look of pain that came from memories of Boston. It was a contented, peaceful look. I knew she was reflecting on the changes that had come to us all, to her, and especially to Pa. Even though no one said anything right then, we all *felt* so complete—a genuine *family*, talking and praying together about the deep and important things in life.

The late-night silence was broken by footsteps as Emily walked out from her room.

"I'm sorry, Pa," she said. "I wasn't asleep, and I couldn't help listening. I was concerned about Katie."

"Come over here, girl," said Pa. Emily walked over to him, and he stretched out his arm around her waist and pulled her close to him. "I'm glad you came out to join us. We're gonna pray for Katie, and I want you to pray with us."

"Thank you, Pa," she said, then sat down on the floor at his feet. Pa kept one of his great strong hands resting on her shoulder.

"After Nick and I were done talking," Pa went on in a moment, "I asked him if he wanted to pray right then with me. I think it took him by surprise, the thought of two grown men praying together like that. But he just nodded. Then he waited to see what I was gonna do. So I bowed my head and reached across and put my hand on his arm, and then I closed my eyes and started praying for him and Katie. Afterward he told me he was surprised to hear me pray in just normal words, without trying to use a bunch of church-words like the Reverend does on Sundays. But I told him, 'Nick, the Lord's not much concerned with a batch of big words that sound like they come out of the Bible. He only wants us to talk to him, that's all, like the people we *really* are, not like someone we're pretending to be. That's what I told him afterwards. But right then I just closed my eyes and prayed for him and Katie, and especially that Katie would come to see that God wasn't her enemy and that he wanted to be her friend. Then I prayed that Nick would find the courage to pray for her and to be the man he was supposed to be. He hardly moved a muscle, and when I finished it was quiet a long time.

"I kept waiting with my eyes closed, 'cause I wanted him to pray, so he could see it wasn't such a fearsome thing after all. It seemed to take him forever to get up the gumption, but finally he said, 'God, I ain't much practiced in this kind of thing. But if you'd give me a hand now and then, I'll try to pray more. So I ask you to help me do what Drum says and pray for Katie. Help me to know what to say to her. And I ask you to make her be able to listen when people talk about you without getting her dander up. Help me to know what to say and do. And help me to be able to listen to you too.'

"Anyhow, that's something like what he prayed," Pa added.

"Good for him," said Almeda softly. "What a wonderful beginning! I know many doors will begin to open for the two of them very soon."

"And now let's pray for them both," said Pa. "Five of us praying, especially five of us who love Nick and Katie—why, that's a powerful lot of prayer for God to be able to use!"

He took his hand off Emily's shoulder and placed it around her little white hand. Then he reached out with his other and took hold of Zack's. Almeda and I joined hands to complete the circle. We all bowed our heads and one at a time prayed for Uncle Nick and Aunt Katie.

*O*ne of the next decisions Pa made as mayor was to announce that there was going to be another town picnic on the first day of spring that year. He told us that he'd been thinking about the gathering we'd had three and a half years earlier at the church's dedication, and thinking it had been too long since we'd done something like that as a community together. So he figured that if he was mayor, he ought to be able to do something about it.

He announced it in church one Sunday early in March.

"On the twenty-first of March," he said, "that's on the Saturday two weeks from today, we're gonna bring in spring with a picnic right out here in the meadow between the church and the town. I want you all to come, and we'll celebrate the day together. That's on orders from your mayor!"

Everyone chuckled, and Pa moved to sit down. For the next two weeks, the whole town looked forward to the chance to get together again. Most of the women—and there were a lot more of them now than there had been in 1853!—spent the time cooking and baking. It was almost like getting ready for a fair!

When the day came, it couldn't have been prettier. There had been rain through the week, and Pa was wondering what to do if it rained on Saturday. But the storm passed on into the mountains and the sun came out Friday afternoon. It was a bit chilly on Saturday, and still a little wet, but *so* fresh and clean!

As I walked into the meadow that afternoon, there was still moisture and dew all about in the shady places, and where the sun shone the grass sparkled. It looked as if the whole area was covered with thousands of tiny glass prisms, all reflecting the sunlight like diamonds.

We were the first to arrive, and as I walked through the meadow, in the distance by the edge of the woods I saw a deer calmly nibbling on the fresh wet grass. She lifted her head and looked around, her tan coat gleaming when the sun hit it as she moved through the shadows. With each movement her velvet-like body shone with the essence of freedom I had always dreamed about.

I looked up and breathed the crisp air with pleasure. The sky was blue with clouds billowing gently across the sky. A whisper of cool wind blew by me, and I smelled again the fragrance of clean, fresh, springtime air.

Gradually more people began to arrive. The women were dressed brightly in colorful spring apparel, the men wearing dark trousers and flannel shirts. A few of the women were carrying parasols and twirling them around—some red, some pink. As the people slowly came and the meadow filled, all the colors and sounds and sights reflected the joy that was felt by everyone.

The men got tables set up and then we arranged food as it arrived and got everything ready. As the crowd enlarged, most of the younger kids went running off, some playing tag and other games.

"What can I do?" asked Becky, as Almeda was preparing one table.

"Hmm . . . let's see," replied Almeda, "why don't you go see if you can pick me some nice wildflowers to use here on the table."

Becky was off in a second, glad to be of some help. "But don't get near those woods again!" yelled Emily after her. Almeda and I both laughed.

After a while we were ready to begin eating. As the men were gathering around the table and the women were spreading out the last of the food, Rev. Rutledge asked if he could say a few words before we began.

"Ye mean we's gonna have t' listen to another one o' yer sermons?" said Alkali Jones, loud enough that everybody could hear.

A great laugh went up from those nearby.

"I will try to make this one as short as possible," said Rev. Rutledge, laughing himself and joining in the fun.

"You know preachers, Alkali," said Pa. "Whenever they see a crowd of people, they immediately start thinking of something to say!"

"And if they don't think of something right off, then they pass the collection plate!" added Rev. Rutledge. His joke got another good laugh out of everybody.

"When I was a child," the minister began as the laughter died away, "my parents always had a celebration like this to start off the season of spring. Most of our friends remembered the coming of spring on Easter, and in the church we went to, Easter was always a busy day. But my parents wanted to preserve Easter as a day spent thinking only of the resurrection and the true meaning of the day. Thus our family celebrated the first day of spring separately, as we are doing now."

The minister paused a moment to look around at the townspeople gathered in the meadow.

"Spring is the season of new life," he went on, "when new things begin to grow and new life bursts forth out of the earth. During springtime we witness the cycles of life and nature emerging in their newness, and all about us we see God's creation alive in the earth. But spring is also the time of year when Jesus Christ rose from the grave. And so the resurrection is the true basis for what spring means. We can let ourselves be reminded of the life that Jesus gave us when we see the new life that nature gives us during this wonderful green, growing, fragrant time of the year.

"So I would like to give a special thank you to our mayor, Drummond Hollister, for arranging this picnic today. As you can see, it is especially meaningful for me. And I would like to thank you all for being here."

Then Rev. Rutledge prayed, and immediately everyone began to eat. I don't know if I'd ever seen so much food before. There was every kind of meat and salad and fruit and bread imaginable. Afterward, people gradually began getting up and going about, visiting, the children playing, men smoking their pipes or chatting and playing horseshoes or discussing their claims and the latest gold prices, while the women worked on clearing up the tables and leftover food.

When no one else was around him for a minute, Mr. Royce walked up to Pa.

"Hollister," the banker said, "I think the time has come for me to acknowledge what you did for me at the town council meeting."

"I meant what I said," replied Pa.

"Nevertheless, I want you to know that I'm extremely appreciative."

"It was for the good of the town."

"*And* for me," said Mr. Royce. "Your vote more than likely saved my bank, and my whole future. And I want to say thank you."

He extended his hand. Pa took it and gave it a firm shake. Then the eyes of the two men met. Pa still held on to Mr. Royce's hand.

"I meant what I said about loyalty, Royce," said Pa. "And about being a friend and neighbor to you."

"I know you meant it, Hollister. You've proved yourself a man of your word. I didn't think I could admit this several months ago, but I have to say now that the best man won last November. Miracle Springs is better off with you as its mayor than it would have been with me."

"Well, I'm just glad you're on the council," said Pa, "and that we can start working together on the same side from now on." He relaxed his grip and let the banker's hand go.

"Well, thank you again, Hollister. And as for the question on interest rates, I'm looking into all that. I want to be fair to the people. If you'll just give me some time to get the details worked out—"

"Certainly, Royce," answered Pa, then added with a smile, "just don't wait too long. The people are all anxious to know what you're going to do."

"I'll move along as quickly as I can, believe me. Just tell the people they can count on me."

"Done!" said Pa. "They will appreciate it, Franklin."

The picnic that day gave us our first sight of someone who would be part of the Hollister future, though we had no idea of it at the time. There were quite a few people at the picnic that I didn't know. New families were coming to Miracle Springs regularly.

After we were through eating, I saw Zack over on the other side of the field throwing a ball back and forth with someone I didn't know, a boy who looked about Zack's own age. Then a while later, when I looked at them again, there were four or five others who had joined them scattered about. The stranger was hitting the little ball with a stick and the others were chasing after it. A few minutes later Zack brought the new boy over to where Pa and Almeda and Emily and I were seated on the grass. He was every bit as tall as Zack, and wearing a straw hat with a white shirt and blue knickers (which I found out later to be of some significance). He had light brown eyes and curly red hair with lots of freckles on his face.

"This here's Mike, Pa," said Zack. "His family just got here from the East."

Pa stood up and shook his hand. "Mike what?" he said in a friendly voice.

"McGee's the name, and baseball's the game," the boy replied. The instant he let go of Pa's hand, he reached into his pocket and pulled out a little white ball, the same one they had been playing with earlier.

"Baseball . . . what's that?" asked Emily.

"What's baseball!" exclaimed Mike McGee. "Why it's just the newest, most exciting game there is. They call me 'Lefty.' "

"Well none of us have ever heard of it," said Pa. "Why don't you tell us about it? Is that stick you got there something to do with it?"

"This stick," said McGee, holding up the rounded piece of wood, "has *everything* to do with it! This is called a bat, and you've gotta hit the ball with the bat."

He took a few steps away from us, then tossed the ball up into the air, slung the bat up over his shoulder as he grabbed it with both hands down near one end. As the ball came back down, he swung the wood around fast. It hit the ball with a loud cracking sound, and the ball went sailing out across the meadow in a big arch, landing over next to the woods.

"Just like that!" he said. Tad, who had just walked up to join us, was off like a flash to retrieve the ball and bring it back to Mike. By now a few more people were gathering around, but something told me young McGee was paying more attention to my sister Emily than all the other people put together.

"You hit it a long ways!" exclaimed Tad, running up puffing with the ball.

"That's nothing. You should see how far they hit it in a real game. My older brother Doug took me to see the first baseball game played between two regular teams. He played for the New Jersey Knickerbockers himself. That was back in '46. I was just eight then. They played against a team from New York."

"How'd it turn out?" asked Zack.

"I was nine before the game ended," replied Mike. "That first game took almost a year because they'd stop and then start again later. Nobody really knew how to play, so there were arguments and disputes through the whole game. My brother was so sick of the arguing, on top of losing the game 23 to 1—"

"Tarnation, boy!" exclaimed Uncle Nick, "that ain't no game, however you play it. That's more like a slaughter!"

"That was the score, all right. And my brother said he'd never play baseball again. So he gave me this here bat and ball and uniform. Now, do any of you want to get up a game?"

"But how do you play?" asked Zack.

"I plumb forgot—none of you know how to play!" he said. "Well, one team hits the ball and tries to run around the diamond and score an ace."

"What's an ace?" asked Emily, looking up into Mike's face.

"That's what it's called when you score a point by running in from third and touching home plate."

"Home plate . . . diamond . . . third? You're not makin' sense!" said Zack.

"And in the meantime," Mike went on without paying any attention to Zack, "the other team tries to catch the ball and throw it ahead of the runner so one of his teammates can tag him out before he gets to the base."

"It sounds mighty confusing," said Pa laughing. "I doubt if you're gonna get many around here to play. We can't understand a word you're saying! How many does it take to play?"

"Eighteen—nine on each team."

"Eighteen! You'll *never* get eighteen people in all of California to make heads or tails of what you're talking about!"

"If nobody knew how to play for that first game, how did anybody know what to do?" asked Emily.

"It sure sounds like one side knew how to play, judging from the score," Uncle Nick said.

"To answer your question, Miss," said McGee, "all the fellers who were there knew how to play, but everybody had their own brand of the game, coming from different places. You see, it was already played a bit before that, but not in an organized way or anything. That's why the game took so long.

The arguments got so fierce they had to keep stopping it and figure out a way to agree on the rules before continuing on. The one game had three different sessions to it, like I said, stretching for almost a year."

"Well that's about the dad-blamdest kind o' game I ever heard of!" piped up Alkali Jones. "Weren't no *game* at all, from the sound of it, but more like a war. Hee, hee, hee!"

Everybody had a good laugh, and after a little more talk, Mike managed to get half a dozen or so of the boys to join him. They walked over to the far end of the field where he began explaining the game to them. Emily followed to watch.

I got up and walked toward the hillside overlooking the meadow, where over three years ago I had looked down on the gathering we'd had to celebrate the completion of the building of the church. That other day seemed so long ago and much had happened since. Yet up there on the sloping hillside, everything still looked the same. It reminded me of how God had watched over us during the years since then.

Wild lilies were in bloom, and the birch trees were just beginning to get their fresh growths of new bark and tiny green leaves. The wildflowers brought back to my mind Rev. Rutledge's words, *"We can let ourselves be reminded of the life that Jesus gave us when we see the new life that nature gives. . . ."*

I walked up the hill, turned around, and looked down on the meadow just at the same spot I had that day three years before. When I was alone, questions about my future always seemed to nag at me. I wanted God to have complete control over my life in whatever I did, but I couldn't keep the fears and anxieties from bothering me from time to time.

Down on the field I watched the group of boys playing with "Lefty" Mike McGee. Every once in a while I heard his voice yelling out some kind of instruction to them, or pointing to get them to go stand someplace else. He didn't seem to be having much success explaining the game of baseball to them. I couldn't help laughing a time or two as I watched.

Zack and Tad were in the middle of it. My eyes followed Zack around. I knew that occasionally he struggled with the same kinds of questions that I did, although being a boy I don't suppose his anxieties went as deep. Boys have a way of being able to take things more as they come, while girls have to think everything out on a dozen levels.

"What are you going to do, Zack?" I asked him once.

"What do you mean?"

"Well, we can't just stay at home and live with Pa and Almeda forever, you know."

"There's the mine," he said. "I figured I'd work the mine with Pa and Uncle Nick."

"No mine lasts forever. Then what?"

"I don't know."

"Don't you find yourself wondering about things, about other places you might go, things to see, people to meet?"

"Not much. I like it here in Miracle. But I reckon you're right, we can't just live with Pa when we get to be adults."

"Hey, I've got an idea, Zack!" I said. "We could go live in Almeda's house in town. It's been empty all this time. Then we could stay in Miracle and do whatever we'd be doing, but it'd sorta be like being on our own."

"You think she'd let us?"

"Sure. She's said once or twice what a shame it is for the house not to be used."

"But what if one of us gets married?" suggested Zack.

"Well *I'm* not worried," I answered. "There's no fear of that about me! *You're* the one some girl will come along and want to grab."

"Nah, not me! I ain't gonna get married."

"Then what are you gonna do if the mine plays out?"

"I don't know. Maybe Little Wolf and I will raise horses like his Pa. And we've talked about going riding together, but I don't know where. I reckon you're right—there is a heap of world to see.

"What about you, Corrie?" Zack asked. "You got plans? What're you gonna do?"

"I don't know. I want to keep writing. But it's hard to say if something is always going to be what God wants for you. I'd like to travel."

This conversation was the most I'd ever gotten Zack to talk personally about himself, and I hoped we'd have the chance to talk like that again.

I didn't stay up on the hillside for too long, just long enough to quiet myself down. I got up from the base of my favorite old oak tree, gave its gnarled trunk an affectionate pat with my hand, and then started back down the slope to rejoin the picnic.

In fact, I thought to myself, maybe I'd go join in whatever Lefty McGee was trying to teach the others about his new game. I'd like to see if I could hit that little ball with that stick!

$\mathcal{D}$oc Shoemaker figured Katie would be due to give birth around the last of April or first of May. He said Almeda would probably follow about two weeks later. So both of them were mighty big around the middle by now and were moving slow, with Pa and Uncle Nick worrying and fussing over them every minute. At the picnic it seemed the women talked about nothing else to Almeda. Katie stayed home. Almeda was still spry enough and went into town every other day or so, but she also stayed in bed longer and took lots of rests. Pa saw to that.

Tuesday night in the second week of April, the doctor had been out that afternoon, had seen both Almeda and Katie, and had left with a smile on his face. "Won't be long now, Drummond," he'd said from his buggy. "Everything looks good. Both your wife and sister-in-law are healthy and coming along just fine."

In the middle of the night I was awakened by a loud banging on the door and shouts outside. I bolted awake and knew in an instant it was Uncle Nick. And from the sound of his voice I knew something was wrong.

I jumped out of bed and put on my robe, but by the time I got out of my bedroom, Pa and Almeda were already at the door and talking to Uncle Nick.

"It's Katie!" he said frantically. "Something's wrong, Drum—she's yelling and carrying on—"

"I'll go right up there," Almeda said as she started to throw a coat around her robe, then sat down to put on her boots.

"You ain't in no condition to—" Pa began.

"Don't even say it, Drummond," she interrupted. "This is a woman's finest hour, and the hour of greatest need."

"But you gotta take care of—"

"I will take complete care of myself," she said. "Katie needs me now, and I am not going to sit here and do nothing. Are you ready, Nick?" she added, standing up and pulling her coat tightly around her. The door was still open and a cold wind was blowing right into the cabin.

Uncle Nick just turned around and hurried back outside into the night. "She's in terrible pain, Almeda!" he said.

"Then you go on ahead, Nick! Tell her I'm coming. And put water on the stove!" Uncle Nick had already disappeared toward the bridge across the creek.

"I'll need the good lantern, Drummond," Almeda said, "so the wind won't blow it out."

"I'll get it lit," replied Pa as he went toward the fireplace. "Then I'll take you up there."

"You must go for Doctor Shoemaker," objected Almeda.

"I ain't gonna let you walk up there at night alone. You fall, and we'd have two women in trouble in their beds! Corrie," Pa said turning to me. "Go see if Zack's awake, and get him in here pronto."

By the time I got back into the room with Zack, who was still half asleep, Pa had the lantern burning bright.

"Zack, you gotta ride over and get the Doc, you hear me, boy!"

"Yes Pa."

"We need him fast!"

"I'll bring him, Pa."

"Corrie, you get out there and saddle up—let's see, who's fastest in the dark, Raspberry or Dandy?"

"At night, probably Dandy, Pa," said Zack.

"Then Corrie, you get to saddling Dandy. Zack, you get dressed and get going!"

Then he turned to the open door, holding the lantern in his left hand while Almeda took hold of his right, and the two of them walked out as quickly as they could to follow Uncle Nick.

In another five minutes, Zack was off, and the sound of Dandy's hoofbeats died in a moment. Suddenly I was left alone. I stoked up the fire with a couple of fresh logs, and lit another lantern. Then I went into the girls' room and woke up Emily, who was already stirring from the noise.

"Emily," I said, "Katie's in trouble. Pa and Almeda are up there already, and Zack's gone for the doctor. I'm going too."

"Should I come, Corrie?" she asked.

"I don't know, Emily," I said. "There probably isn't anything we can do to help, but I've gotta know if Katie's all right. You stay here with the others, and if they need us, I'll come and get you."

I was glad Pa had gone with Almeda! A storm had blown in while we'd been sleeping, and the wind was howling fiercely. I had trouble keeping my lantern from blowing out.

By the time I arrived at Uncle Nick's cabin, it seemed like an hour had already passed! Things were happening fast, and I could feel the tension the minute I walked in. Pa stood at the pot-bellied stove watching a kettle of water that was nearly boiling. Alongside, a pot of coffee was brewing. Uncle Nick paced around with a horrified look on his face. I'd never seen him like that before—so helpless, so concerned, wanting to help yet looking like a lost little boy who didn't know what to do. Even though it was his house and his baby being born, it looked like he felt out of place.

Both of them glanced at me as I came in but hardly took any other notice. Just as I closed the door, I heard a scream from the other room. Uncle Nick spun around. "Oh God!" he cried. He took a couple of quick steps toward the bedroom, then stopped. Pa went over and put an arm around Uncle Nick's shoulder, and from the slight movement of his lips, I knew he was praying hard.

O God, I breathed silently, *whatever's going on, I ask you to be close to Katie and take care of her. And Uncle Nick too.*

"Anything I can do, Pa?" I said.

He gave me a wan smile that showed he appreciated my being there. "Could you check on Erich? He's sleeping in the other room," he answered. "And pray that the Doc'll get here in a hurry."

Almeda came in from the bedroom. She was so obviously pregnant, walking with a bit of a waddle, and her face was a little pale. But otherwise you'd have thought *she* was the doctor! Still wearing her robe, she had her sleeves rolled up. Her hair was loose and hanging all out of place. And you could see the perspiration on her forehead. She looked like she'd been on the job working with Katie for an hour already.

She came up to Uncle Nick and attempted a smile. "You have nothing to worry about, Nick," she said. "The baby's just a few weeks early, that's all."

"Why's she crying out and screaming then?" said Uncle Nick, still looking frantic.

"That's what labor is like, Nick," she answered. "You weren't here when Erich was born, were you?"

"No, you and the Doc made me and Drum get outta here."

"And this is exactly why," said Almeda, smiling again. "It can be harder on the husband, who's fretting and stewing in the other room, than for the woman herself."

"But is Katie . . . is she all right?"

"Of course. She is fine. Labor is a long and painful process, Nick. It hurts, and sometimes we can't help crying out. It might not be a bad idea again for you and Drum to go down—"

Before she could finish, another shriek came from the other room. A horrified look filled Uncle Nick's eyes. You could tell the sound pierced right through to his heart.

"It's another contraction!" said Almeda, turning to return to Katie. "Drummond, why don't you take Nick down to our place? And take little Erich with you."

"We oughta at least wait till the Doc's here."

"We'll be fine. Corrie, come with me."

Nick bundled up little Erich, still half asleep despite all the commotion, and he and Pa took the lantern and started down the hill to our house.

I followed Almeda into the bedroom. Katie lay there with only a sheet over her. She yelled out again just as we came in. I was frightened, but Almeda walked straight over to the bed and took Katie's hand.

"Go around the bed, Corrie," she said to me. "Take her other hand so she has something to squeeze. It helps with the pain."

I did as she said.

Katie was breathing hard, her face wet and white. Her eyes were closed and a look of excruciating agony filled her face. Just as I took hold of her, she cried out again and lurched up in the bed. She grabbed on to my hand like a vise and held it hard as she pulled herself forward. The pain lasted ten or fifteen seconds, then she began to relax and lay back down, her face calming, her lungs breathing deeply. Still she held my hand, but not as hard. Slowly she opened her eyes a crack, glanced feebly at the two of us, managed a thin smile, then closed her eyes again. It was the first smile either of us had had from her in a long time.

Almeda left the bedside and wrung out a towel that had been soaking in a bowl of hot water. She pulled back the sheet and laid it over Katie's stomach just below where the baby was.

"Corrie," she said, "we need some more hot water. Go in the other room and fill this bowl from the kettle on the stove."

"That feels good," I heard Katie murmur as I left the room. "Thank you, Almeda," she added, and then all was quiet.

I got the hot water and went back into the bedroom. Katie was resting peacefully for the moment. Almeda sat by the bedside holding her hand. The look on my face must have been one of anxiety, because Almeda spoke to me as if she were answering a question I hadn't voiced.

"Don't worry, Corrie. This is just going to take some time, and Katie's not done hurting and crying out. She needs us to be strong for her."

Just then another contraction came. Katie winced and held her breath for a minute, then suddenly let it out in a long wail of pain. She lurched forward, holding her breath. I hurried over to the other side of the bed and took her hand. She grabbed on to it for dear life until the pain began to subside a minute or two later.

It went on like this for a while. In between contractions Almeda changed the hot towel while I wiped off Katie's face with a cool cloth, went to get water, or did whatever else Alm-eda said. It must have been a half an hour or forty minutes before we heard the outside door open.

"It's Doc Shoemaker," a voice called out. Doc walked into the room, carrying his black leather case. "How is she?" he asked.

"The contractions are coming about every two or three minutes now, Doctor," Almeda replied.

"She's getting close then," he said with a sigh that didn't sound too enthusiastic. "Three weeks early," he mumbled to himself as he approached the bed. "Hmm . . . don't suppose that's too worrisome in itself."

I stood aside and the Doc spoke softly to Katie, then put his hand on her stomach where the baby was. He held it there a long time with a real serious expression on his face. He didn't say anything.

Another contraction came. Katie winced and cried out. The doctor kept one hand on the baby and with the other took hers. I stood on the other side of the room watching. The Doc's face was expressionless.

When the contraction finished and Katie fell back on her pillow, the Doc let go of her hand and again felt the baby, this time with both hands. Still I couldn't tell a thing from his face. Almeda too had her eyes fixed on him, looking for any sign that might betray what he was thinking.

He looked over at Almeda, then back down at Katie, then glanced up in my direction.

"Corrie, do you mind if I have a few words with Almeda," he said, "alone?"

"Sure," I said. "I'll go put some more water on the stove."

I left the bedroom, wondering what the matter was. I scooped out some water from the big bucket Uncle Nick had pumped up from the stream and added it to the kettle sitting steaming on the stove. Just as I was putting another log or two on the fire, I heard Katie cry out again. It wasn't quite as loud as before, but the tone sounded so painful, more like a wail than a scream. It shot straight into my heart and a shiver went through me. I heard the Doc's voice too, though I couldn't make out anything being said. I hurried and shoved the wood into the stove. Then I tried to find something else to keep me busy, but there wasn't anything to do but pace around the floor.

Another scream came from the bedroom. It had been less than a minute since the last one! I was getting worried, and I wished they'd call me back in instead of making me wait outside.

Almost the instant the cries and sounds stopped, the bedroom door opened. It was Almeda. Her face was pale.

"Corrie, go get your uncle."

"Is everything—"

"Just get Nick, Corrie," she said. "Get him now!"

I didn't wait for any more explanations. I turned around and ran from the house, hearing another mournful cry from Katie just as I shut the door. I was halfway back to our place and stumbling along the path beside the stream before I realized I'd forgotten both a lantern and my coat. I would have known the way blindfolded—and I might as well have been because of the dark! The wind was still howling. Finally I saw the faint glimmer of light from one of our windows. I crossed the bridge, still running, and ran straight up to the house, tore the door open, and ran inside.

"They want you, Uncle Nick!" I said, all out of breath.

"Is the baby born?" he asked, jumping up and throwing on his coat.

"I don't know. They just said to get you quick."

He was already out the door at a run.

"What is it, Corrie?" Pa asked.

"I don't know, Pa. They made me leave the bedroom, then Almeda told me to go fetch Uncle Nick."

He had his coat on now too, then grabbed the lantern and headed out the door after Uncle Nick. I followed, running after him, although the bobbing light ahead of me got farther and farther away as we made our way up the trail along the creek.

By the time I reached Uncle Nick and Aunt Katie's place, I was breathing hard. The door to the cabin was open, and Doc Shoemaker was standing in the doorway. Nick was trying to get by into the house but the Doc was holding on to him trying to talk to him.

"Not yet, Nick!" he said. "Give her a few minutes."

I didn't see Almeda. Pa was standing beside Uncle Nick. He saw me coming and stretched out his arm to put around me. I came up close and he drew me to him tight, but just kept looking at Uncle Nick.

"I gotta go to her!" said Uncle Nick frantically. "I gotta know if she's—"

"She's fine, I tell you, Nick. But she's just been through something awful, and you must let her—"

"Get outta my way, Doc!"

"Please, Nick, just wait for two or three minutes until you calm—"

"I ain't waiting for nothing!" said Uncle Nick. He pushed the doctor aside and ran inside.

"Nick, please!" Doc Shoemaker called after him. But it was too late. Uncle Nick was through the door and the tromping of his heavy boots thudded across the floor toward the bedroom.

The doctor sighed, looked at Pa with a helpless expression, then followed slowly after Uncle Nick.

"What is it, Pa?" I said finally, feeling a great fear rising up inside me.

"The baby's dead, Corrie," he answered. I'd never heard such a sound of grief in his voice in my life. He squeezed me tight with his arm again. I felt the sobs tugging at my breast even before the tears came to my eyes. Pa knew what I was feeling. I knew he had tears in his eyes too, even in the darkness, even without looking up into his face. I just knew.

Slowly we walked inside. Pa closed the door. The next moment Almeda emerged from the bedroom. Before she got the door shut behind her, I heard the sound of the doctor's voice again, and Nick's. Uncle Nick was crying.

Almeda walked toward us. She was very pale, her face covered with sweat, with splotches of blood on her robe. Her eyes met Pa's, and they looked at each other for a few seconds, almost as if they were wondering in the silence whether something like this was in store for them in the near future.

Then Almeda glanced at me, and gave me a thin smile. Pa put his arm around her and Almeda embraced us both. The three of us held on to each other for a long time. I knew Almeda was crying, too.

"God, oh God!" Pa said after about a minute. "They need your help now more than they ever have. Be a strength to them."

"Yes, Lord!" Almeda breathed in barely more than a whisper.

Again they were silent. Slowly Pa released me and led Almeda to a chair and made her sit down. He turned toward the kitchen and found a towel, dipped it in the bucket of cold water, then gently began wiping Almeda's face and forehead with it.

She sat back, closed her eyes, and breathed in deeply.

In another minute Doc Shoemaker came back from the bedroom. He walked over to Pa.

"Drum," he said softly. "You've got yourself a mighty brave woman there. But she's in no condition for all this. This has taxed her more than I like. You get her home and into some fresh things and to bed."

"Yes, Doc."

"Then you send one of your kids—Zack or Corrie, or if you want you can go yourself—but one of you go into town and get Mrs. Gianini. You'll have to rouse her, but she'll come right out when you tell her I need her. She'll spend the night with Katie and help me clean up and get the baby ready for burying."

"You need any more help, Doc?" Pa asked.

"She'll know what we need, Drummond. Don't you worry about anything but that wife of yours. She's put in a hard night's work. If we need anything, I'll get one of your girls. As soon as things are in order here, I'll come down and check on Almeda."

"I'll be fine, Doc Shoemaker," said Almeda softly.

"I will check on you anyway. And, Drummond," he added, again to Pa, "fix me some place to spend the night. The barn will be fine. I want to stay close."

"You can have my bed," I said.

"Doesn't matter to me," replied the Doc. "I appreciate it, Corrie. But I'm sure I'll be able to catch a little sleep anywhere!"

Pa helped Almeda get slowly to her feet. Then we began our way home, both of us helping her so she wouldn't stumble in the dark. It was a slow walk, but within half an hour Almeda was in her own bed and sleeping peacefully.

lmeda was tired the next day, but otherwise fine. She stayed in bed the whole day except for about an hour when we had the funeral for Uncle Nick and Aunt Katie's little still-born daughter.

Mrs. Gianini helped get everything cleaned up and tended to Katie through the night. Then in the morning she got the baby ready. Once the new day came, Uncle Nick showed what a strong man he had become. His tears were now past, and he did everything he could for Katie, being tender and serving her when he could, being brave and in charge when that was necessary too.

Doc had spent the night getting what sleep he could, but checking on both Katie and Almeda every hour or two to make sure they were all right. Katie was weak and stayed in bed all the next day, although Doc Shoemaker said she would recover and be fine in a week or two. She didn't even get out of bed for the burial.

A few people came out to pay their respects to Nick and to stand with him at the graveside—the Shaws and Miss Stansberry and a few others. Rev. Rutledge, of course, took care of things, read from the Bible, and prayed before the tiny box was lowered into the ground. Pa had dug a grave not far from the apple trees Katie had planted from Virginia. The little cross marker on the grave, so near the trees that were a symbol of hope and new life, became a poignant reminder that things don't always go the way we expect or want them to, and that frontier life in this new state sometimes brought hardship along with it.

I cried. So did the other women—Becky, Emily, Almeda, and the others. Pa and Uncle Nick were pretty straight-faced and serious. Afterward people shook Uncle Nick's hand and tried to say encouraging things to him. They wanted to go in and pay their respects to Katie too, but she wouldn't see anybody.

Doctor Shoemaker went home after the funeral, got some fresh clothes, and came right back out. He wanted to spend the rest of the day near both ladies. They were all right, so he managed to get a good bit of sleep during the afternoon. After checking on them early in the evening, he went home. He kept coming out every day for a while.

Almeda stayed in bed for another day or so. She said she felt fine, but the doctor had told her to rest, and she complied with his wishes. Katie hardly got out of bed, except when she had to, for two weeks. We all admired the way Uncle Nick tended her. But through it all Katie was sullen and cross, hardly speaking, even to him. She just lay there in her bed, either sleeping or staring straight ahead across the room, not even noticing when people came and went.

Pa and I tried to help Uncle Nick, and after a few days Almeda went up to visit Katie. I went with her. We took a pot of soup and some bread we'd made. Little Erich was glad to see us, but the look on Uncle Nick's face made it clear he was feeling awkward about Katie's moodiness. We went in to see her. Almeda tried to be as cheerful as she could, but sensitive too.

"I'm so sorry, Katie," she said, sitting down beside the bed and taking Katie's hand. Katie continued to stare straight ahead. Her hand just lay limp in Almeda's. She didn't act as if she was even aware that anyone was in the room. She didn't move a muscle to acknowledge us.

"Is there anything I can do for you?" Almeda asked. "Anything you need or would like to eat or drink?"

Katie said nothing. There was a long silence.

"Would you mind if I prayed for you?" Almeda asked at length. Suddenly Katie's eyes shot wide open and her nostril's flared. She yanked her hand from Almeda's and turned on her with red face.

"How dare you talk to me about prayer!" she shouted angrily, as loud as her condition would allow. "After God's just taken my baby, and you want to pray to him?"

"It's impossible for us to understand his ways," said Almeda softly, smiling sadly down on Katie.

"I suppose you're going to tell me next that I ought to thank him for what he's done!"

"We just can't know what's in God's heart, Katie. All we can know is that he loves us more than we can imagine, and that everything he does can work for *good* if we allow it."

"Good! Ha!" she shot back, seething now. "I suppose if he takes *your* baby, you will smile and give him thanks—is that what you're telling me?"

"I would try to have a heart of gratitude, in spite of the pain I'm sure I would feel."

"Well, you're a foolish woman, Almeda!" said Katie bitingly. "You're more of a dimwit than I took you for! Don't you even know what it's like to feel a woman's worst grief? I don't think you have any feelings at all, Almeda!"

Almeda turned away. The words stung her to the heart. Her cheeks reddened, and hot tears rose to her eyes.

"Katie," she said, looking back toward the bed, "I'm so sorry. I didn't mean to sound unfeeling. I understand the pain you must feel, and I want you to know—"

"*Understand!* What could you understand about what I feel? Spare me your sympathy, Almeda. I don't need you feeling sorry for me any more than I need your idiotic prayers! Just leave me alone!"

"Oh, Katie, please let us—"

"Get out, Almeda! You and Corrie just go. I don't want to see you . . . or anybody!"

Again Almeda turned quickly away, fighting back emotion. Slowly she rose and without any further words the two of us left the room.

We closed the door behind us. I think Uncle Nick had heard everything because he was standing close by. The look that passed between him and Almeda was enough. They both seemed to understand what the other was thinking and feeling.

"You come get us if there's *anything* any of us can do, Nick," said Almeda. "Fixing something to eat, cleaning up, taking Erich for a while . . . anything."

Uncle Nick nodded, then went into the bedroom. We left and started the walk home in silence, going slowly on account of Almeda's condition. I kept hold of her arm. We were barely out of the clearing toward the creek when we heard Uncle Nick running up from behind. We stopped.

"She's crying," he said. "She won't say a word. She's just sobbing."

"Did she ask for us?" said Almeda.

"Not exactly," replied Uncle Nick. "But I can tell she's sorry for how she treated you. Won't you come back and try to talk to her?"

"It's got to be in her time, Nick."

"But she's hurtin' something terrible, Almeda."

"I know. Anybody can see that, Nick. But she's so angry and bitter toward God that she can't hear anything we try to say, and she can't receive any love we try to offer her."

"But won't you just try?" His voice sounded almost desperate.

"Of course we'll try. We'll be back every day. We'll do all we can. And yes, I'll come back and try to talk to her. But right now, Nick, I just don't think she's open to anything I have to give or to say. Come down this evening and let us know how she is. If you think she would like to see me, you know I'll be on my way that very minute. Corrie too—any of us. We'll stand with you through this, Nick, whatever comes."

"But what do I do for her in the meantime?"

"Pray for her, Nick. She is fighting against some things that have been with her for a long time. God is moving closer and closer to her heart, but she is resisting him. She needs your prayers now more than ever."

"I'll try," sighed Uncle Nick, turning back toward his cabin.

"You pray, and then you serve her and love her every minute," added Almeda. "When she finally breaks, it will be your love that will see her across that unknown gulf she's so afraid of."

"I'll try," repeated Uncle Nick. He walked back to the cabin, frustration showing in the slump of his shoulders. We turned and continued our way back down the slope toward the creek.

Remorse and Confusion
CHAPTER FORTY-FIVE

Almeda was quiet the rest of the day. It was hard to hear the kinds of things Katie had said to her. She had done so much for Katie, only to be spoken to so rudely because of it. I have to admit, as sorry as I was about the baby and for the grief Katie was feeling, her angry words toward Almeda got me more than a little riled. But Almeda kept saying, "It's not me she's angry at, Corrie. She needs our patience and our love now more than ever. The Lord is pushing aside her outer shell, and she needs us to stand with her until he breaks through to her."

She asked me to go back up that evening to ask about Katie. Emily and I went. Uncle Nick came outside with us.

"She's calmed down and is feeling better," he said. "She slept most of the afternoon."

"That's good," I said. "Almeda said to tell you that if you think she wants to talk again, to come get her."

"I wish she would," he replied. "I don't ever know what to say when she's feeling down and upset like she gets."

We took Erich back down to our place with us for the night so Uncle Nick would be free to look after Katie and get some sleep. He looked tired.

Nothing much happened for another day or two. Uncle Nick was still downcast from worrying about Katie. Doc Shoemaker came out again. He pronounced Katie fit and said she could get up and about for a few hours a day if she wanted. But she remained glum, and stayed in bed.

He told Almeda to take care of herself. "Only three or four weeks for you now, Almeda," he said. "Don't you go getting any ideas about going back into town or doing anything around this house. You've got three daughters for all that. You just keep yourself rested, you hear?"

"Of course, Doctor," she laughed.

The next day, early in the afternoon, Uncle Nick came running down to our place. His face looked more full of life as he came through the door than I'd seen it in weeks. Pa was outside, but he came straight to me.

"She asked to see you!" he said out of breath.

"Katie?" I said.

He nodded.

"Me?"

"You and Almeda."

In an instant I was off to tell Almeda in her room. She was dressed but lying in bed. She got right up and came out to where Uncle Nick was still standing. The look on his face was bright and excited.

"Did she really ask to see us, Nick?" Almeda asked.

A sheepish expression crossed his face. "Well, we were talking," he said, "and I happened to say as how I thought she'd been a mite hard on the two of you last time. She was pretty quiet, you know how she's been of late. Then she just kinda nodded and said, 'I suppose I was at that.'

"So after a minute I said, 'What'll you do if Almeda or Corrie comes calling again? You gonna send 'em away like you never want to see them again?' I reckon it was a hard thing to ask her, but doggone if she wasn't beginnin' to try my patience with all her surly scowls and irritable talk."

"She can't help it, Nick," said Almeda softly.

"I figured that," replied Uncle Nick. "Well, anyhow I said it, and she didn't say nothin' for a while, then she said, 'No I wouldn't send them away.' I figured that was about as good an invitation as you was gonna get, so I came down when she fell asleep to tell you."

Almeda looked at him for a moment with a blank expression. Then her face broke into a laugh. "You are something, Nicholas Belle! You really love that wife of yours, don't you?"

"I reckon so. I just can't cotton to you and her being apart and for her to be angry with my own kin. Will you come?"

"Of course we'll come," she replied with a smile. "You go on home. We'll come up for a visit sometime this afternoon."

A couple of hours later we walked up. I had made some shortbread to take, which I knew was one of Katie's favorites.

Uncle Nick met us at the door and took us straight into the bedroom. Katie was awake. I told her I'd made her some shortbread. She tried to smile, but it was one of those smiles that showed there was something on her mind behind it. I think she was embarrassed about what had happened before.

"How are you feeling, Katie?" Almeda asked.

"Oh, better, I suppose. You?"

"Very well."

"How much longer?"

"The doctor said probably three weeks."

"I hope . . . I hope it goes well for you," said Katie. It was hard for her to say.

"Is there anything you need?" Almeda asked after a minute. Her voice was so full of tenderness and compassion, and her eyes so full of love as she stood beside Katie's bed. Katie looked up at her and her eyes filled with tears.

"Almeda, I'm sorry for the things I said before," she said.

"Oh, Katie, dear, think nothing of it." Almeda sat down on the chair at the bedside and took Katie's hand.

"It's just that I was so afraid of dying," Katie went on, trying to maintain her composure. "When I was lying here having the baby, it hurt so bad! I was more worried about myself than . . . than my little daughter! Every time I screamed out, I was sure it was going to be the last breath I breathed. It was so much worse than with Erich!"

"There, there," said Almeda, running her hand gently along Katie's head and smoothing down her hair. "It's all right, dear."

"And then when she came out, and the doctor told me she was dead," Katie said, sobbing now, "I felt . . . I just felt so guilty! All I had been thinking about was myself! And all the time, even while she was inside me . . . my poor little daughter was—"

She couldn't even finish the sentence, but let out a mournful wail of such bitter remorse that it went straight into my heart, and my eyes filled with tears. Poor Katie!

"She was dead!" sobbed Katie. "Dead, and the whole time I was worried about *myself*! I can hardly bear the thought of how selfish I was! O God, why couldn't you have taken me instead of her?"

I could hardly keep from crying. I wondered if I should leave and let Katie and Almeda be alone. But when I looked at Almeda as she stared down into Katie's forlorn face, I could tell she was praying even though her eyes were open. I had seen her pray for others like that and I always knew when she was talking to the Lord. Then I thought maybe it would be best for me to keep sitting right where I was.

I closed my eyes and began praying for Katie myself.

"He wanted you to live," said Almeda softly.

"But why? Why should he want me to live, instead of my baby?"

"I don't know, Katie. He loves you, Katie. I know that. He loves you, and your baby."

"O God!" Katie wailed again as if she hadn't even heard. "How could I think of myself at a time like that?"

Almeda didn't reply. Katie was sobbing.

"I've always thought more of myself than anyone else," she said. "Nick's so considerate to me, but I don't show him half the love he does me! I've acted dreadfully to you . . . to both of you! I'm so selfish! I hate the person I've become! I'd rather it *had* been me that had died! You'd all be better off without me!"

"Don't say such things, Katie. Don't you know that we love you?"

"Love me! How could you love me? Look at me! There's nothing to love!"

"God wouldn't have made you if you weren't special to him."

"That's ridiculous! Why should God care about me? I've never given him a thought! Why should he love me?"

"He loves us all."

"You, maybe. But I've always told him to keep away from me."

"Don't you remember all I told you, Katie? I used to be further from him than you could ever be."

"I don't know if I believe half what you told me, Almeda."

I opened my eyes. One look into Katie's face told me the old anger was coming back. Her voice had changed, too.

"Oh, Katie, I would *never* tell you something that wasn't true."

"Well, I don't care anyway. I never had any use for God, and I certainly don't mean to start now."

"Oh, but Katie . . . dear! You need him now more than ever."

"I won't need him! I refuse to need him," she snapped back. "If he's going to take my baby, then he's not going to have me! He took my parents from me! He's taken everything I ever cared about. I've had to make my own way. It's little enough he's ever done for me! And now he's taken my daughter! I won't need him, I tell you!"

"Perhaps he took your little girl because he loved her so much he wanted to have her near him," said Almeda after a moment, still speaking calmly.

"That's absurd, Almeda!" said Katie angrily. "If there's a God at all, which I doubt, then what right has he got to toy with our lives like that?"

"He doesn't toy with us, Katie. We just can't see how much he loves us. But everything works for good if we will only let—"

"There you go again, saying it's good that my baby died!" interrupted Katie. "I suppose you'll tell me next that it's good I'm such a hateful and selfish person! If that's your God, Almeda, then curse him! I hate him, too . . . I hate you all . . .I hate myself . . . God . . . just go . . . leave me alone . . . just let me die!"

She turned over in her bed, sobbing bitterly.

Almeda looked over at me, sick at heart. She closed her eyes again. Then after a moment she sighed deeply, rose from the chair, and together we left the room. Katie was still weeping.

"Your dear wife really needs you, Nick," Almeda said to Uncle Nick. "Love her, Nick. Give her all the love you can. She's more alone right now than she's ever felt in her life. God is right at the threshold, but she doesn't know it. That tough self-sufficient outer layer is nearly broken. And when it does break, she's going to need you there to help her."

Uncle Nick nodded. We left the cabin and started home.

We had nearly reached the bridge over the creek when Uncle Nick overtook us. This time he had a message directly from Katie's lips.

"She told me to get you," he said. Almeda looked him intently in the eyes. "She *wants* to see you," he said.

We turned around at once and walked back up the trail. Almeda took Uncle Nick's arm, and I followed behind them.

*O*nce again we walked into the bedroom. This time Uncle Nick went in with us.

Katie was sitting upright, propped up by several pillows. Her face was red and her eyes puffy, but she wasn't crying any more, and there was a look of determination on her face.

"Please forgive me, Almeda . . . Corrie," she said. "Please have patience with me for my rudeness."

"You are forgiven," said Almeda softly, smiling at Katie. I walked over to the bedside, leaned down, and gave Katie a hug. She put her arms around me and squeezed me in return. The feel of her arms around my shoulders filled me with such happiness I started to cry again. I pulled back and sat down across the room. Almeda again sat down next to the bed.

There was a long silence. Finally Katie spoke again.

"Do you *really* believe that God intends everything for our good?" she asked. For the first time her voice sounded as if she genuinely wanted to know.

"Oh yes, Katie," smiled Almeda. "He is more wonderfully good, and his ways are more wonderfully good than we have the faintest notion of."

"Then why did my parents die . . . why did he take my baby?" said Katie, starting to cry.

Almeda took her hand. "I don't know, Katie," she replied with tenderness. "There's so much we *can't* understand about life. Corrie lost her mother also. I have had to struggle with all of the *whys* of my past life. There are hurts every man and woman has to face and wonder about. There are disappointments. We can be lonely. We lose things and people who are precious to us. But there is one thing I've learned in the years since I gave my heart to the Lord, and I think it's just about the most important lesson our life in this world has to teach us. Do you know what that lesson is?"

Almeda stopped and waited. Finally Katie spoke up. "I don't suppose I do," she said.

"It's just this, Katie," Almeda continued, "that when life's heartaches and hurts and disappointments come, running *to* God, not *away* from him, is our only hope, our only refuge."

"Is that what I've been doing—running away?"

"I'm not sure, Katie. I don't know that it's my business to say. Only you would know for certain. But you haven't been running *to* him." There could be no mistaking the love in Almeda's voice, in spite of the directness of her words. I knew that at last Katie realized Almeda loved her and wanted to help her. She began to weep softly.

"I know you've suffered hurts and losses, Katie," Almeda went on. "But they've made you bitter and resentful toward God, when actually he was the one you should have gone to for help. He would have borne the pain *for* you. But by keeping him away, you had to bear it all alone.

"Katie, I'm so sorry about your daughter! I grieve with you! But don't you see, the only place for the pain to go is into the hands of Jesus. Otherwise it will tear you apart inside. Instead of turning *from* him, and blaming him, and crying out *against* him, he is the one you must go *to*. He did not take your daughter to inflict hurt. He loves that precious little girl, who is now radiantly alive in his presence, more than any of us ever could! And he loves you, Katie! His arms are wide open, waiting for you to run into his embrace. He is waiting to en-fold you in his arms and draw you into himself, waiting to pour out his love in your heart, waiting to fill you with his peace."

Still Katie wept softly.

"I'm ready to listen to what you want to tell me," she said finally, her voice barely above a whisper. "But I don't know what to do, how to do what you say, even if I want to."

"There's nothing to do, Katie, except to receive the love he offers, the love his arms are waiting to wrap around you."

"How do you receive his love?"

"Just by telling him you want to be his."

"You mean . . . praying?"

"It doesn't matter what you call it, Katie," said Almeda. "God is a friend we can talk to. He is also our Father. We can crawl into his lap and let his arms wrap us up tight, and we can tell him we're tired of being wayward children and we want to stay close to him from now on. Whatever you say, however you say it, he understands. And once you open up your heart to him like that, he will be with you from that moment on, for the rest of your life. With you, and *inside* you! The Bible says that he actually takes up residence inside our hearts and lives with us forever. It's what Jesus calls being born again. That's what it means to give your heart to God. It's what Mr. Parrish helped me to do, and it changed the whole course of my life forever."

A long silence followed.

Without another word, very softly Almeda rose from her chair. With the slightest gesture of one hand she motioned for

Uncle Nick to take her place beside Katie's bed. Uncle Nick got up, a momentary look of confusion on his face, not exactly sure what she meant. As he approached Katie and sat down in the seat where Almeda had been, Almeda and I quietly left the bedroom and closed the door. Then we left the cabin and started toward home.

"I'm glad Erich is down at our place," Almeda said after we were a ways along the path. "The two of them need to be alone for a while."

"Why did you get up so abruptly to leave?" I asked.

"Was it abrupt? I didn't mean it to be. I just knew there was nothing else for me to say right then. The next step was Katie's to make, and I felt it was best she have some time to reflect on everything I'd said. God's timing cannot be rushed."

"I know," I said with a smile. "You've taught me that."

"Katie has finally stopped fighting against God. That is a good beginning. How far she goes now, and at what pace— that will be up to her. But I would never want to push someone too fast. We do great harm when we impose our own timetable on the work of the Spirit."

We walked on to the creek and alongside it in silence.

"What do you think will become of Katie and Uncle Nick?" I asked finally.

"Oh, Corrie," said Almeda excitedly, "life is just beginning for them! Everything that's happened up till now has just been preparing them for this time, getting them ready to walk with God in a new way. I truly believe that!"

"And the baby?"

"Sometimes I don't understand God's ways any more than Katie does. But he turns all for good—when we let him. The two of them losing their daughter is no exception. If they allow him to use it in their lives, it will draw them both closer to him . . . and to each other."

We walked the rest of the way without talking again. When we got home, Almeda lay down.

About an hour later I saw Uncle Nick coming toward the house. Pa was out in the barn. I'd been talking to him and was just coming out when Uncle Nick came up. He had a great big grin on his face and his step was lighter than I'd seen it for several days.

"Where's Almeda?" he said.

"In bed."

"And your Pa?"

"In the barn."

"Well, get Almeda up and I'll go fetch Drum. We'll be inside in a minute."

"What for?" I asked, dying of curiosity.

"Never you mind! I'll tell you all at once," said Uncle Nick, heading off in the direction of the barn. "I got news, that's all I'll say." He was still smiling.

A few minutes later Pa and Uncle Nick walked into the house, Pa's arm around Uncle Nick's shoulder.

Uncle Nick scooped his son up in his arms. "Well son, your ma did it!"

"Did what, Nick?" asked Pa. "Come on, out with it!"

Uncle Nick was beaming, both from embarrassment and pride all at once. "She prayed, just like you said she ought to, Almeda," he said. "Dad blame if she didn't grab my hand the minute you two left and say, 'Nick, will you pray for me? I want the life that Almeda and Corrie and Drum and the others have. I don't want to be like this anymore!' Then she started crying, and I didn't know what to do. 'Please, Nick,' she said, 'you've got to help me! I don't know what to do, but I want to live with God. I don't want to live alone in my heart anymore.'

"So I just got up what courage I could muster. Except for that one time with you, Drum, I've never prayed out loud before, but I just said, 'God, you gotta help us, 'cause I don't know what to do. So I ask you to just help Katie, like she said, and show her how to let your arms go around her.' "

"Well, at that, she starting bawling as if she couldn't stop, and I just sat there wondering if I'd said something wrong, getting kinda worried. She just kept crying. But then all of a sudden she burst out praying herself, and she prayed on and on, asking God to forgive her for being so ornery all this time, and for being angry and resentful and for treating people rude and for being selfish. She was crying out how she had hurt so deep inside, saying things I never thought I'd ever hear her say. It was like she was a different person once the shell around her broke apart. There was a look of pain on her face worse than when she was having the baby. She seemed far away in a place all alone—it was a place even I couldn't reach her, though I was sitting beside her holding on to her hand. She was talking to God like I'd never imagined anyone doing, as if he was sitting on the other side of the bed from me— saying . . . all kinds of things."

He stopped and took a deep breath.

"And. . . ?" said Almeda expectantly.

"I guess you could say she and God were having their own private time together. She said, 'God, I've been so lonely, my heart has felt so cold . . . but now I feel like a little girl again. . . . O God, why did you take my mother and father from me . . . why did you leave me all alone? I felt so unloved, God . . .

no one needed me or wanted me. And now my baby's gone! Was it because of me that you didn't let me keep her . . . wasn't I good enough? O, God!' And then she really started to wail—stammering out stuff about being mad at him and getting angry when people would talk about him, and resenting people who went to church. She cried, 'Nobody ever really understood me, Lord . . . no one wanted to be near me, and I took it out on you . . . oh, forgive me—please, Lord! I don't hate you. . . . I'm not angry at you anymore. . . . I *need* you. . . . I want so much to trust you . . . so much to feel your love, to know that your arms are wrapped around me like Almeda said. O God, I want you to hold me like my daddy never could!' "

Again Uncle Nick stopped. All the rest of us were silent, hanging on his every word. It was such a moving story, there was nothing to say!

"That was about it," he said, but then a sheepish expression came over his face. "After she was done praying," he continued, "she opened her eyes and looked over at me with a smile, just about the happiest look I'd ever seen on her face. Then she said, 'Oh, Nick, you've been standing with me a long time, and putting up with a lot from me. How can I possibly thank you?' "

"Well . . . what did you say?" asked Pa when Uncle Nick stopped.

"Aw, not much. I just told her I loved her and that it weren't no big thing I done. Then she opened up her arms to me, still smiling, and I sat over on the edge of her bed and leaned over and gave her a hug. And, tarnation if she didn't nearly squeeze the insides out of me! That's when I knew she'd got back most of her strength!"

"Hallelujah!" said Almeda quietly. "God *is* good!" She closed her eyes, and I knew that inwardly she was giving praise to God.

We were all awestruck at what we'd heard.

"God bless her!" said Pa. "I told you if you prayed for her, everything would come out right in the end, Nick."

"What happened to Aunt Katie?" asked Tad, not quite understanding all that was being said.

"The angels in heaven are singing, boy," said Pa, "that's what."

"Your Aunt Katie just gave her life to Jesus, Tad," said Almeda.

"What did you two say to each other after that, Uncle Nick?" I asked. Another sheepish look came over his face.

"Well, if you wanna know," he said, "I prayed again. You see, I'd been sitting there listening to everything you said, Almeda, and it was going down mighty deep into me too. Now you all know I went to church when I was a kid, and that was fine as far as it went. But then I went my own way for a lot of years, as you know better than anyone, Drum. And now I been trying to live my life a mite different, now that I'm married and got myself a family. And I been praying like you said, and trying to remember what I used to know about being a Christian.

"But while you was talking, Almeda, it just sorta dawned on me all of a sudden that I didn't know if I'd ever actually done what you was talking about—prayed, you know, and told God all that about wanting to be different and have him live in my heart. I reckon what I'm saying is that I didn't know if I'd been what you called born again *myself*. I just couldn't say for sure. So I figured it couldn't do no harm to pray all that again, even if I was already on my way to heaven.

"So I did. I prayed it just like Katie'd done. I was still holding her hand, and I closed my eyes and told God I wanted him to live with me too, just like Katie, and I asked him to help me, and to help us both do what he wanted us to, and to be the kind of people he wanted us to be for a change. And when I was all done I stopped, and then I heard Katie whisper a real soft *Amen*. I looked down at her and her eyes were closed again, and the most peaceful look was on her face. I just sat there a long time, her hand in mine. And pretty soon she was asleep, with just a faint smile still on her lips. So I slipped my hand out from hers and came straight down here to tell you what we done."

Our house was so quiet! The only dry eyes in the place were Tad's and little Erich's.

Pa's hand was on Uncle Nick's shoulder again. "You done good, Nick," he said. "You done what you needed to do. It takes a real man to do what you did, to stand up in prayer for himself and his wife. Aggie and your ma and pa'd all be proud of you." He paused just a second or two, then added, "And I'm right proud of you too!"

"Amen!" said Almeda.

I was so happy! We all were. And even though nobody said anything for another spell, all I could think of were Pa's words. And I knew he was right—there was rejoicing going on right then in heaven!

God's Little Community
CHAPTER FORTY-SEVEN

The next few days were a joyous time. Uncle Nick's and Almeda's faces showed that a weight of concern had been lifted from them. And among all of us there was a sense of calm and peace, a good feeling, that would erupt every so often in laughter. Pa played with Tad like I hadn't seen him do in a long time, and Emily asked if she could invite Mike McGee to the house for dinner the next Sunday afternoon. Uncle Nick could be seen bounding all over the property and up and down between the two houses with Erich on his shoulders, laughing and carrying on like they were two little kids. There was really a change in him. How much had to do with Katie, and how much had to do with what he'd done himself, I didn't know.

It didn't matter. A new spirit was suddenly alive among us all because Katie had opened up her heart—and it was wonderful!

Almeda remained quiet. I knew she had to take it slow on account of the pregnancy, and every time Doc Shoemaker came to the house he would say, "Now you just don't let yourself get excited about anything, you hear me, Almeda?" But I think her joy went deeper than it did for anyone else. She probably knew in a more personal way how hard it had been for Katie, and knew more of what Katie was feeling because she had felt the exact same things herself. She had shared her own life with Katie, painful as all the recollections were, and endured the emotional pain over what Katie had said. After all that, and the loss of Katie's child, to have Katie finally say that she wanted to know God's love for herself meant more to Almeda than she could have expressed.

She went up to see Katie the next morning. I asked her if she wanted me to go with her.

"Walk me up to the creek, Corrie," she answered. "But then you can come back down here. I want to talk to Katie alone."

She was there a long time. When she got back home she was clearly tired but there was a peaceful smile on her face. Pa asked her what had happened.

"We had a long talk," Almeda said. "A more personal time than we've ever had. She opened up whole new areas of her life to me. She's really a changed woman! I think we're at last ready to be sisters. And then we prayed together, for the first time, and when I left *she* hugged *me*."

There were tears in Almeda's eyes even before she was through telling about it. She turned and went inside and straight to her bed. Pa just put his arm around my shoulder and gave me a squeeze, and said nothing for a minute.

"The Lord's really up to some unexpected things around here, ain't he, Corrie?" he said finally.

"You can say that again!" I said.

"Nick's just as changed inside as Katie," he said. "And I aim to sit him down like Almeda's done with Katie, and talk about some things and get him to praying too. It's time all ten of us—well, at least the nine of us except for little Erich—it's time we all started praying together and bringing God into *everything* we do around this little community of ours."

"Community, Pa?"

"Yeah, Corrie. Don't you see—we got two houses, two families, nine or ten people, however you count them—"

"Soon to be eleven," I put in.

"Yeah, well I reckon you're right—eleven. But you see, here we are a little community within the bigger community. And if all of us—this nine or ten or eleven of us dedicate ourselves to live in what we do by what God tells his folks to do, then it just seems to me that other folks around might sooner or later stand up and take notice, and say, 'Hey, I want to be part of living that kind of life too.' You see, Corrie, it's gotta start someplace, people joining themselves to live together like God's people. I've been thinking a lot about this, and now with Katie and Nick doing what they've done, I figure God might be about to do some new things among us that we haven't seen before."

"That sounds exciting, Pa," I said. My mind flashed back to my talk with Zack at the picnic, and I wondered if I *wanted* to leave this little "community," as Pa called it, of the Hollister-Belle families. Pa made it sound like there couldn't be a better place to be than right here in the middle of where God was at work. "What do you think he's going to do now?"

"How could I know that?" he answered. "I'm not about to start trying to figure God's ways out ahead of time. I'd have never figured a bunch of people like us would be all together like this. Almeda's from Boston, and Katie's from Virginia! But God's got a way of bringing folks together from places about as far apart as we can imagine, and then, *boom*—there they are together and he starts working among them. So how could I try to figure what he's gonna do *next?*"

"I see what you mean, Pa."

"But I'm sure of one thing."

"What's that?"

"When God sets about knittin' folks together—just like weaving threads to make a piece of cloth—when God starts doing that, then good things happen. Just like all of us here— good things are gonna happen, Corrie, I can just feel it. Other folks besides Katie and Nick are gonna find out what it really means to live like God's people."

"How will they find out?"

"Who can tell? They just will. I don't doubt my being mayor's got something to do with what the Lord's up to. It's no accident I got elected when nothing could have been further from my mind. And your writing, Corrie. People read the things you write."

"But I don't write anything about God or what's happened here in our family."

"You might someday. And when you do, people are gonna pay attention to what you say. They're gonna listen, and they're gonna say, 'Hey, I want to live the kind of life Corrie Belle Hollister talks about. . . . I want to be a Christian like that. . . . I want to pray and know God's love.' You see, Corrie, there's all kinds of stuff God's gonna do with all of us, and with lots of other people too. We've only just seen the beginning!"

*K*atie was up and out of bed within two days. Everything about her was changed. You'd have never known she just lost a baby. It was as if she had made a decision to be different from now on—which she had!—and was determined to act accordingly. And of course, God living inside her made the biggest difference of all!

All of a sudden, she was down at our place all the time. It reminded me of the time before Pa and Almeda had been married. There was Katie again in our house, bustling about the kitchen, helping with everything. Now Almeda was being pampered and cared for—with Katie and the three of us girls all taking care of her. I usually went into town to handle the business at the freight office. Doc Shoemaker came out every day. Pa wandered about, not able to get much work done for nervousness, but hardly able to get near Almeda—as much as he wanted to help—for all the women tending to her!

After all that had happened, the birth of Pa and Almeda's baby came almost as a routine event in our lives. It was, of course, one of the greatest things that had ever happened, but there was no huge crisis like there'd been with Katie. One morning about two and a half weeks later, Almeda calmly said

to Katie, "I think my labor's begun. You'd better send Drummond for the doctor."

The birthing wasn't routine for Pa! He scurried around
like a nervous old lady! He sent Zack for Doc Shoemaker. He
didn't leave Almeda's side for a second until the Doc came
and shooed everyone out of the bedroom.

Almeda's labor lasted about five hours. I don't know
whether it was as painful as Katie's, but she didn't cry out
like Katie had. About the middle of the afternoon, all of us
except Doc and Katie were gathered in the big room. Suddenly we heard some shouts and exclamations, followed by
the cry of a baby.

Pa jumped out of his chair and was off to the bedroom
like a shot! The doctor tried to keep him out for a few more
minutes, but it was no use.

For the next hour the whole house was like a beehive—
nobody could sit or stand still for a second. There were kids
and men and women, the doctor and Katie and Uncle Nick—
everyone moving to and fro, cleaning and congratulating and
laughing and talking. Mrs. Gianini was there too—there was
hardly a birthing for miles around Miracle Springs that she
didn't attend.

Late in the afternoon, after things were more or less back
to normal, Doc Shoemaker let us go into the bedroom one at
a time and have a visit with Almeda and to see her and Pa's
little daughter. Almeda gave me such a smile when I walked
in! For the first time in my life, I found myself wondering what
it would be like to become a mother.

"What do you think of your new baby sister, Corrie?"
she said.

"She's wonderful." What else could I say? She truly was!

They named her Ruth. "Ruth has long been one of my favorite Bible women," said Almeda. "God took a foreigner from a strange land and grafted her into the royal line of his people. That's just how I feel to be married to your father," she told me. "So blessed of God beyond what I deserve. Our daughter's name will always remind me of God's goodness in bringing me, like Ruth, from a distant place to give me a new life here."

There was a bit of a dispute over little Ruth's middle name, with both Pa and Almeda showing that they wanted to honor the *other* above themselves.

"*Parrish* has gotta be her middle name," said Pa.

"But I was only a Parrish for a few years," objected Almeda. "How can we name *our* daughter after my first husband?"

"Ain't no different than naming her after my first wife." Almeda wanted to use the name *Agatha* in honor of Ma.

"That's completely different," said Almeda. "Your Aggie is the mother of *my* children now. I love her because of them."

"That may be," said Pa. "But I'm still mighty grateful for what Mr. Parrish did for you. If it hadn't been for him, you wouldn't be walking with God now, and wouldn't be my wife. I owe the man plenty, and some day I'm gonna shake his hand and tell him so. Besides, I first knew you as a Parrish, and I kinda like the name!"

In the end they compromised and used both names. She became Ruth Agatha Parrish Hollister.

The rest of the spring and then the summer passed quickly.

What a difference a little baby made to life in our little community! There was new life all around—on Katie's face, in little Ruth's crib, in Uncle Nick's walk, and in Pa's stature as a leader in town and among his acquaintances. I could see what Pa had said to me happening—that people would be taking notice of the life that was flowing out on the Hollister-Belle claims.

I had done a lot of thinking about what he'd said about my writing too. And so later that summer I started devoting myself to it again. I didn't write any major articles, but I started spending more time thinking about stories I could write, and dusting off some of my old ideas. I sent some stories to Mr. Kemble, and he printed them all in the paper and was always encouraging me to write more. As I did, I found myself thinking more and more about how I could work God into what I wrote in a way that Mr. Kemble would still find newsworthy. I wanted people who read my articles to know that I was living my life as a daughter of God, not as a person who never thought about him.

I also kept writing in my journal. I wrote about Rev. Rutledge's and Miss Stansberry's wedding. Rev. Rutledge asked Pa to perform the ceremony, and then the men in town *really* started teasing Pa about being a preacher! But he didn't mind. And pretty soon Harriet was expecting a baby too!

I also filled several pages of my journal with the story about Emily and Mike McGee. He didn't just come for dinner that Sunday. He started coming out to the cabin nearly every day. And just before Christmas later that year, he came to see Pa and asked if he could marry Emily. Pa was shocked! Everybody liked Mike, even though he always talked about that new game he liked to play. But *marry* him! "The girl's only just seventeen!" Pa must've exclaimed three dozen times.

But the most important entry in my journal came in March of 1858. It was my twenty-first birthday, and in a lot of ways it was a day when something inside me said, "Well, I suppose I'm getting close to being grown up now."

I wanted to do something special, something I would always remember. For several weeks I'd been considering the idea of taking a ride up into the high hills east of Miracle Springs, maybe even as far as the lake region by Grouse Ridge or Fall Creek Mountain. I didn't really have any definite plans—I just wanted to get high up so I could see the sunrise over the Sierras farther east.

It was still dark when I got up, and for the first hour of riding I had to make my way slowly until the faint gray light of dawn gradually began sending the darkness away. In the distance, as I climbed higher and higher over the rugged terrain, gnarled weathered oak trees sat on the horizon, silhouetted against the clear early morning sky that was gradually brightening in the east. Everything was so still and quiet—

just a horse and rider moving as one through a smooth grassy
meadow of the foothills, dotted sparsely with massive trees,
then suddenly encountering the steep rockiness of the mountain region.

Of all the horses I had known and ridden, Raspberry remained my special friend. He was a golden brown color, except
for his white stockings and the blaze of white running from
between his ears forward to his nostrils. His bulging muscles
glistened with sweat. *What a magnificent beast he is,* I thought
as he glided with liquid ease, responsive to my every change of
the reins, alert to everything around him. I think he enjoyed
the morning's ride as much as I did! We galloped across the
gently sloping meadows, then slowed to ascend steeper paths
upward, and I almost felt Raspberry knew what I was thinking
ahead of time!

For an hour we rode, many thoughts passing through my
mind, the beauty of the surroundings giving way to reflec-
tions on what this day symbolized. What was it that made
this, my twenty-first birthday, different from all the ones that
had come before? I didn't *feel* any different . . . or did I?

Perhaps it was a deeper sense of accountability—accountability toward others . . . toward God . . . an accountability for
my *own* life, my own self.

Even though there were still areas of my life where I felt
like a little girl—tentative, unsure of certain things—people
would look at me from now on as a "grown up" adult. I was no
longer a young girl, but a woman. On this day I was stepping
over a threshold into being totally responsible for my own actions, my own thoughts, my own attitudes—accountable for
my own decisions, and responsible for making good and right
decisions.

God had brought me so far!

Such a short time ago, it seemed, I hadn't known much of anything about what life truly was. I didn't know about God and how he was involved in people's lives, how he wanted to be intimate with us. I hadn't known much about who I was or where I was going, or even who I wanted to be and where I wanted to go.

Yet God had given me such a sense of purpose, so many desires of who and what I wanted to be and become as a person, as his daughter. I wanted to be pure before him. I wanted to love God with my whole being. I wanted to be able to love others with his love. I wanted to be able to tell people about him, about my life with him, about the thoughts and feelings that were in my heart toward him. I wanted to meet and know people who shared that same commitment, those same desires—people who were also on that same road of life.

When I found my thoughts drifting toward marriage, I surprised myself. I didn't think such things very often, and usually figured I'd never marry. But on the occasions when it did cross my mind, I wondered what kind of man God might have for me to share my life with. I'd even fall to imagining about it sometimes. And then I'd realize that in spite of what I'd said to Zack, I did have certain feelings and ideas about the man I would marry, *if* I did. He would be strong and sensitive and loving. But strong in an inward way, not strong the way boys and men talked about strength. *Strong* to me was the quality of character that made someone willing to stand up for what they believed, even to make sacrifices to do it. Almeda was strong in that way. So was Pa. And *sensitive* to me meant the kind of man who could tell what another person, especially a woman, was thinking. Sensitivity meant respecting the thoughts and feelings of others, a gentleness, and especially the ability to talk and share and be open with feelings. Women didn't have much trouble doing that kind of thing, but men usually did. I wanted to marry a man who knew how to talk and share and feel—a man who knew how to cry and wasn't ashamed to be an emotional, open, tender man. That was sensitivity to me. I wondered if such men even existed! As hard as it had been for him at first, Pa was learning to be that kind of man, and I loved him so much for it!

And of course *first* of all, such a man would have to be a Christian, sharing with me the desire to follow God with all his heart in *everything*. How could a man and woman be friends for a lifetime if they didn't share that most important thing of all? And if marriage was something God had for me, I didn't want to just be a wife, and have a husband. I wanted to have a best friend to live the rest of my life with!

Raspberry stumbled momentarily on a rock in our path, and suddenly my thoughts were jolted back from marriage to the present. We were climbing pretty steeply now. It was completely light, and over the mountains ahead of us hues of pink were starting to spread upward from the horizon. The summit up ahead looked like a good place to stop. From there I'd be able to see the sun rise over the peaks in the distance. I urged Raspberry on.

But in spite of the difficult climb, I couldn't keep my thoughts on the ride itself. I found myself thinking about myself and what kind of person I was—the kind of thoughts you usually keep to yourself and don't tell anyone, even your parents or closest friends.

God had given me certain talents and strengths, although sometimes it was hard to admit good things, even to myself.

But I knew I had done a lot of growing up in the five and a half years since we had come to California. I'd been fifteen and a half then, and so young. Now here I was looking at life as an adult would. And I wanted so badly to put to good use all that God had given me. I wanted to use the gifts and abilities and strengths he had put inside me to help other people, to grow still closer to him, and to glorify him.

"O Lord," I found myself praying, "help me to cultivate what you've given me. Don't let me waste anything. Help me to grow to the fullest, so that I can be the person you want me to be!"

Even as I prayed I realized how much he had already done within me. The growth hadn't all been easy. I'd cried a lot of tears since Ma's death out on the desert. I'd cried with Almeda. I'd cried with Pa. And I'd cried alone. Yet I had grown and matured so much through it all!

And I wasn't the only one who had changed. I'd seen so many other relationships develop and deepen, from Pa and Mr. Royce to Uncle Nick and Katie, Little Wolf and Zack. Mr. Lame Pony was having more to do with people in the community. Rev. Rutledge had changed and become a friend to our family. I saw so much growth in so many people.

I thought about what it was like to toss a pebble into a pond. The rock starts a motion of ripples that spread outward in concentric circles, which eventually goes the entire length of the water in every direction. I was reminded of Almeda, one woman, left alone at her husband's death, yet with faith alive and growing inside her heart, like a rock thrown into the middle of this community.

Then we had come. And through Almeda's walk and life with God I saw something I desired to share, something I wanted and knew I needed. As I searched for the truth, with

Almeda helping and guiding and teaching me, our friendship developed and deepened, as did my faith. I became a daughter to her in many ways.

Then Pa was gradually drawn by the same thing I had felt. His faith in God began to grow deeper too, not just from Almeda, but maybe even from me and seeing Rev. Rutledge reach out to him. God was already spreading his life out into the community through more than just one or two.

After Pa and Almeda were married, the circles of deeper faith continued to widen. As Zack and Emily and Becky grew, we all started praying more together as a family. Then things began changing for Uncle Nick. And then God, in his mysterious ways, worked through tragedy to bring Katie into the ever-widening circle.

God, O God, I thought, *you have transformed me and the people around me in so many extraordinary ways! Where will it go from here? What are you going to do next? Whose life will you change . . . whose heart will you get inside of next?*

As we crested the peak, Raspberry struggled up the final bit of the steep climb. Then the path leveled out and continued along for some distance over the high ridge.

I reined him in and sat still in the saddle for another moment or two, glancing around in all directions. What a beautiful view! The long ride, the climb . . . it had all been worth it for this one moment!

Slowly I dismounted, taking the reins in my hand, and walked to a lone tree, growing by itself on the high plateau. I tethered Raspberry to its trunk and patted the red splotch in the middle of his white forehead, the reason for his name.

I walked on farther, climbed onto a big boulder, and sat down on top of it. The sky in the east was now full of vivid colors, all melting into each other as the brightening flame on the horizon gathered in intensity.

Suddenly, from behind a snow-capped peak in the distance, a sliver of the sun shot into view. The intense ray pierced my eyes like a blinding arrow. In a second the whole eastern horizon was changed as brilliant, flashing rays spread out in all directions. All other colors instantly vanished in the core of blinding orange fire.

I turned around and looked in the direction from which I had come. Down in the distance the early morning haze still clung to the trees and ridges and hollows, some of which wouldn't see the sun for several more hours. And then, still farther off, I could just glimpse the big valley into which all the rivers of these mountains poured.

I am twenty-one, I thought to myself. *Twenty-one!* It hardly seemed possible! What would my future hold? I wanted so much to do what God wanted me to. I wanted always to be growing in my knowledge of him, growing in what the Bible called righteousness. I never wanted to let myself relax in my faith and take the easy way. I wanted to hold on to the standards that God had established, the way he wanted his people to walk.

"God," I prayed as I sat there, "I want my whole self to belong to you. I give my all to you. Show me how to do it. I know I can only do it with you beside me and in me."

I could feel the warmth of the sun's rays on my back. I sat still for a long time. Everything was still and quiet. The only sounds to meet my ears were the songs of birds celebrating the sun and the springtime.

Seized by a great surge of joy, I wished I could soar like those birds. I had grown in the years since coming to California from a timid and uncertain young girl into a confident, though occasionally still struggling—could I actually *say* the word?—into an—*adult*.

As I sat there basking in the sunrise, the dawn reminded me of the day Almeda shared her story and her feelings with Katie. Almeda had said that Mr. Parrish gave her a place to stand. I remembered her words, and I could almost hear her voice when she said, "*Not only was he giving me a place to stand, it was a place of warmth and smiles.*"

I got down off the boulder and walked back to the tree where Raspberry was waiting patiently for me. I mounted and we moved on for a short distance in the other direction, gazing toward the mountains, then back westward toward the valley below, where the sun's rays were now probing the hollows and caressing the ridges above them.

Suddenly the overpowering radiance of the sun became a revelation to me. *I have been given a place to stand, too,* I thought. *A place right here, a place in this new state, "the sunshine state." God has given me a place in the sun!*

A sense of calm and peace and assurance flooded over my being. Even as I felt the sun's warmth on my arms and back, I felt God's presence wrapping around me.

I sank to my knees on a patch of nearby grass. Lifting my face toward heaven, I was filled with a heart of gratefulness.

"Thank you, God, for being so near to me, so present with me. Thank you that I am here. Thank you for bringing me to California. Thank you for the place you have given me to stand . . . and to walk. And thank you for everything my future holds . . . whatever it may be."

I lingered a while longer on the grass, soaking in everything I was feeling. Then I slowly stood.

The sun was already climbing into the sky, its fiery beams waking up every inch of the sleepy earth. I walked back toward Raspberry, gave his nose a pat, untied him, and remounted.

"It's time we headed back, my old friend," I said.

Down the way

we had come, we made our way toward home. I knew my family would all be up by now and wondering where I was. I smiled at the thought. I probably should have told someone where I was going. But I had wanted to be completely alone, even in the knowledge of where I was!

My heart was still welling up within me, full of God's peace and love. My thoughts and prayers seemed to take up where they had left off on the ride up.

"God," I prayed again, "help me take care of the good things you are doing inside me. Never let me take for granted all you've given, and the life you've put within me. I give my life to you, Lord, and place into your hands whatever my future holds."

About the Author

MICHAEL PHILLIPS is perhaps best known for reawakening interest in the writings of George MacDonald. In the 1980s Phillips embarked on a campaign to reacquaint the reading public with the works of the forgotten Victorian novelist and Scotsman. Phillips edited and published more than fifty of MacDonald's works in twenty years, including his own acclaimed biography of the man. Combined sales total two million copies, inaugurating a renaissance of interest in MacDonald's work. Phillips also began writing fiction of his own, and now it is as a novelist he is primarily known. He has authored and coauthored (with Judith Pella) more than seventy titles in addition to his volumes of MacDonald. His best-known novels include those of the Phillips-Pella writing team, THE STONEWYCKE SERIES, THE JOURNALS OF CORRIE BELLE HOLLISTER, and THE RUSSIANS, as well as his solo THE SECRET OF THE ROSE, AMERICAN DREAMS, and SHENANDOAH SISTERS. Michael Phillips and his wife, Judy, alternate their time between the U.S. and Scotland, where they are attempting to increase awareness of George MacDonald and his work.